"Why are you apologizing to me?"

Rachel brought Utah to a stop. Ahead of her, the road was choked with weeds. "We hate each other."

She'd brought him as far as she'd said she would. He slid to the ground and moved to Utah's head, rubbing behind the gelding's forelock beneath the browband. It was the kind of gesture a cowboy would give to a beloved horse, and at odds with the ridiculous jogging clothes Ben wore.

Utah leaned into his touch. Without realizing it, Rachel leaned forward, as well.

"I don't hate you, Thompson." Ben stared up at her. "You're one of the few people in town who had the courage to tell me the truth on my wedding day."

The way he said it...as if her shouting at him in the church aisle all those years ago was a good thing. The way his blue eyes looked at her...as if she was the only person in town he could trust.

Dear Reader,

I'm the youngest of a large, blended family—three brothers and two sisters. We're all very different but share many of the same family traditions and values. We drifted apart when we were younger—seeking our own paths, healing perceived family hurts, trying to figure out who we are. But we're closer than ever now.

The Blackwell family has drifted apart, too. Ben Blackwell wasn't proud of his first win as an attorney back in Montana. That victory changed the fortunes of the Blackwell Ranch and the Double T, and it drove Ben away. So the last thing he wants to do is return to the family ranch, admit what he's done to his brothers and face childhood friend Rachel Thompson of the Double T in court. He doesn't know the path to forgiveness runs through family.

I hope you enjoy this installment of the Return of the Blackwell Brothers, as well as the other books in the series. It was a joy working on another project with my writing sisters—Carol Ross, Cari Lynn Webb, Amy Vastine and Anna J. Stewart. Yes, this wasn't our first writing rodeo, so to speak. And yes, we're something of a family.

Happy reading!

Melinda

HEARTWARMING

The Rancher's Redemption

USA TODAY Bestselling Author

Melinda Curtis

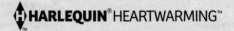

Recycling programs
for this product may
not exist in your area.

ISBN-13: 978-1-335-63381-1

The Rancher's Redemption

Copyright © 2018 by Melinda Wooten

Printed in U.S.A.

Award-winning, *USA TODAY* bestselling author **Melinda Curtis** is an empty nester married to her college sweetheart. However, she didn't feel old until her oldest son and his wife became pregnant during the writing of this book. Topics at family gatherings eventually turned to what Melinda wanted to be called by her grandchildren. *Grandchildren!* Her three children eventually came up with a name for her: *Grandma Overlord*, a name derived from her mastery of all things, or at least her ability to fake it on the page. *Is that supposed to be a compliment?* Now they lovingly refer to her as *GO* (pronounced "gee-oh"). Check in with Melinda a few years from now to see if the "endearment" stuck.

Melinda writes sweet contemporary romances as Melinda Curtis (Brenda Novak says *Season of Change* "found a place on my keeper shelf") and fun, sexy reads as Mel Curtis (Jayne Ann Krentz says *Fool for Love* is "wonderfully entertaining").

Books by Melinda Curtis

Harlequin Heartwarming

A Harmony Valley Novel

Visit the Author Profile page
at Harlequin.com for more titles.

To Carol Ross, Cari Lynn Webb, Amy Vastine and Anna J. Stewart. I know I often scare you with my writing ideas—*"Come on! Let's write connected cowboy stories!"*—and I admire your courage for falling into step with me... And then having my back so I don't face-plant on a public sidewalk. Love you, ladies!

CHAPTER ONE

NEVER LOOK BACK.

That's what Ben Blackwell's grandfather, Big E, always said.

At least, that's what he used to say. Back when he and Ben used to talk. Back before Big E eloped with Ben's fiancée. Back before Ben left behind trail dust and boots and Montana to be a top public utilities lawyer in New York City.

And now, Ben was doing more than looking back—he'd gone back. Home to Falcon Creek and the Blackwell place, which had been a cattle ranch for five generations, but was now also a dude ranch.

"Big E wants us to call it a *guest* ranch," Ethan, Ben's twin, had corrected Ben when he'd muttered something about *dudes* on the phone last week.

Seemed like Ben had been muttering ever since—about his bossy older brother, Jonathon, who wanted him home ASAP; about his younger twin brothers, Tyler and Chance, who couldn't seem to be bothered to help at the family homestead; about the grandfather whose picture was in the dictionary under *selfish*; and about the small-town attorney who was suing the ranch for water rights.

At thirty-two, Ben was too old to be dragged back into the family drama that orbited Big E and the Blackwell Ranch.

Too big for your city britches, more like.

That was his grandfather's voice in his head. That voice had been talking nonstop since Ben had agreed to return to Falcon Creek.

You have arrived, big shot.

And he had.

Ben got out of his Mercedes, punched his arms into his suit jacket, ignoring the stifling feeling from being buttoned-up in the early afternoon heat. He'd flown from New York to Montana, and then driven to Falcon Creek without stopping. He didn't plan to stay more than a few days—a week, tops.

Across the street, Pops Brewster looked up from his chess game on the Brewster Ranch Supply porch to get a good look at the city slicker. Annie Harper slammed too hard on her truck brakes as she pulled up to the stop sign, gaze ping-ponging between Ben and the intersection. In the Misty Whistle Coffee Shop parking lot, Izzy Langdon tipped his straw cowboy hat up, the better to ogle Ben's ride.

Rachel Thompson opened the door to the law office of Calder & Associates, crossed her arms over her chest and glared at Ben. "Late as usual, Blackwell."

"Welcome home," Ben muttered, walking around a knee-high weed bending over the sidewalk. He stopped in front of the steps of a white clapboard shack, which had probably been built over a hundred years ago when the town had been founded. "Traffic was gridlocked, it was impossible getting out of Bozeman." That was like saying traffic in the Mojave Desert was bumper-to-bumper.

Overexaggeration. Hyperbole. Sarcasm.

It was completely lost on Rachel. She spun on her high heels without so much as a roll of her eyes.

Reluctantly, Ben followed. It took him two tries to get the front door closed behind him. The building had settled, and the doorframe was no longer plumb. He slammed it home, earning a dry, "Really?" from Rachel.

"Really," Ben said airily. "You should run a planer on that door." *And think about practicing law elsewhere.*

The narrow, rectangular building was divided into two offices and a waiting area with a black couch that was so old it had butt impressions in the cushions. The building's hardwood floor was worn to the nails that kept it in place and there was a crack in the ceiling plaster that spoke louder of foundation issues than the ill-fitting front door.

Everything about the office screamed struggling law practice, from the receptionist's bare desk to the unread magazines perfectly fanned on the coffee table.

Rachel settled behind a large oak desk in her office, which had a clean blotter and a few neat, low stacks of paper.

By contrast, when Ben had left his office at Transk, Ipsum & Levi, his credenza had piles of depositions and his desk had been buried in briefs and court filings.

Ben paused in the doorway to Rachel's office, assessing his adversary for any apparent weaknesses other than inadequate resources.

Rachel was still easy on the eyes, and still favored suits that lacked the sophistication and designer cachet most of his female opponents in New York wore into battle. Joe Calder was probably behind the closed door of the other office. He had to be ancient. When they'd met in court five years ago, Joe had shuffled into the courtroom slower than a turtle in deep sand.

Beware! Remember the tortoise and the hare, boy.

Well, this hare had won the last go-round, but not without a bit of finagling of the race-course.

That's what lawyers are supposed to do, boy, bend the law.

Ben ran a hand over his hair. "Where's Joe?" He leaned back to see if the other office door was opening. "Will he be joining us?"

"Joe died last winter." Rachel's tone indicated she didn't think she needed Joe. "He left me the practice."

It looked like Joe hadn't done Rachel any favors.

Ben dusted off the seat of a chair across from her before he sat down, but his gaze never really left Rachel.

They'd known each other since kindergarten, both raised as ranch kids on bordering properties. His grandfather hadn't much cared for the Thompsons and hadn't encouraged a friendship.

Ben had targeted Rachel in dodgeball in the fifth grade, because she wasn't much of an athlete beyond being able to ride. She'd asked him to the Sadie Hawkins dance in the seventh grade, but they'd both been awkward about it, because what did you do with the opposite sex when you were almost thirteen? When Ben was fourteen and in high school, he had the answer to that question, but he'd moved on to dating Rachel's best friend, Zoe Petit. Back in the day, Rachel and Zoe were always made-up and dressed-up, looking like they went to school in a Beverly Hills zip code.

After Ben graduated law school, he and Zoe had made wedding plans. Rachel had been Zoe's maid of honor—meaning she was supposed to stand up at the altar, smile serenely and hold Zoe's bouquet while the preacher said his words. Instead, Rachel had stood up to Ben in the church aisle, smiled like she wanted to kill him and then told Ben that Zoe had run off with a wealthier Blackwell—Ben's grandfather.

Kind of made it hard to look at Rachel's pretty face after that.

Today, Rachel wasn't so put-together. She'd straightened her blond hair, but missed a long lock on the side. The eyeliner beneath her left eye was heavier than the line beneath her right. And the pink blouse beneath her navy suit jacket was wrinkled with a stain near the neckline. He wasn't so principled that he didn't take a little pleasure in seeing how far the mighty had fallen.

"Lookin' good, Rach." Ben ran a hand over his hair once more. Behind her on the credenza was a picture of a baby, a cute one as babies went. Round face, big brown eyes, a thatch of blond hair. Brought to mind another baby and another court case. Ben didn't let his gaze linger. He gave Rachel a peacemaking smile and reached across the desk to shake her hand. "Is that another one of your sister's babies?"

"Still the charmer, I see." Rachel's fingers were small and cold. They convulsed around Ben's hand before she drew back, rubbing her palm over her skirt as if he had germs.

No surprise in that handshake. As adults, the Blackwells and the Thompsons were about as friendly as the Hatfields and the McCoys.

Ben flattened his smile out of existence. Best get to the point. "I hear there's an issue over river water rights." That's why he'd returned to Falcon Creek. At his twin's urging, not his grandfather's. Big E had apparently gone on drive-about in his thirty-foot mobile home and wasn't taking calls.

For centuries, ranchers in Montana's high country had been fighting over water rights. Water nourished crops. Crops fed cattle. Cattle was sold to pay bills. Limited water meant skinny cattle, small herds and limited income. Permission to divert river water for agriculture or to communities was determined in court and by the state water board, and was based on several factors, including historical use and legal precedent. Properties and towns were assigned allotments and priorities. Those in first position had first rights to river water even if they were farther downstream. Ben and Big E had won the first position from the Double T five years ago with a slick piece of legal wrangling that should be iron-clad.

"The Double T has decided it's time to revisit *your* rights." Rachel opened a thin manila folder. "I've done some research with the water district and it appears the Blackwell Ranch hasn't been using their allotment of water, which—*as you know*—means the claimant with secondary rights can divert more river water. And the ranch with second rights—*as you know*—is the Double T."

She'd done research?

Ben was surprised, but not worried. This was Rachel Thompson. She used to copy off his test in Mrs. Whitecloud's science class. There'd be no competition here. He'd graduated from Harvard and practiced law in New York City. Rachel had graduated from the University of Montana and only ever practiced in Falcon Creek.

Rachel thought she could break the deal Ben had drawn up five years ago? Not on her best day.

He gave her a pitying smile. "I haven't seen your brief yet, but—"

"I have a copy for you here, along with Exhibit A, the Blackwell Ranch's year-to-year river water usage." Rachel handed Ben a few pages, a challenging spark in her brown eyes.

For the first time since arriving in Falcon Creek, Ben felt like doing more than muttering.

He sat up straighter and scanned the brief. But his mind was chugging along an unpleasant train of thought. Both ranches relied on the river for water. The Blackwell Ranch also had rights to an underground reservoir, although it was their practice to use aquifer water only if the river was low. But there was a third player in the water game. Decades ago, the Falcon County Water Company had won legal access to the metered pumps monitoring river water use on both ranches, claiming someday the community's needs might supersede theirs.

Rachel shouldn't have the Blackwell Ranch's water information. She shouldn't have filed a lawsuit with the court either. There were new housing developments south of Falcon Creek. Unused water would make the water company salivate. There were legal firms out there being paid to watch for opportunities just like this.

He should know. Up until last week, he'd worked at one and as soon as he wrapped things up here, he hoped to work for another.

And then Ben noticed something odd in her brief. Battle alarms went off in his head, ringing in his ears. "Why are you mentioning aquifer rights? I thought this case was about river water use."

Rachel's smile contradicted the wrinkled blouse and frizzy lock of hair. "We'd like to establish with the court that the aquifer provides you with more than enough water. More than enough," she repeated.

More than enough as in...more than enough to share?

There was something about Rachel's attitude that made Ben wonder...

Is she going to make a run for aquifer access?

She couldn't. Not without a land ownership claim. And to do that, she'd have to suspect the Double T had rights to the property above the reservoir. Or she'd have to have proof of…

The alarm bells rang louder.

She knows.

Ben sucked in thin mountain air.

She couldn't know. Big E may be the worst grandparent on the planet, but he was one of the best businessmen Ben knew. The proof Rachel needed to obtain aquifer water rights was in Big E's safe.

Or it had been five years ago.

A lot can change in five years, boy.

Ben wanted to tell his brothers this was nothing serious.

But there was something about Rachel's smile that made him nervous.

And nervous lawyers didn't run.

RACHEL THOMPSON'S HANDS SHOOK.

She clenched her fingers and tucked her hands beneath her arms, watching Ben pull away in a black Mercedes blanketed with dust that dulled the expensive car's shine.

Ben Blackwell was going down, along with the rest of his swindling family.

Thanks to her anonymous guardian angel,

Rachel thought she had what she needed to get the Double T's river rights back and to put the Blackwell Ranch in secondary position for water from Falcon Creek. Her confidence should have been unflappable.

And yet, her hands shook.

Because Ben Blackwell was intimidating. Perfect walnut brown hair. Strong chin. Cold blue eyes that judged her just as harshly as she'd judged others as a teenager. Tailored suit and red silk tie. Ben spared no expense to look like a rich and powerful attorney who'd crush the opposition beneath his fine Italian loafer.

For heaven's sake, those shoes cost as much as the used truck she was driving.

He'd looked at Rachel as if she was a speck of dust, an inconvenience that ruined his shine, just like the dust on his car.

Five years ago, she'd been a speck of dust. She'd been a young, green lawyer paired with a crotchety old man who'd been no match for Ben. The Blackwells had stolen their river resources, forcing Dad to sell off some of their land or pay through the nose for water that should have been theirs. Three years later and the stress of the struggle to keep the Double T alive had sent Dad to an early grave.

Win back the water rights.

Set the ranch to rights.

Those were her mantras lately.

A shiny red truck parked in front of the office where the Mercedes had been. Rachel's ex-husband got out of the vehicle that used to be hers. Ted Jackson was uncouth, compact and cowboy rough—everything Ben wasn't. Everything that shouldn't throw Rachel off her game. She repeated her mantras, adding one:

Win back the water rights.

Set the ranch to rights.

Get a signed custody agreement.

Everything threw her off her game lately, especially the thought that she should add more to her list of mantras.

Rachel opened the door to the June heat with a hand that still trembled. "The custody papers are ready for you to sign."

Ted paused on the porch, staring at her with bloodshot gray eyes. "I didn't say I'd sign. I said I'd look."

She wanted to slam the door and shut Ted out of her life. She wanted to press the reboot button and start her adult life over. It'd taken her three months to get Ted to sign the divorce papers. Three more to get this close to him signing the custody papers. No way was she dividing custody of her nine-month-old baby equally with this drunk.

And yet, if he didn't sign that was exactly what the court demanded.

Rachel gave Ted her lawyer smile, polite but withdrawn. "Let's review the papers and see what you think."

He came inside and waited for Rachel to shut the out-of-kilter front door before following her back to the office, not taking off his straw cowboy hat. "One weekend a month. That's what we agreed to."

"Only at your parents' house." His mother watched Poppy sometimes. She was a capable and trustworthy adult.

"That'll work since I don't change diapers." Ted slouched in a chair and stared at her with a lecherous smile.

Rachel's stomach did a slow, sickening roll. Ted was proof the pickings in Falcon Creek were slim. A ticking biological clock, a night of dancing, and she'd been convinced she could make her father's handsome, blond ranch hand into something. She hadn't counted on a prior, much stronger claim being staked by whiskey. Whiskey made Ted something else. Something sour and dangerous.

She clicked the point on a pen and slid it

with the papers across her desk. She'd flagged the places Ted needed to sign with red sticky notes. If he agreed to this, she'd file the agreement at the county courthouse within the hour.

Ted didn't reach for the paper or the pen. "I was talking to the boys down at the Watering Hole…"

He'd been taking advice from his drunk buddies at the bar again? Rachel straightened her spine and cleared her throat of angry responses that would do her no good.

Ted pointed at the custody agreement, still not touching it. "I want you to put in there that you can *never* take Poppy away from Falcon Creek."

Rachel's neck twinged. She was a fool for once telling Ted she'd like to try life outside of Falcon Creek.

"I want that moving bit in there because I deserve to watch my daughter grow up." Ted stood, scraping the chair across the wood floor. "I deserve things, you know."

He did. He deserved a stay in a rehab facility or dry out in a county jail cell. He didn't deserve Rachel's truck, her money, her daughter or her freedom.

"I deserve things," Ted repeated, spinning in slow motion until he found his bearings and headed toward the door. He yanked it open and slammed it on the way out.

Rachel tried to breathe normally. She shouldn't feel trapped in Falcon Creek. This was home. It always had been. It was just...

She had dreams. She sometimes wondered. What would it be like to be a lawyer in California or Florida, someplace it didn't snow? Or even New York, where...

It was foolish to think she was good enough to practice law in New York. It was foolish to think about anything but this life—managing the ranch, handling a few small cases, raising Poppy.

She had to be strong for the Thompson legacy, for the Thompsons left. Mom and Nana Nancy. Her sister and her kids. Poppy.

There was a noise in the second office. A thin wail. Poppy was waking up. The sticky front door had been slammed too many times.

Rachel squared her shoulders. Dreams were for sissies. She had to accept the consequences of her choices and be strong.

If not for herself, for Poppy.

CHAPTER TWO

THE BLACKWELL FAMILY RANCH.

That's what the new, grand metal arch over the gravel road proclaimed. Ben's childhood home.

Family? Not hardly. The only Blackwells who lived there were Big E and Zoe. Mom and Dad were dead. All five Blackwell brothers had vamoosed.

Ben drove the Mercedes down the road with a speed that matched his reluctance to return.

A new green metal roof rose above the rolling pasture, lifted by log framing. But it wasn't a simple log cabin. It was a huge building. Two stories. Two wings. An imposing porch. Twenty or so vehicles parked in front. This must be the guest lodge.

Farther behind the lodge, a huge gazebo shaded several wooden picnic tables. Beyond that sat a fire pit big enough to roast a pig in. Adults and kids milled about in T-shirts, shorts and flip-flops. In a nearby corral, two mares and two foals watched the afternoon proceedings with bright eyes and ears cocked forward, as if they couldn't believe the West had been invaded by suburbia.

Where were the blue jeans? The plaid button-downs with pearly snaps? The boots?

"So much for the *dude* ranch," Ben muttered.

At the fork in the road, he steered to the right and drove on to a much smaller, white two-story home with green shutters and a wraparound porch. He took his foot off the gas and slowed to a crawl. The house was surrounded by lawn on all sides. He'd bet the big elm in the backyard still held the tire swing and that there'd be a picnic table and two benches near a modest fire pit, a place the Blackwells had enjoyed gathering around over the years.

"Listen." Mom had tucked Ben under one arm and Ethan under the other as the red flames crackled in the darkness. "Can you hear the owl hoot? He's telling you he's out hunting for food tonight."

"Boo!" Ben's older brother, Jon, dug his fingers into Ben's and Ethan's shoulders from behind, like an owl striking its prey.

Ben and Ethan screamed. But their screams

turned into laughter as Jon ruffled their hair and handed them marshmallows to toast.

"Jon, you need to take care of your little brothers." Dad handed out sticks sharpened for s'more making. "And not wake up the babies." The babies being Tyler and Chance, asleep upstairs.

"Let the boy have his fun," Big E said, smoking a cigar at the picnic table. "Ranch life has a way of making boys into men before you know it. And then they'll have too many responsibilities to laugh."

His grandfather had been right. When Ben was twelve, his parents had drowned in a flash flood as they tried to cross Falcon Creek in their truck. After that, there wasn't a lot of joking in the house for quite some time. Jon had taken on the burden of mother hen. Heaven knew the women Big E married, one after another, hadn't been able to fill a mother's role. Big E resumed running the ranch after his only son had died.

Ben parked between two trucks in front of the white house—one newer and one on its last legs. Ben got out, grabbed his designer suitcase and expensive silver briefcase with his laptop inside and moved up the walk.

"Late, as usual." Ethan stood on the porch,

looking like a true ranch hand. Dirt-smudged blue jeans, dusty boots, sleeves rolled up on a blue chambray button-down. The junker truck had to be his. Ethan tilted his worn blue baseball cap back and surveyed Ben as if he was one of his veterinary patients with an unknown illness. "You sure you don't want me to roll out the red carpet? You might get those fancy shoes of yours dirty."

"Never joke about your lawyer's shoes." Ben climbed the porch steps, stopping one riser away from the top, just short of the shade. The last time he'd been on this porch had been the day he was to be married. They'd taken pictures—five brothers and the old man who'd finished raising them, who'd guided them, who'd betrayed each of them in turn. Ben had worn a tux that chafed his neck and shoes that pinched his feet. He should have known those uncomfortable clothes were a sign that his marriage wasn't meant to be.

"We can't joke about our lawyer's shoes? Is that kind of like saying never joke about a man's cowboy's hat?" Jonathon appeared in the doorway, a black-and-white dog at his side. He had the Blackwell dark brown hair and was dressed similar to Ethan, except he didn't look as dirty. He stuck his gray Stetson on his head, looking the part of a respectable rancher.

Jon had his own spread farther north and two twin girls he'd been raising alone until recently. Gen and Abby had to be about six by now. Ben's assistant sent them birthday and Christmas gifts every year. With any luck, Ben would be breaking in a new assistant before long and instructing them to add the girls to his gift list.

"Shoes say a lot about a man." Ben gave his brothers a hard stare and let it drift down to their footwear. The last time Ben had faced these two, they'd tried to convince Ben that Zoe jilting him at the altar was a good thing.

"She was only interested in your money," Ethan had said.

"If nothing else, her running away with Big E proves it," Jonathon had added.

"But you knew they were eloping," Ben had spat back.

It hadn't been enough that Ben had suffered through the humiliation of standing at the altar as friends and family filled the church. His brothers had known their grandfather and Ben's fiancée were running away together. And they hadn't said anything!

They'd let Rachel tell him.

Rachel.

For the love of Mike, she was Zoe's best friend and his opposing counsel even then.

Rachel had tossed her blond ringlets over one shoulder and glared at Ben. Gone was the casual camaraderie they'd had as teenagers; not surprising given she'd just lost the Double T's water rights the day before. "Did you honestly think Zoe would move away from her family and friends to live with you in New York City?"

Ben had to keep himself from shouting, *Yes!* Instead, he'd said through stiff lips, "Marriage to me seemed more likely than my twenty-seven year-old fiancée eloping with my seventy-two year-old grandfather."

Big E, Zoe, Rachel, Jon, Ethan. Five people he'd thought were family. Five people he'd never trust again.

He'd done little more than exchange text messages with his brothers in five years. Even then, his replies were often brief—I'm fine. Can't get away. Not coming home for Christmas.

And then ten days ago, Ethan had texted and left voice mail, and then texted and left voice mail again: Big E has run away from home. Double T taking us to court over water rights. Help.

Ethan's second text and voice mail had come on a bad day. Ben had been coming down from the sixty-seventh floor in the elevator, escorted by Transk, Ipsum & Levi security, carrying a box with his personal belongings. His stomach had long since reached the lobby, having plummeted there when his boss told him he was being removed as lead counsel on a big case and—oh, by the way (as if it was an afterthought)—fired for unethical practices.

Unethical practices? Being a lawyer was about bending the law to justify your client's stupidity. The utility company had broken federal laws regarding safety standards and people had been killed. In their homes, no less. Leaving husbands without wives and kids without fathers. Ben had been broker-ing generous settlements with survivors, ap-parently, not to the client's satisfaction.

A cherubic face drifted through his mem-ory. Big brown eyes. Gummy smile. That baby didn't know what it meant to be orphaned yet.

That child had made Ben rethink what con-stituted a fair settlement in a legal case that was spinning out of control, spun faster by

Ben's actions to make things right. And coming down in that elevator, he'd felt the need to lean on someone.

In that moment of weakness, he'd stepped out of the building in midtown and called Ethan back, agreeing to return to Falcon Creek to defend the ranch.

Now here Ben stood, back where the cow pie had hit the fan five years ago, staring at the faces of the brothers who could have warned Ben he wasn't getting married.

"You think Ben convinced Rachel to back off?" Ethan said to Jon.

"Nope." Jon eyed Ben like the time he'd caught him trying to feed his beets to the family dog under the table.

Ethan tsked. "Then he's going to need a pair of jeans and boots."

"He's your size, not mine." Jon knelt and rubbed his dog's black ears.

"I'm standing right here, *gentlemen*." Ben shook his head. "I'm not going to be staying long enough to wear boots."

"He'll be in boots by sunup." Jon gave Ben a half smile.

"Definitely." There was nothing half about Ethan's smile. It was wider than a pregnant heifer's hips.

The sun beat down on the back of Ben's neck. He sighed and shook his head once more. He had things to do. The latest in Montana water rights to research. And the legal precedents behind those rights. "I don't have time to play home on the range."

"He wants us to think he hasn't forgiven us for being right," Ethan said smugly.

"I haven't," Ben said as darkly as any villain.

Jon ignored him, continuing to pat his dog on the head. "But we know better, because there's no other reason he'd show up in Falcon Creek." Ben's older brother was far too smug when he added, "Family means forgiveness."

Ben scowled, possibly with his entire body. "When you apologize for humiliating me, then I'll forgive you."

Five years ago, Jon and Ethan had presented their case for letting the revised wedding plans and ensuing drama play out. They'd thought Zoe was wrong for him. And sure, Ben had probably dodged a bullet when Zoe chose to marry a wealthier Blackwell, but he lived by the strict rules of the court. He'd been wronged. Restitution had never been made. His brothers owed him a sincere apology and a reason to trust again.

"You're lucky I'm here at all." Ben lowered his chin. "I wouldn't have come if Big E and Zoe were home."

"That solves where he's sleeping." Ethan pointed toward the henhouse near the main barn.

Jon chuckled, albeit briefly, and then stood. "But seriously, Ben, I'm glad you came home. All hands on deck tonight. We'll need you to bus tables for the ranch guests. Mrs. Gardner is helping us out and making tamales."

"I'm not the hired help," Ben said firmly, despite the prospect of homemade tamales. "I'm your lawyer." For two weeks and two weeks only.

"Prima donna, more like," Jon muttered. "I suppose your pride won't let you come inside until you've had a poke at someone. Go ahead. Give it your best shot, little brother." He angled his jaw Ben's way.

Ben's fingers clenched so hard around the handles of his briefcase and suitcase, his knuckles popped.

Ethan hurried to stand between the two. "Or we could go inside, have a beer and give Ben a chance to get even with a couple hands of poker." Ethan wasn't smiling when he turned to Ben. "I told you. Big E and Zoe have run away. The ranch is in trouble, both financially and in terms of resources. Primarily, water resources. We need you."

Without another word, Ethan and Jon walked inside their old family home. With one inquisitive look at Ben, the black-and-white dog followed, leaving Ben little choice but to do the same.

Ben crossed the threshold and stopped. "What the—" He nearly dropped his bags. He turned, looking outside to make sure he was still in Montana. There were the Rockies. No mistaking those peaks. He turned to take in the interior once more.

The house looked like a Wild West boudoir. Red velvet wallpaper. Crystal chandeliers. Furniture that wasn't for flopping on at the end of a hard day on a ranch. The chairs and sofa were white and prim, not to mention they weren't made for anyone over six feet in height. A black lacquered table with gold pinstripes sat in the dining room in front of a large gilded mirror that looked like the one the evil queen used in Snow White.

"Zoe redecorated." Jon sounded disgusted.

"You should see the master bedroom." Ethan sounded horrified.

"Or not," Ben murmured.

Both brothers turned to Ben, who was trying to remember what the place had looked like when he'd left. Blue plaid couch. Brown leather recliner. Coffee table scarred with circles from glasses of ice tea and cold cans of beer.

"You dodged a bullet," Jon said.

"In other words…" Ethan slung his arm around Jon's shoulders and grinned at Ben. "You should thank us."

Jon tipped his hat back. "Yep."

"Nice try, but you're missing the point." Ben didn't want to come inside, but he did anyway. Far enough in that he could see the kitchen, with its white marble counters, pink-trimmed cabinets and sparkly pink tile backsplash.

"He's not forgiving us," Ethan said, hanging his head.

"Not yet," Jon said.

Not ever. That's what Ben wanted to say.

But the words stuck in his throat as firmly as that red velvet wallpaper was stuck on the wall.

THE DOUBLE T was quiet when Rachel pulled up in front of the main house after she'd left her office.

The late afternoon heat lingered, but would

soon give way to the evening mountain chill.
Rachel took a moment to study the ranch
house, seeing beyond the white clapboard that
needed paint to how it must have looked in
the 1920s when it was new. Dormered windows. Black shutters. Gray metal roof. Great-
Grandpa Thompson had built the house for
his bride.

When Rachel was growing up, at this time
of day, there would've been ranch hands finishing up their chores, preparing to go home
or to cook something in the bunkhouse. Today,
only Henry, the ranch foreman, and Tony, a
part-time ranch hand remained. And the yard
was empty.

"Ga-ga-ga-gahhh," Poppy said from the rear
seat of the truck. How Rachel's baby loved the
sound of her own voice.

"Yes, sweetheart." Rachel smiled as she
walked carefully around to open the door. She
was still wearing her suit and heels, not having time to stop at her little house on the other
side of town and change. She had a number
of chores to do here before Poppy's bedtime.
"We're going to see your grandma and mine."
Her mother would feed Poppy and give her a
bath while Rachel did some ranch paperwork.

She freed Poppy from her car seat and grabbed her diaper bag.

"Na-na-na-nahhh." Poppy clapped her little hands and then pointed to the house, a regal command that made Rachel laugh.

"You're a princess, just like I was." She'd had the best of both worlds—a cowgirl with Daddy's credit card. Although nowadays, she wished she'd been raised differently. If Dad had demanded she work on the ranch, she'd be better equipped to run the Double T.

She drew her daughter closer, breathing in the scent of baby powder and shampoo. Poppy was so perfect, sometimes Rachel never wanted to let her go. Those blond curls. Those big brown eyes. Those chipmunk cheeks. If her marriage had to fail, at least Poppy was more than worth it.

And what was the silver lining to her legal practice failing?

There didn't seem to be one. Divorces. Living trusts. She barely cleared enough to earn a living wage. Pride made her keep the office open.

And the Double T? Things were just as grim here. Water was going to make or break her family's ranch. But this time, she was going to beat the Blackwells. She was sure of it.

Ben's handsome face came to mind. He represented everything she resented about the Blackwells. Ben and his brothers were raised to be ranchers, but they didn't care about their family heritage or tradition. They'd all moved on, coincidentally after stealing the Double T's water all those years ago. Even Zoe, who was only technically a Blackwell, had little sympathy for the struggles of the Double T.

Rachel opened the white picket gate surrounding the ranch house and carried Poppy toward the front door. The heat and her load made Rachel sweat. She kissed the top of her daughter's golden head. "I love you, sunshine."

Poppy grinned up at her. "Ma-ma-ma-mahhh."

This was real. This was good. Mommyhood. Caring for family. Going to bed every night knowing she was making a difference.

A sound had her looking back. A white-faced heifer poked its head around the barn.

"How did you get out?" Rachel asked, hurrying to get Poppy indoors where it was cooler. "Remind me to text Henry," she said to Poppy, hoping that saying it out loud would jog her memory once she got inside. Her memory lately was spotty, and Henry was ancient.

He didn't work after dinner, which was fast approaching.

Win back the water rights.

Set the ranch to rights.

Get a signed custody agreement.

Learn how to be a better rancher.

Her list was daunting.

"Ga-ga-ga-gahhh," Poppy breathed, pointing at various items, including the comfortable brown sofa and matching recliner. She loved her grandma.

The small living room was empty. As was the kitchen, which had been remodeled in the 1980s when Rachel's parents married. Oak cabinets. White ceramic tile counters. Flowery linoleum nearly worn away in front of the sink. The room may have been dated, but it was filled with the warm smell of something good in the oven. Nowadays, Rachel appreciated someone else cooking for her.

"Hey! Where is everybody?" Rachel dropped her diaper bag near the front door.

"Back here," Mom called.

With Poppy on her hip, Rachel went in search of the family.

Mom was pinning quilt pieces on the bed in the master bedroom, bright red-and-green material that formed pinwheel blocks. Fanny,

Mom's white toy poodle, leaped off her dog bed and began yapping at Rachel and Poppy. She was hard of hearing and had to make up for the pair sneaking up on her with faux indignation.

Mom shushed Fanny and muted the TV. "We've been crafting to avoid the heat." She stood on the other side of the bed wearing a blue-flowered blouse and black capris. Her highlighted blond hair was cut in a front-slanted, fashionable bob and her makeup was flawless. Lisa had married a rancher but had never quite embraced the wardrobe.

Rachel suspected her own makeup had melted off sometime after lunch when emotions had run higher than the heat. She'd prepped Nelly O'Ryan for a court appearance tomorrow, while Nelly's toddler, Alex, and Poppy had played with plastic blocks on the floor. Nelly was seeing her soon-to-be ex-husband for the first time in a month and was scared to death that Darnell would take out his frustrations on her afterward.

There had been tears, not all of them Nelly's.

When Rachel was younger, she'd been unflappable. Crying in public? That wasn't her thing. Now that she had Poppy, her hands shook when she got nervous and she cried at every Hallmark commercial.

"Good thing you're here," Mom said in the overly bright voice she'd been using since Dad died. "We're arguing over which is better—the BBC production of *Pride and Prejudice*, or the movie with Kiera Knightley." The movie was playing on the television. "You can be the deciding vote."

"You should pick Colin Firth and the BBC if you want a Christmas gift this year." Nana Nancy was knitting in a chair in the corner. Rachel's grandmother was short, short-haired, short-tempered and, like her knitting needles, slender and pointed.

"There can be no penalties for voting." The cheer in Mom's voice was tested. "I'm sure Rachel knows that the movie version empowers Elizabeth."

"I'm as neutral as Switzerland." Rachel looked for a place to set Poppy down where she'd be no trouble.

"Ga-ga-ga-gahhh." Poppy bounced impatiently, extending her arms to her grandmother. Rachel set her down and she crawled over to Lisa's feet, using her grandmother's capris to bring herself to a wobbly stand.

Fanny circled, wagging her pom-pom tail as she sniffed Poppy for stray crumbs.

"Poppy only goes to you first because you feed her." Nana didn't like coming in second to anyone. "See?" She caught Rachel's eye. "Your mother just slipped Poppy a Cheerio and yet she didn't want me to bribe you for your vote on *Pride and Prejudice*."

"Babies get low blood sugar if they don't eat regularly." Mom had the cereal stored in covered containers in the living room, kitchen and bedroom, reminiscent of the way Dad used to keep kibble around to train their ranch dogs.

Rachel loved her mother and grandmother, but neither woman asked how Rachel's day went or about her meeting with Ben. Didn't they care about the Double T? Didn't they care that generations of Thompsons were weighing heavily on Rachel's shoulders? Didn't they respect her for taking on the reins of the ranch? She knew she shouldn't say anything, but how could she not? Their fate was in her hands. "I go to court tomorrow against the Blackwells. They won't win this time."

"Water," Mom grumbled. "That's what broke your father's heart. We should—"

"Don't start about selling the Double T." Nana clicked her knitting needles angrily, looping purple yarn faster than a drummer hitting a cadence for a marching band. "This land has been in our family for seven generations."

"And it'll be in it for seven more," Rachel promised, mentally crossing her fingers and knocking on wood.

Mom lifted her gaze heavenward. "At least, tell me you got Ted to sign the custody agreement."

Rachel's smile fell. "He wants another stipulation."

"What is it this time?" Nana put down her knitting needles. "Does he want you to be his designated driver on Saturday nights?"

"It's nothing." Rachel bent to pin a fan of the pinwheel together, unable to look at her family.

"From the expression on your face—" Nana thrust a finger in Rachel's direction "—your nothing means something awful."

"It's not." It shouldn't be. "Ted wants me to agree to stay here to raise Poppy."

"As if you'd leave us." Mom picked up Poppy and gave her another Cheerio from her stash. "We wouldn't know what to do without you."

"We sure couldn't get Stephanie to run the ranch." Nana harrumphed. "Your little sister is more interested in the color of her nails than in the color of a healthy heifer's tongue."

Rachel grimaced. She wasn't sure she could confidently state the correct color of a healthy heifer's tongue, either. And she resisted looking at her nails. She hadn't had a manicure in who knows how long. Or a pedicure. Or gone shopping for clothes for herself. Or had highlights put in her hair. She missed the days when she could pamper herself, like Stephanie, who had two beautiful girls and a handsome architect husband in nearby Livingston.

Poppy giggled and patted her palms on Mom's cheeks. "Ga-ga-ga-gahhh."

Guilt wrapped around Rachel's chest and squeezed. With such an adorable daughter and a loving family, Rachel shouldn't resent Ted's restriction.

The sound of wood cracking and snapping could be heard outside. She hurried to the window and peered out on the backyard. "Shoot. It's that heifer." She'd forgotten to text Henry. The cow had pushed her way through the pickets to the vegetable garden. "I'll get her." And now she could add fixing the garden fence to her long list of to-dos.

Rachel rushed to the mudroom, slipped out of her heels and into Mom's pink and gold-trimmed cowboy boots. She grabbed Dad's lariat from a hook on the wall and then ran out into the heat wearing her best suit and pearls. "Git! Git!"

The heifer looked up. The green feathery tops of Nana's carrots dangled out of one side of the cow's mouth. She didn't budge, most likely because she didn't consider Rachel a threat.

The cow lowered her head and resumed her grazing.

"Hey! Hey!" Rachel slapped the stiff rope against her boots and then ran down the porch steps, charging the heifer. "Get out of there. Git-git-git!" She sounded like Poppy, except not as happy. She swung the loop of rope at the heifer's front flank.

Startled, the heifer rolled her eyes and backed up a few steps, reevaluating Rachel much the same way Ben had earlier.

"That's right. Git!" Rachel swung the lariat in front of the cow's face. "Back up. Get out."

That worked. The heifer made a sound like someone had sat down hard on a whoopee cushion. She wheeled and trotted out through what was left of the fence posts, kicking up dirt clods at Rachel. Slimy mud spattered her good jacket and skirt.

A guttural wail filled the air.

That wail… It was hers.

Rachel had three court suits that fit her mommy hips.

Well…now only two.

Her mother tapped on the bedroom window glass, her face hovering above Nana's. "Are you all right?"

Rachel nodded, even though she wasn't. She marched across the ravaged carrots and torn-up grass, scrunching her eyes against the threat of tears, because ranchers didn't cry. Not over ruined wool and silk.

The heifer headed behind the barn.

Rachel took off after her, rounding the corner only to find the escapee ambling down the weed-choked road that separated the Double T from the Blackwell Ranch, tail swinging happily as if she was high on carrots.

The gate was open, which gave rise to many questions. Why was it ajar? Who'd been careless enough to leave it open? How had the heifer escaped the large pasture? Was another gate open? A fence down? Were other livestock roaming about? The herd was supposed to be summering across the river in higher, greener pastures.

Rachel latched the listing gate, closing off

the road and shutting the heifer in. Someone would have to saddle a horse and ride the property line to find how and why the heifer was free.

Personally, she'd like that someone to be Henry. She hadn't expected to do anything but paperwork today and hadn't brought a change of clothes. Although her clothes were already ruined, she reminded herself.

Rachel turned toward a small house behind the barn. It was the original one-room homestead. It had no front yard. No fenced backyard. No driveway. But a well-used green Ford pickup was parked near the front door.

"Come in," Henry called after she'd knocked.

The tiny house had somber walls and exposed beams. A twin bed was in one corner next to a tall pine dresser. The doors to the closet and bathroom were ajar. The kitchen had a collection of empty soda cans on the brown Formica countertop. A burgundy recliner and television filled out the space, the latter perched on an old kitchen table with spindly wooden legs.

Henry sat in his recliner, an empty microwave container of macaroni and cheese in his lap. His scuffed boots were discarded near the door, as if he'd needed to take off his shoes first thing to pamper his aching feet. He muted the television. "What can I do for you, little lady?"

Is it too much to ask that he call me Rachel?

Probably, since he'd seen her as a toddler running through the front yard sprinkler naked.

Hoping to garner some respect, Rachel tugged down her blouse and buttoned her jacket. Her efforts to look like a presentable boss—one worthy of a title better than *little lady*—resulted in a fair amount of dung sprinkled on the floor. "There's a heifer loose. I shut her in the road leading to the river, but there's a break in the fence somewhere."

"I'll get to lookin' tomorrow." Henry was seventy-five if he was a day. He'd been with the ranch since he was in his twenties. Nothing upset him. Not loose heifers or flooded pastures. "Thanks for letting me know. If she continues to be a problem, we'll have to make steak out of her."

Rachel had never been good at eating animals she'd had a face-to-face with. "Let's hope it doesn't come to that. Let's make sure none of the rest of the herd is loose."

"Little lady." Henry slid his glasses off his nose and stared at Rachel. "After your father died, we made an agreement. Unless there's an emergency, I don't put in more than my eight hours, or I retire."

The last thing Rachel needed was to upset Henry enough that he'd retire. But still, she worried. They had so few cattle left. "What about Tony?"

"He left early to have a root canal in Bozeman." Henry's gaze drifted back to the television. "He won't be in tomorrow by the way."

Shoot. She'd forgotten. But still… "This needs to be done tonight."

"Ain't no hurry, little lady. We don't live in a time of cattle rustlers." Henry cast a disparaging glance at Rachel's pearls and then at her mother's pink-and-gold trimmed boots. "The Blackwells raise Black Angus. They aren't going to confuse white-faced cows on their land with their own." He unmuted the television. "You can't run a ranch in heels and pearls. Now, you worry about taking care of that baby of yours and I'll worry about the ranch."

Rachel left, feeling as if she'd been given a glass of water, a pat on the head and then shooed toward her bedroom.

Little lady.

Rachel's anger increased with every step

she took. Dad wouldn't have waited until morning. There was nothing for it. This little lady was going to have to ride out to the fence line herself.

Now all she needed was something to wear.

CHAPTER THREE

BEN SPENT THE rest of the afternoon and early evening at the kitchen table of his childhood home researching water rights and occasionally staring up at the pink-feathered chandelier above him.

He'd seen a lot of high-end apartments decorated by celebrated designers in New York, but he'd never seen the likes of that chandelier. Big E had to be going blind. There was no way his grandfather could sit underneath pink feathers and drink his morning coffee every day.

Watch out, boy. Men bend over backward for love.

His grandfather had told Ben that years ago. And now? Big E was like a pretzel.

When Ben had proposed to Zoe, he'd been naive. He'd thought his high school sweetheart wanted the same things he did—the finer things city life had to offer. He'd thought his grandfather wanted what was best for Ben when he'd made sure Zoe didn't need to worry about spending on the wedding.

"Your grandfather took me shopping in Bozeman," Zoe had said on the phone one night when Ben was in New York.

"Why?" Ben's attention was still half focused on the wording in the legal brief he was crafting.

"Because he wants me—and you—to have the very best," she'd replied in a stately voice.

Later, when Ben had asked his grandfather about his generosity, he'd scoffed and said it was nothing.

Today, looking around the remodeled kitchen with its frivolous decor, it looked like the Blackwell Ranch had money to burn. According to Ethan, that was far from the truth. But then, when had Big E been a proponent of the truth?

Ben had worked hard in law school, spent summers interning in Boston, passed the bar in New York on the second try and in Montana on the first, returning home to help Big E protect the ranch's water interests after practicing law in New York for a few years. He should have known Big E had personal interests of his own.

"We have to disclose this to opposing council," Ben had said when Big E showed him a yellowed piece of paper referring to the thin strip that divided the Double T from the Blackwell Ranch. "This says the land above the aquifer was traded by Mathias Blackwell to Seth Thompson in 1919 for a prize bull." In which case, the Thompsons would have rights to the aquifer, not the Blackwells.

"No, not necessarily." Big E closed the door to his study, affording them some privacy. "For all we know, there's another deed for the parcel. Folks in this valley bartered back and forth with land all the time. The Blackwells have been paying taxes on that strip for decades. I don't care what that paper says. It's our land."

"We won't know for sure until I do a title search." Protecting Blackwell assets required due diligence.

Ben was in a precarious position. He didn't want the Double T to go under, but they might if their river water was restricted. If the Thompsons owned the strip of land and the aquifer rights, the river water would matter less.

"No title search." Big E dragged the cigar chair to the left of the fireplace out of the way. He leaned down and pried a board up with a letter opener, revealing a small safe. He put the yellowed piece of paper inside. "This is a small county. You search for a title and pretty soon everyone knows we're looking for something, and then someone will want to know what it is we're looking for." Big E got to his feet with a creak of bones and put his hands on his hips. "Next thing that happens is we've got less land and a need for water. Are you a Blackwell, or not? Are you going to be our lawyer, or not? Think about the repercussions before you betray attorney-client privilege."

Ben hadn't wanted to let the issue go, but he had in the end. Eventually, they'd won the river water rights, but Ben had felt guilty about the victory because his father wouldn't have approved the means, and Rachel was his friend. Of course, he'd only had twenty-four hours to feel guilty about it before Zoe ran off with Big E, and Rachel tossed that in his face, along with their friendship.

"Hey, where were you?" Ethan returned to the house after dinner. He'd showered and changed into a clean pair of jeans and a green button-down. "Dinner service at the guest ranch was an hour ago. We were expecting you to lend a hand."

"I've been busy." Ben closed his laptop and the article about the revocation of rural water rights in nearby Gallatin County. "And before you get on me, I don't take calls or answer texts when I'm preparing for court." Ben glanced around the kitchen and at Ethan's empty hands. "Didn't you bring me something to eat?"

"No." Ethan scowled. "You have to earn dinner. We're all pitching in until Big E gets back."

Ben pointed at his laptop. "I am pitching in." He let annoyance trickle into his tone. "I've been working on something more important than making sure Zoe's guests give the ranch a good rating on social media."

Ethan crossed his arms over his chest.

"Come on, Ethan. Are you sure Big E went on vacation on impulse? Coincidentally right before the guest ranch opened its doors?" Ben hooked his arm over the back of his chair, not about to be a busboy in Zoe's little side business. "Are you sure Big E didn't take off because he didn't want to be the host of a bed-and-breakfast? This could be a ploy to get someone else to do all the work."

"This isn't like the time he hid our truck keys until we fixed the roof on the barn." Gone was the humor Ethan had greeted Ben with earlier in the day. "He and Zoe and the motorhome are gone. Big E's voice-mail box is full. No word from them. No ransom note either, in case you were wondering."

"There has to be some clue in Big E's office as to where they went." Ben got up and walked down the hall to their grandfather's study.

"We searched in there already," Ethan grumbled, following him.

"Is it normal for Big E and Zoe to take off like that?" Ben stepped into the room, trying to remember which floorboard his grandfather hid his safe under. "The sheriff doesn't suspect foul play?"

"No." The way Ethan said the word, the sheriff had probably laughed him and Jonathon out the door.

The study was the one room on the ground floor where nothing had changed. The same wide-topped solid oak desk. The same metal, olive-colored file cabinet. The same dark wood floors worn in front of the fireplace where Big E liked to pace.

And there, to the left of the hearth, was the leather cigar chair that stood guard over Big E's floor safe. Was the paper documenting the land trade still inside? All Ben needed was the combination to find out.

"According to Jon, Big E and Zoe travel

regularly in the motorhome." Ethan moved to stare out the window, sounding preoccupied. "But this time they left without telling Katie or Lochlan or anyone where they were going or how long they'd be gone. And Big E didn't move enough funds in the bank accounts to cover the checks Katie needed to write, like for feed and payroll."

Ben stared at a photo of Big E on the mantel. He wore a dark suit and black bolo tie. He'd shaven and his peppery hair was neatly trimmed. Zoe leaned in to kiss his cheek. Her straight blond hair was framed by a white bridal veil.

Ben expected to feel pain in his chest, somewhere around the spot his heart was supposed to be. Jealousy. Loss. Betrayal.

He felt nothing, except…confusion.

His grandfather looked happy. And Zoe looked like a joyful, blushing bride.

Ben's image of them had been clichéd. He'd pictured Big E with a depraved, triumphant attitude, as if he'd successfully pulled one over on Ben. He'd imagined Zoe with a cold look in her eye as she calculated the spending limit on the credit card Big E gave her.

"We should be worried," Ben said reluctantly. "Couples in love don't just disappear.

I'd wonder about his sanity if he didn't have Zoe with him." And wasn't that a change? Ben paying a backhanded compliment to his ex.

"I need to tell you something." Ethan turned, looking as if he was about to go on the witness stand in a contentious case.

His brother's heavy expression seemed to require lightening. "If you tell me you killed Big E in the library with a candlestick, I'm going to be very disappointed in you."

Ethan's mouth was a flat line. This was either something grim, or Ethan had indeed killed their grandfather.

Ben swore. "Seriously, I would have studied criminal law if I knew you had a violent side."

"It's not that kind of news." His twin shook his head. "I'm getting married."

"To Sarah Ashley Gardner?" *Please say no.* Ethan had been dangling from Sarah Ashley's string since he was thirteen.

"No. To her kid sister. Grace." That wasn't concern lining Ethan's face. It was defensiveness. "I love her. We're going to have a baby."

Ben had the strongest urge to close the distance between them and hug his twin. He glanced at the photo of Big E and Zoe and didn't budge. "Congratulations."

"Jon's getting married, too, in case you

hadn't heard. Her name is Lydia and she's great for Jon."

Ben's chest tightened. He felt like an outsider. They hadn't told him their good news earlier. Of course, he'd refused the offer of a beer and a game of poker, during which they might have told him. "I'll congratulate Jon next time I see him."

"Grace has been helping at the guest ranch," Ethan said. "But she's tired and if you helped out—"

"If I helped out," Ben cut his brother off, "I wouldn't be prepared to defend the ranch's water rights in court." He had to be ready for whatever Rachel threw at him. "I'm here for one reason and one reason only. As your attorney."

"Which is important to me. I want to start a veterinary practice here on the property once I get licensed in Montana." Ethan rubbed a hand through his hair, still looking defensive. "Right now, I'm practicing under Norman Terry at the clinic in town. Most of my patients are pets of friends, our ranch livestock and the petting zoo animals."

"A zoo?" Had he heard Ethan right? "When did a zoo open in town? And who was the fool who thought that was a good idea in Falcon Creek?"

"It's a *petting zoo*. It was Zoe's idea. And the guests really like it." Ethan's gaze swept the photos on the mantel. "I hate to admit it, but there might be something to the guest ranch. It could help the place stay afloat. You know, diversify income. That's why the water rights are so important."

Ben studied his brother the way he scrutinized an opposing counsel's witness, looking for sincerity and certainty. Finding both, he asked, "Do you know why Rachel brought this lawsuit now?"

Ethan shook his head.

"Someone gave her the history of water use here on the ranch." Ben couldn't imagine Big E going that soft. Unless she'd gotten her figures from someone at the water company, the only other people with knowledge of and access to the water bills were Zoe, Katie Montgomery and her father, Lochlan, the ranch's foreman. Lochlan had been managing things on the Blackwell Ranch for years and was as loyal as they came. Same for his daughter. "Now that Big E is acting irrationally, my money's on Zoe."

"Regardless, you'll handle it," Ethan said stiffly.

Standing so near his twin, the loss of their close relationship was an ache in Ben's chest.

"Jon wants to sell the ranch," Ethan blurted. "Combined, we can get a majority stake in the ranch and could wrest control from Big E. Jon's going to call a vote. I want to stay. I'm staking my livelihood here. My future." The words stopped tumbling out of his mouth, slowed, were given weight. "For the future of my child, Ben."

Ben drew back. He knew what Ethan was asking. He wanted Ben's vote to keep the Blackwell Ranch within the family. "And if I lose the water rights? What then?"

"Don't talk like that. Dad wouldn't want us to walk away from our heritage." Ethan placed a hand on Ben's shoulder. "Maybe roots and family aren't important to you, but they're important to me. Think about the memories we had growing up here. Riding the range. Camping under the stars. Running around a safe little town. When you have kids someday—"

"Big E ruined that for me." Ben brushed Ethan's hand away. "The ranch, the town, my life."

"I notice you didn't say anything about a broken heart," Ethan said softly. "Let it go, Ben. Move on."

Never look back, boy.

"It's kind of hard to move on when you've returned to the very spot where you started." Ben hated that he sounded pathetic.

"Do you want me to say I'm sorry that I waited until I knew for sure they'd eloped? Because I will." Ethan didn't sound resentful or pompous. He sounded earnest. "I'm sorry I made sure you couldn't catch up to the woman who didn't love you. I'm sorry that meant you heard about their elopement from someone else in front of an audience. And…" Ethan shuffled his booted feet. "And I'm sorry we haven't been close since then."

"I…" Ben swallowed. An apology. It was what Ben had waited for. And yet, he didn't know what to do.

Outside the window, the tire swing spun in the breeze.

"Higher!" a six-year-old Ben had demanded of their grandfather.

Ethan sat inside the tire swing while Ben stood on top of it. With each push from Big E, the wind had whistled past Ben's ears almost as fast as when he rode Cisco, Jon's bay mare.

His parents were cutting birthday cake for Tyler and Chance on the picnic table. Tyler swiped a glob of frosting and flung it in

Chance's dark hair. They giggled even as they tussled, trying to reach more cake.

Laughter. Smiles. The feeling that all was right with the Blackwells' world and that they were invincible. When was the last time Ben had felt that way? He couldn't remember. His life was a series of court cases where Ben protected big utility companies from greater consumer liability. Gas leaks. Energy surges. Fires sparked by downed power lines.

And the subsequent loss of life. There was no joy in putting a dollar figure on death. No laughter when negotiating with an attorney sitting next to a grieving, tear-stained mother holding a baby who'd never know her dad.

"I apologized," Ethan said to Ben now, the light dimming in his eyes. He turned to go.

"Wait." Ben had no idea what to say. The very air between them felt taut with tension. "Thank you."

Ethan gave a jerky nod. "Now that we've dealt with that... I need you on my team. The way we used to be." His words were stilted, as if he hadn't practiced what he'd say and didn't know how to say it now. "I can buy you out later." He grimaced. "Well, not for a couple years. Student loans and..." Ethan drew a deep breath. "Just...don't make a decision on selling now. Stop and think about it, for my sake." He walked out.

Ben sank into the leather cigar chair. Ethan was getting married. He was going to be a father. He had his life planned out. Hopefully he was headed for happiness. A part of Ben wanted to crow with ironic laughter. And yet…

In rolled jealousy like a toxic tide, eating his insides.

Ben was thirty-two. Jobless. Wifeless. Childless. Back where he started. Back where everything went bad.

Never look back.

He wanted to side with Jon and sell the ranch. He wanted to put the ranch and the past behind him just like he was putting Transk, Ipsum & Levi in his rearview mirror.

They gave you the boot, boy.

Enough!

Ben moved the leather cigar chair to the left of the fireplace out of the way, pried the floorboard free and stared at the safe. Someone besides Big E had to have the combination. Katie or Lochlan were the most likely candidates.

His stomach growled. It was past dinnertime. He replaced the floorboard and went to the kitchen.

Ben surveyed the contents of the pantry and then the fridge. There wasn't much to eat, not a fresh vegetable in the house. Canned green beans. Canned pork and beans. Canned chili beans. Even though there were low-salt and no-salt versions, everything was processed.

In New York, he'd have ordered something delivered. Beef stir-fry with quinoa sounded good. Sushi. Chicken chop salad.

You've gotten weak, boy.

No. The fact was he'd never learned to cook like an adult.

Big E's idea of providing for five boys was to tell them to make something for themselves. He'd assigned them days of the week to cook dinner. Ben and his brothers had spent many nights in the kitchen baking frozen pizza and boiling hot dogs. Some of the Blackwell brothers had progressed to a cookbook. One winter, one of Big E's wives had taught Jon the rudiments of the spice rack. Ben had survived college on dorm food, fruit, fast food and peanut butter sandwiches. Without take-out or delivery, he'd be resorting to the same.

Ben stared at the sparkly pink backsplash, the pink trimmed cabinets with glass knobs, the pink-feathered crystal chandelier.

Who's gotten weak, old man?

He'd skip dinner. He'd go for a run.

Ben grabbed his suitcase and headed upstairs toward the bedroom he'd shared with Ethan growing up. He stopped in the doorway, nearly dropping his suitcase for the second time that day.

Zoe hadn't contained her redecorating to the common areas.

Instead of bunk beds and two old oak dressers, there was a queen-size bed buried beneath a mountain of frilly pink pillows. The walls had gold-striped wallpaper. The curtains were sparkly silver and draped into a pool on the floor.

How much did this cost?

For the first time in five years, Ben almost felt sorry for his grandfather.

Ben slung his bag on the end of the bed and withdrew his running clothes. The sun was dropping low on the horizon. The wind would be picking up on the high plains, whipping down through the mountains. He dressed for chill temperatures.

A few minutes later, he ran down the steps and cut across the series of pastures that separated the ranch buildings from the river. This wasn't a run in Central Park on smooth pavement. This was uneven ground, dotted with cow pies and prairie dog potholes. There were dips and rises blanketed with brown grass. The wind filled his ears and his lungs. It whipped through his hair.

Betrayals didn't matter. Water rights didn't matter. Past mistakes didn't matter.

He climbed a metal gate and dropped into the north pasture. This was June and there wouldn't be any cattle here. By now, they'd have been moved up the slopes across the river where the grass was greener.

Ben could see Falcon Creek in the distance and how it had carved its way through the land. The banks were at least fifteen feet high and lined with a few lush elms. The tributary may have been called Falcon Creek, but during the winter and spring, it ran high and fast, like a river. And during the spring and summer, rain in the mountains could turn it into a raging torrent, sometimes with little warning. This time of year, the water was low and slow, dancing around rocks exposed to air.

Ben kept his gaze from drifting south toward the remnants of the old bridge where his parents had died in one of those flash floods. He concentrated on losing himself in the run.

He had a good stride going. Steady.

His heartbeat was strong. Steady.

He felt his equilibrium return. Steady.

But then he heard something rumble. Fast. Uneven. Angry. Like gathering thunder.

The sky was the gentle pink-orange of approaching sunset. Not a cloud was visible. But the sound was growing louder.

Ben glanced over his shoulder and swore.

An Aberdeen Angus bull was barreling down on him, hide as black as night, eyes filled with a deadly rage.

The beast was sixty feet away and closing fast. The riverbank was thirty feet ahead. It seemed like a mile.

Ben picked up the pace. Strike that. He sprinted for all he was worth. Nothing was steady anymore. Not his stride. Not his heartbeat. Not his chances of seeing another sunrise.

His only hope was to scramble up the nearest tree before that bull tossed him onto the rocky creek bed.

RACHEL'S ROAN GELDING, Utah, was ungainly but trustworthy. Nothing spooked him. Not her mother's yappy poodle. Not Poppy pulling on his mane.

Not even the sight of Ben Blackwell being chased by a charging bull.

Rachel was spooked, though. Her hands trembled and air stuck in her throat. Life on the range wasn't like living in the suburbs. She'd witnessed ranch hands gored by bulls during branding, struck by hooves while training horses, lose fingers to hay balers. Lacerations. Broken bones. Internal injuries. People got hurt on a ranch. People died.

She might not like Ben, but that didn't mean she wanted him to be trampled.

On the road separating the two properties, Rachel urged Utah into a fast trot toward the gate that opened onto Blackwell land. She freed a length of rope from her saddle as smoothly as if she was reaching for her cell phone. She loosened the noose.

Like I'm gonna rope that bull?

She wasn't that good with a lasso. A shiver of fear ran through Rachel, originating in concern for Ben. And then another shiver startled her, one brought on by the image of her roping the bull and watching helplessly as he bolted for the river. She'd be pulled off Utah's back, dragged into the pasture and serve as the bull's doormat, one that read Little Ladies Not Welcome Here.

Little ladies weren't cowboys. Little ladies didn't run ranches or track down escaped heifers or save grown men. Rachel breathed raggedly as Utah carried her closer.

Dad wouldn't cower in fear.

The Double T had survived generations because of strong Thompson leadership. It was why she'd come after the garden trampling, suit ruining heifer, because she was running things now and she couldn't rely on anyone else. Although, to be honest, this little lady had eaten dinner before embarking on her heifer search. Consequently, the cow had a big head start and was nowhere to be found.

Rachel squared her shoulders. Not that the heifer mattered right now. This rancher had other priorities.

Ben reached the trees before the bull and swung up into the branches like a monkey. He looked more like a rodeo clown in red running tights beneath black shorts and a neon yellow nylon jacket. No wonder the bull was chasing him.

The bull charged the tree, bumping the trunk without reaching Ben or knocking him down. He continued to patrol, clearly hoping to catch any straggling rodeo clowns.

Erosion and the river created a natural

"fence." The pasture was about fifteen feet above the river and a narrow, rocky bank. Tree roots prevented the pasture from eroding any farther.

Spotting Utah and Rachel, the bull took a run at the gate.

"Whoa." Rachel pulled up ten feet away and stood in her stirrups, twirling the rope above her head. This was her chance. Rope the bull and hold him long enough for Ben to escape.

She should have felt confident. The animal was a big fella and there weren't any horns to get hung up on. In short, he'd be hard to miss.

Instead of feeling like an experienced cowboy, she felt like a first-timer, afraid to let go for fear of what she'd have to do next.

The bull rammed the metal gate with his beefy shoulder, testing the barrier to see if it would give. It didn't. Thank heavens Big E kept the ranch in tip-top shape. Utah pawed the ground, refusing to back down.

Heartened, Rachel spun the rope higher. Now was the time to prove she was a rancher, not the rancher's princess daughter.

"Do *not* taunt that bull, Rachel."

"The superhero in red tights is giving me advice?" Rachel threw the rope.

It landed cockeyed on the bull's forehead

and over one ear, which seemed to annoy the beast. He shook his head and pranced on the other side of the gate, snorting. The rope fell to the ground.

Rachel sat back in the saddle and coiled the rope for another try. "My mother would say you're in a pickle, Blackwell." Her mother would tell Rachel to get her sweet patooty out of there and get help.

Rachel might have done that a year ago, before Dad died, but now things had changed. She'd changed.

"It's June," Ben griped from his position in the tree. "This pasture should be empty. The cattle should be over on higher ground across the river."

Hearing Ben's voice, the bull turned and charged the trees. He wasn't the brightest steak-on-a-hoof. He slammed into the wrong tree.

"Quit taunting the bull." Rachel's heart was having palpitations to rival the ones that killed her father. "A true cowboy would've asked where the livestock was before he took off in his pretty running clothes."

"I'm not a cowboy anymore. I'm a lawyer." Ben clung to the tree trunk and shouted at the bull, *"A lawyer!"*

"Calm down, Blackwell. You'll be reduced

to bits of superhero tights if that bull has its way with you." If she rescued him, maybe he'd be so shaken up he wouldn't show up in court tomorrow.

A girl could dream.

But this girl had a former cowboy to save first. How was she going to get him to safety?

Roping the bull was too much of a crapshoot (she wasn't that great of a roper). Riding into the pasture to Ben's rescue was too risky (for her and Utah). She tugged her cell phone out of a pocket, but there was no signal. They were in a dead zone. Literally.

She laughed. Somewhat hysterically, if truth be told.

"Go ahead," Ben said. "Have your fun."

Rachel wasn't going to explain she was losing her composure. "I'll keep him distracted and you shimmy down that tree and jump to the bank below. Chances are, if he notices you, he won't want to leap down a fifteen foot cliff." Not unless he had a very big grudge against Ben. "From there you can walk to the road." The one she and Utah were on. "And I'll escort you back to safety."

Oh, this was good. Ego-bruising good. Almost as good as the day Zoe had jilted Ben at the altar. For which—sometimes, late at night—Rachel was sorry.

But not sorry. He'd undercut the Double T's livelihood.

On Ben's wedding day, Rachel had come out of the bridal vestibule at the back of the church, wearing a red satin gown so tight she could barely breathe. Or maybe she hadn't been able to breathe because she'd lost her court case the day before to Ben.

Looking sophisticated and handsome, Ben had walked down the aisle toward Rachel, ignoring the murmurs and stares of his patiently waiting wedding guests. "Have you seen Zoe? I'm worried. She should have been here by now."

At the altar behind him, his brothers hung back in their black tuxedos. *Cowards.* At least two of them knew where Zoe was. Rachel had sworn to keep her friend's elopement a secret for as long as she could. Did she need to postpone things any longer?

"Rachel?" Ben had bent to peer into her eyes when she didn't answer. "Are you okay?" Here was the Ben she'd grown up with, always watching out for Zoe and Rachel, so unlike the heartless man she'd faced in court over the past few weeks.

Rachel had tried to tug Ben away from prying eyes. "Ben, I want to renegotiate the water rights." She sounded desperate, maybe because she was. Her father hadn't spoken to her since the verdict came in.

"Not now, Rachel." Ben glanced over her head, clearly searching for his bride.

"Yes, now. This can't wait."

"Rachel." In the middle of the aisle, in the middle of the church, Ben blurted, "If you have to ask now, the answer is no."

"You're an idiot." Rage as red as her dress pummeled Rachel's veins and caused her to raise her voice. "Zoe eloped with Big E an hour ago!"

The assembled gave a collective gasp. Ben paled.

Only then did his brothers move, rolling toward them like a fast, incoming tide. They swept Ben out the door, leaving Rachel to face the crowd alone.

"Go get help!" Interrupting Rachel's thoughts, Ben settled into a sitting position in the tree by the river. His red-clad legs dangling down from the branch he'd chosen. "I'll be here when you get back."

"Where's your backbone, Blackwell?" She urged Utah closer and leaned over to rattle the gate to get the bull's attention. Reluctantly, the bull ambled toward Rachel, huffing unhappily.

With Ben safe, Rachel's gaze drifted toward the river. How many memories did she have at the end of this road with Ben? Too many to count.

This was where Rachel came to sort out her feelings. It was where Ben came to escape his large family. By unspoken agreement, this was where they weren't Thompsons or Blackwells. This was where they could just be Rachel and Ben. This was where they could be friends without Zoe being jealous or his brothers teasing him. This was where—

Ben began to climb down the tree, quiet, like a rainbow-clad ninja.

The bull didn't notice.

This is going to work.

The light dimmed as the sun disappeared on the other side of the mountain range, leaving the world in a blue-gray twilight. Rachel needed to pick up Poppy and put her to bed or she'd be a bear tomorrow, worn out from lack of sleep. She needed to prepare the quarterly tax paperwork. She needed to refill Nana Nancy's weekly pillbox. She needed to read through her brief for court tomorrow because solid preparation was going to make her a better lawyer.

She rattled the gate some more.

A few minutes later, Rachel's rope was secured on her saddle, the bull fidgeted on the other side of the fence, and Ben stood in front of Utah, stroking the gelding's neck. "Hey, what's that platform for?" Ben gestured toward a wooden structure by the river. It looked like a dock built too high above the water.

"Zoe calls it the observation platform. It's on the website as being ideal for watching the sun rise or doing yoga." Rachel doubted Zoe had done any of those things, either. And as far as Rachel knew, Zoe didn't understand the significance of the end of this road to Ben and Rachel.

"Zoe built it?" Ben studied it with more attention than Rachel thought it deserved.

She wondered which memory came to his mind first. For her, it was always senior prom. He'd been out riding the morning after that dance and had found Rachel huddled on the bank wearing baggy sweats and no makeup with a nose stuffed with tears.

"Andy broke up with me." Rachel hadn't been able to look at Ben when she'd said it.

He hadn't said anything in response. He'd just settled down beside her, slung his arm over her shoulder and watched the sun come up over the Rockies. Back then, she'd thought he was the best Blackwell ever.

It had taken nearly a decade to prove that wasn't the case.

"The platform was Zoe's idea." Best make that clear. "She paid a ton to have it built." Rachel turned Utah toward home, pausing to add, "And you can thank me for saving you and letting you traverse Double T land without having you arrested for trespassing." The ingrate.

"Actually, this part of the road belongs to the Blackwells," Ben said in an odd voice. And then he ran a hand over his hair and jogged ahead of her.

On the other side of the fence, the bull trotted next to him, like a loyal two-ton dog.

Dismissed, Rachel held Utah back, casting one last look over her shoulder toward the river, glimmering in the sunset. Now that Ben was safe, she could think about the rescue with more detachment. Replay Ben running from a raging bull as if he was running with the football, a pack of defenders at his heels.

In high school, Ben had played all sports. He was still in good shape and looked as if he could pick up where he'd left off on any playing field.

The playing field will be my courtroom tomorrow.

Rachel smiled. Now was the time to get into her opponent's head. "Do you really go out looking like that back east?"

"Yep." He was pulling away from her in an easy stride.

Down here, the road wasn't overgrown the way it was on the section from the Double T to the first Blackwell gate. Traffic from Blackwell ranch hands, and now ranch guests, kept the weeds to a minimum.

She kicked Utah into a trot, bringing them alongside Ben. "Must be a city thing."

His white teeth flashed. "You mean my running clothes don't do it for you?"

"No." Couldn't he have developed a tick? Grown straggly gray hair? "I've seen people dress in tights before." She let that sink in before adding, "Ladies doing Zumba at the community center in Livingston, for instance."

"You've spent a lot of time commenting on my legs." He sent her a sly glance. "The only reason I can see is that they must please you."

"Still got that ego, I see."

"I call 'em as I see 'em, Thompson."

Thompson. He'd called her that in the seventh grade when he'd accepted her invitation to the Sadie Hawkins dance: *Okay, Thompson.*

"Okay, Thompson. Let's do this," he'd said again, as he led her to the dance floor, his tone as serious as if they were heading into battle against overwhelming odds.

She felt the same tummy shimmy now as she had then. Of course, years ago her nerves were from not knowing what would happen next. Would he accept her invitation? Would they slow dance? Would he try to steal a kiss?

A kiss...

She watched Ben's athletic stride, thinking about how much she missed kissing and being held in a pair of strong arms. His arms looked rather strong.

Ridiculous.

Rachel put a halt to her wandering thoughts. She wasn't interested in men right now or Ben ever. She had a ranch to save and a baby to raise. Not to mention Ben was opposing counsel at their hearing tomorrow, her best friend's ex and completely off-limits. Her mantras echoed in her head:

Win back the water rights.

Set the ranch to rights.

Get a signed custody agreement.

Learn how to be a better rancher.

Her excuses didn't make a difference. The tummy shimmy persisted.

Ben and Utah kept pace with one another. Neither was winded. If their situations had been reversed and Rachel had been jogging, she would've quit by now, clutching a deep stitch in her side. The last time she'd gotten her heart rate up in the red zone, she'd been in labor.

"Speaking of fancy dressers…" Ben half glanced Rachel's way. "I see you've got your Montana date clothes on."

"Date clothes?" Rachel had forgotten she was wearing her mother's overalls. They were too short and hit the top of her mother's fancy boots. Not to mention Mom had embroidered white poodles on the bib. *Très chic.*

"Are you planning to escort me to my door and kiss me good-night, too?" Ben laughed.

Laughed! Rachel sputtered.

The bull huffed, as if he couldn't believe Ben's ego either. Utah just kept trotting. He had a smooth gait, which probably prevented Rachel from falling off in shock.

Ben stopped jogging. "Why don't you give me a lift?"

"A lift?" Rachel squeaked. She'd barely touched the reins and Utah planted his hooves.

Traitor. She would've liked to have kept right on going.

"Or you could hurry on home to your Mama just like you did that time we stole some beer from Big E on the Fourth of July." Ben gave Rachel a wry half smile that pressed in on her chest like a hot humid day.

"We weren't alone." She huffed, at a loss as to why Ben was having such an effect on her. "I was with Andy, and you were with Zoe." There. Reminding him of Zoe ought to burst his bubble.

Or not.

Ben continued speaking as if she hadn't brought up his ex. "But if I get lost, or Ferdinand here breaks through the fence and tramples me, you're going to have to explain to the judge why I didn't show up for court in the morning. And if I don't show, there will be a continuation, and you'll look heartless for having left me out here in the cold, possibly injured."

"Geez, Blackwell." She sounded as if she was enjoying their banter. Rachel regrouped with her most serious tone. "I know this line of yours doesn't work on women in New York City."

"It could." His grin was classic Ben, delivered with intent to charm. "I haven't met many horseback-riding women in Central Park, particularly ones wearing such stylish poodle-trimmed overalls."

Rachel's cheeks heated. "And you wouldn't. Not wearing those superhero tights of yours."

He glanced down. A rumbling sound rippled through the air between them. It was so loud, even Utah turned his head toward Ben.

"Was that your stomach?" Rachel laughed. Why was she knocked off-kilter by Ben? He was a thirteen year-old jokester in a grown man's body.

"I'm hungry. There was nothing to eat in the ranch house." He tried to look forlorn.

"You're pathetic, Blackwell." And harmless. Rachel took her booted foot from the left stirrup and held out her left hand. Ben clasped her wrist, put his sneaker in the stirrup and swung up behind her, settling on the saddle blanket.

Utah didn't even look back to see what was happening.

Ben placed his hands on Rachel's hips, which was so unexpected she nearly jumped out of the saddle. Instead, she heeled Utah forward and lurched against Ben's solid chest.

She was wrong. Ben wasn't harmless. He

was handsome and charismatic and dangerous to single ladies.

Rachel shivered.

Ben's chin brushed her shoulder. "Are you ticklish?"

"No."

"Cold?"

"No." His touch made her lonely, made her regret wearing her mother's overalls and made her want to touch up her makeup. "Let it go, will you?"

He was silent. For most of a minute. "Have you been inside Big E's house lately?"

She chuckled, only because she imagined the look on Ben's face when he'd walked into his old home. "It's a bit over the top, isn't it?" Not wanting to seem disloyal, she quickly added, "I mean, it's quite an upgrade from what it was. Zoe was much more traditional in her design choices when she decorated the guest lodge."

"I haven't seen the place." And by the tone of his voice, he didn't plan to.

Another round of silence ensued. She hoped it lasted to the last Blackwell gate.

"Are they happy together?" His question was spoken so low, she almost thought she'd imagined it. Until he added, "Rach?"

"You mean Big E and Zoe? Sure, they're happy. They've been married five years." The words didn't quite ring true. Zoe was too proud to say much, but Rachel had sensed a change in her friend the past year or so. Remodeling the house hadn't been enough. Building the guest ranch hadn't been enough.

Ben sighed. His palms settled more comfortably over Rachel's waist. "What did you have for dinner?"

Did he think she was fat? He had his hands on her post-baby love-handles. She never should have eaten dinner.

"You really want to know?"

His stomach growled an answer. "Excuse me, but yes. It's like food porn. Give."

She laughed. "It's not exactly haute cuisine." Nothing like he probably ate in New York. "Chicken casserole. Steamed veggies. Homemade biscuits." Not exactly wise, given she wanted to lose that last ten pounds of baby weight. But there was nothing in the world like hot buttered biscuits to make your cares seem less important.

Ben pounced. "Was it your mother's chicken casserole? The one with the fried onions and cheese?"

"Yes."

"She used to make that for the sports banquets." Ben's stomach rumbled once more. "Her chicken casserole was better than Ms. Gardner's tamales. Better than Ms. Castillo's chicken and dumplings. Better than Ms. Maeda's stir-fry."

Rachel's mother would be thrilled with the praise and… "Hold up." This wasn't about Rachel's baby weight. "Are you trying to mooch food off me?"

"Well, if you're offering…" It seemed as if he leaned in closer. His breath was warm over her ear. "I will gladly accept your hospitality."

"Ben Blackwell." He was trying to get under her skin before tomorrow, just as she'd been trying to do with him. And he was doing a better job of it than she was! "You are *not* coming to my house. My family loathes you for stealing our water. My grandmother is convinced you're the reason my dad had a heart attack."

Ben had no comeback for that.

She took his silence to mean remorse. Which was silly. Blackwells never had regrets.

The bull finally grew tired and stopped following them. Or perhaps Ben's talk about food had made the animal hungry. He began to graze.

"I didn't know about your dad." Ben's voice

was deep and sincere. "I'm sorry. Is he going to recover?"

"No. He *died*." Rachel forced the words past a throat that wanted to close. "Nearly two years ago. I've been running things at the Double T ever since."

"I didn't know," Ben said again as they reached the gate leading to the main Blackwell property. The guesthouse roof and glowing windows stood out on the distant horizon. "I'm sorry."

"Why are you apologizing to me?" Rachel brought Utah to a stop. Ahead of her, the road was choked with weeds. "We hate each other."

He slid to the ground and moved to Utah's head, rubbing behind the gelding's forelock beneath the browband. It was the kind of gesture a cowboy would give to a beloved horse, and at odds with the out-of-place jogging clothes Ben wore.

Utah leaned into his touch. Without realizing it, Rachel leaned forward as well.

Ben stared up at her. "I don't hate you, Thompson. You're one of the few people in town who had the courage to tell me the truth on my wedding day."

The way he said it…as if her shouting at him in the church aisle all those years ago was a kind thing… The way his blue eyes looked at her…as if she was the one person in town he could trust…

Don't let him get in your head.

And stop thinking about kissing him.

Heart pounding, Rachel sat back in the saddle. "This isn't a Kumbaya moment, Blackwell. My best friend dumped you." Rachel had to remember where her loyalties lay.

Ben didn't so much as flinch. "How long before the wedding did you know?"

Rachel had wondered if he'd ever ask her this question. "Too long," she admitted. She'd tried to talk Zoe out of her infatuation with Big E, but the old man had dazzled Zoe with expensive gifts and undivided attention. "They love each other, really." Weird as it was, it had turned out all right in the end.

It took him a moment, but Ben nodded. "Do you have any idea where they are?"

Rachel shook her head. "Big E likes to go camping off the grid. And in return for Zoe's patience, he takes her on a shopping spree." Rachel was amazed Zoe had any tolerance for her husband's whims, which were so different from her own. But Rachel supposed shopping without worrying what things cost was a good incentive.

Ben chewed on Rachel's answer, testing its validity, as any good lawyer would. "They left eight or nine weeks ago."

"They were gone for three months last spring." After Rachel had told Zoe she was pregnant, news her friend hadn't exactly been pleased to hear. "Don't worry."

"Thanks for the insight." And then Ben smiled, his gaze never leaving Rachel's face as he backed away from Utah. "Good luck in court tomorrow, Thompson."

"Ah, come on, Blackwell. You don't mean that."

He laughed and shook his head, handsome and charming and confident. "I don't mean that."

Rachel gave Utah full rein and headed for home.

But she could feel Ben's eyes on her as she rode off, and she could feel his hands on her waist for a lot longer.

CHAPTER FOUR

"ARE THOSE PANTYHOSE?"

Ben stopped foraging in the guest lodge's refrigerator and bumped the door closed with his hip, having found a cold beer and a container with Mrs. Gardner's leftover tamales. He placed his food on the black marble-topped island and stared at Katie Montgomery, smiling at her verbal jab.

From what Ethan had told Ben, Katie was Big E's young, right hand "man" lately, more so than her father, Lochlan, the ranch foreman. Ben supposed it was because Lochlan was Big E's age and slowing down.

Katie entered the kitchen. She had fiery red hair, which contrasted against her white T-shirt and nearly threadbare pale blue jeans.

Rachel had been right. The finishes in the guesthouse were much more traditional— white Shaker cupboards, whitewashed wood tile flooring. The light fixtures had no feathers and there was no pink anywhere. In fact, there was nothing overtly feminine in the kitchen.

Nothing as overt as the feminine curve of Rachel's hips. He'd originally asked for a leg up to unnerve Rachel, to shake her confidence before court tomorrow. It was low, but he was playing catch-up in this case.

Surprisingly, once he was riding behind her, the case had been the furthest thing from his mind. His hands had rested on her waist with surprising ease. He'd enjoyed teasing her and had been disappointed when he was denied her mother's leftovers, only to be saddened to hear of her father's passing. It was tough to lose a parent.

Seeing Rachel at the end of the road to the river had brought back too many memories, including the day he'd learned his parents had died. He'd saddled his horse, taken a bedroll and tried to head for the hills, but the bridge was out. So he'd come to the end of the road and cried. He was twelve and he wasn't supposed to cry anymore, but there had been no one there to witness his sobs, except his horse, Rodrigo.

And then he'd felt a warm body at his side. It'd been Rachel. She didn't say anything. She took his hand and laid her head on his shoulder. They sat like that for a long time, until Jon rode up and told Ben he had to come home.

"Oh, sorry, they're not pantyhose." Katie came to stand beside Ben, still staring at his legs.

Like Ben, Katie had grown up on the Blackwell Ranch. She was five years younger than Ben and as close to a sister as he could have. Reality was, they were related, since her older sister had married Ben's younger brother Chance, although she'd died a couple of years ago, leaving Chance a single dad.

"For your information," Ben said, pushing thoughts of Rachel to the back of his mind, "these are running tights."

Katie grinned. "You know, I've only seen women wear things like that in—"

"Livingston? At the community center? For Zumba class?" At her amused nod, Ben added, "Just so you know, on the East Coast, men wearing tights is a thing."

"Interesting." Katie filled a tray with small containers of sugary toppings, chocolate chips and a variety of syrups. She removed a tub of vanilla ice cream from the large freezer. She was either very hungry, or the ranch guests were having sundaes.

Ben was more interested in dinner than dessert. He glanced around the lavish kitchen. "Where's the microwave?"

Katie showed him a cubby on the side of the gigantic island. Before he realized it, she'd dished out a plate of tamales, set the microwave to work and returned the leftovers to the fridge.

Ben thanked her. "Hey, what's a bull doing in the north pasture?"

"Chasing after runners in red tights?" Her eyes glinted with mischief. "Honestly, he's a slippery fella and I wasn't able to move him by myself. It's been a challenge fulfilling our commitments to the guests and the ranch with limited staff."

"Isn't he needed for breeding season with the herd? Never mind." Ben shook his head. He didn't need to worry about ranch business. "I have to open the safe in Big E's study. Can you do the honors?"

Katie leaned against the counter and crossed her arms over her chest. "Whatever you want probably isn't there. Big E is more careful with his money and paperwork nowadays."

"His secrets, you mean. Regardless, there's a document he kept in there that I need." To reassure himself that the corners he'd cut five years ago weren't going to be the downfall of the Blackwell water supply.

Voices carried from the common room.

"The safe will have to wait until tomorrow." The front doors opened wide and Katie gestured toward the folks congregating behind her. "I've got to take care of the guests."

Ben frowned. "I want it tonight. Tell me the combination."

The noise level swelled. "I don't remember what it is." Katie put an ice cream scoop on the tray.

"I'll ask your dad then."

Katie leveled a hard gaze at him. "It's too late."

Ben drank some beer and considered her words. "I just heard about Dave Thompson's passing. Lochlan isn't—?"

"He's very much alive." Katie turned back to the tray, her spine rigid. "He's off the clock is all."

Her father must have aged quite a bit in the time that Ben had been away from the ranch. Maybe there'd been medical issues, too. "The Ziglers are having an ice cream social tonight," Katie continued. "I'm the only one working. I'll be here for another two hours, unless you want to make sure they have enough nuts and sprinkles for their sundaes. And then I've got to make the rounds, put the mares and the foals in the barn and lock things up. I've had to prioritize my time since Big E left."

The tug to help was strong, but Ben was used to hardening his heart where the ranch was concerned. "I can wait until morning." The microwave beeped. Ben removed his dinner and sat on a barstool. "But only if you can open the safe by seven. I have to be at the county courthouse by nine thirty tomorrow."

"Normally, I'd say that's no problem." Katie hefted the tray to her shoulder and then picked up the tub of ice cream. "But things have been crazy lately and my schedule is never what it's supposed to be."

"Seven, Katie," Ben said firmly.

"I'll try," she said, looking more worn out than her blue jeans.

THE NEXT MORNING, Ben made it to the county courthouse with a few minutes to spare.

He'd waited too long for Katie, who'd been a no-show. When he finally got her phone number from Ethan, who was living in town with his fiancée, Grace, Katie had texted back that she'd overslept and couldn't stop by because she was prepping breakfast for the guests.

During the thirty-minute drive, Ben had told himself not to worry. Worst case, Rachel might be given more of the ranch's river water. She couldn't have the yellowed piece of paper documenting the land trade. She was an honest lawyer, the kind of lawyer he'd once thought he'd be. Working with clear-cut goals for honorable clients. People with vulnerabilities that needed defending, not corporations set on limiting liability for their own mistakes. The image of a baby being held by her mother resurfaced, along with a previous courtroom experience.

"Mr. Blackwell, maybe you should remember which party you represent in this hearing." Judge Scarpetti's rebuke a few weeks back hadn't gone unnoticed by the powers that be at Transk, Ipsum & Levi. Their lawyers weren't supposed to have hearts or show sympathy to plaintiffs.

Ben shook off the memory and walked the narrow marble hallways of the county court, dodging cowboys who paced nervously in their best boots and blue jeans, and lawyers in dark suits with bolo ties. He spotted Rachel in a gray jacket and matching skirt outside the door to Courtroom Three.

"Good morning." Ben had consumed a strong cup of coffee on the drive over, but to unnerve Rachel, he plucked her coffee cup from her hand and took a sip. He nearly spat it right back out. "This isn't coffee."

"It's an organic protein drink." Rachel smirked.

Her blond hair was in a tight bun and she wore black-rimmed glasses, undoubtedly trying to make herself look more deserving of a judge's respect. It might have worked if she hadn't had a series of wrinkles on her collar and a wisp of blond hair hanging over her shoulder.

"I see you're going with the Clark Kent persona this morning." At his questioning look, Rachel added, "A suit. No tights."

"Not even a superhero could drink this stuff." He thrust the cup back at her, swallowing a bitter aftertaste. "Out of curiosity, what are you going to do with the water if you win?"

"Not that it's any of your business, but we're going to plant hay and alfalfa in the pasture near the river and irrigate it." She dug a tissue from her purse and wiped the lip of her mug where his lips had touched it. "More feed equals more fat cattle."

"Smart." Existing pipes. Land sloping toward the river for good drainage. Even as he analyzed her intentions, Ben's gaze roamed the hallway, looking for someone who would help him create a seed of doubt in Rachel's mind. Someone who looked busy and bored and...kind of like Ben—out of place, not your typical Montana lawyer. "Did you consider mediation with the Blackwells before filing?"

Bingo. A middle-aged man with a gray receding hairline wearing an expensive suit was checking something on his phone. He looked like he could be a Montana water company lawyer.

"Mediation?" Rachel's slender brows drew low. "Big E would never bargain with me."

"That's too bad." Ben edged closer to her and lowered his voice. "Big E would've haggled with you to fly under the radar of the water company. The Falcon County Water Company would like nothing more than to take water away from both our ranches. They're here to watch." He nodded toward Mr. Middle-Age Phone Checker.

Sometimes he wondered if he was going to hell for all the truth-stretching he did in a routine workday.

"Nice try." Rachel turned her back on him to face the courtroom doors, not buying Ben's ploy.

"That's not a water company lawyer. Besides, the water company doesn't need our water."

She was as naive as she was beautiful.

And thoughts like that would lose him this case.

Ben shrugged and checked the time on his watch. "If you say so."

The bailiff came out of the courtroom. He was a reedy, older man with thinning white hair and thinning patience, if his skeletal smile was any indication. "You here for the case of Double T versus the Blackwell Ranch?" At their nods, he indicated they should come in.

"Good luck, Thompson," Ben said to Rachel.

She glared at him. "You don't mean that, Blackwell."

"I don't mean that," Ben agreed, grinning. He opened the door but went through first. Rachel needed to understand who was top dog around here.

The courtroom hadn't been redecorated in decades—dark wood paneling, dark wood theater-type seating, dim lighting. The judge's bench was nearly six feet tall and stained a deep brown. The top edge was worn where lawyers usually approached for a private word, as if they'd clung to the edge of the bench in desperation.

And look. It was Ben's lucky day. The middle-aged man with the cell phone had come in and taken a seat in the back. Ben caught Rachel's eye and directed her attention to the man.

She frowned, but it wasn't a frown of disagreement. There was doubt in her eyes now.

"All rise. The court of Falcon County is now in session. Judge Edwards presiding."

Ben stood, processing the name just announced. *Edwards...* Why did he know that name?

A door behind the judge's bench opened. A wisp of white hair was visible and then the judge mounted the steps to her elevated seat, revealing in stages white hair tightly pulled back, a wide forehead, beady eyes devoid of makeup, a hook nose, thin lips framed in disapproving wrinkles.

It can't be.

Ben forced himself not to grip the table in desperation.

It was.

The judge was Myrna Edwards, formerly Myrna Edwards Blackwell. One of his grandfather's ex-wives. Back then, she'd been a lawyer. She'd lasted five days as the wife of Big E. One day for each Blackwell brother.

This was not good.

Myrna should have recused herself from the case. The fact that she hadn't was a bad sign, one in a long string of bad signs.

"Be seated." Myrna opened a file she'd brought with her, glanced at it and then at Ben, who was reminded of the last time he'd seen her.

She'd wanted to take the ranch's new truck since Big E had driven her car into town, but Ethan, with Ben's approval, had disconnected the spark plug wires. The truck wouldn't start. The boys had been attempting to drive her crazy since Big E had brought her home from their courthouse wedding.

"Boys, can you find Jon?" Those beady eyes had drilled Ben's gaze with a chilly combination of anger and restraint. "I need his truck. I have to get to court."

Ben and Ethan had laughed and disappeared into the main barn, watching her from the hayloft with Tyler, Chance and Jon. Myrna was nothing if not resourceful. She'd discovered the tractor Jon had left to the side of the house, which still had the key in it, and she'd driven to court, never to return.

This was really not good.

"Well, well, well. What have we here?" The way Myrna smiled made the pulse throb in Ben's temple. "Slumming it, are we, Mr. Blackwell?"

Ben turned on the charm. "So nice to see you again, Judge Edwards."

Myrna wasn't buying it. She shuffled some paperwork. "Are you licensed to practice in Montana, Mr. Blackwell?"

"I have my Montana certificate of good standing." He produced it immediately from his hard-sided, silver briefcase. Heaven only knew why he'd kept his license current in the state.

The bailiff took it and handed it to the judge.

"How fortuitous for the Blackwells." Myrna frowned and turned her attention to Rachel. "Ms. Thompson." Her voice was as hard and sharp as fresh icicles after a New York blizzard. "The issue of water rights between the Double T and the Blackwell Ranch was settled five years ago. Why are we here today?"

"Your Honor." Rachel stood. She was confident. Trusting in the law. Completely undeserving of having her water stolen by Big E.

By me.

Ben tamped down the slow churn of guilt in his gut and ran a hand over his hair.

"The Blackwell Ranch hasn't been using their allotment of river water." Rachel shoved her glasses up her nose. "Which brings up the question of positions in terms of river water rights."

"Your Honor, I move for a continuance on this issue." Ben barely drew a breath before pressing on. "Elias Blackwell has been out of town for two months and I only saw the brief when I arrived yesterday. I'm sure that Ms. Thompson and I can come to an equitable agreement outside of the courtroom." And wasn't that what every judge wanted?

"Objection." Rachel didn't quite roll her eyes, but they did circle to the ceiling above Myrna's head before coming to rest on the judge. "The Blackwells were given five business days to review the brief. Just because Mr. Blackwell didn't prepare—"

"Objection. I was busy working other cases in New York."

Licking your wounds after being fired, more like, boy.

"Can I get a ruling in?" Myrna demanded in a raised voice.

"Please," Ben murmured.

Rachel gripped her pen. "But Your Honor—"

"Silence." Myrna held up a sheaf of papers. "According to your brief, Ms. Thompson, you're wanting to reinstate your first position rights, plus ten percent additional volume to make up for the previous five years' losses."

"Yes, Your Honor." Rachel released her pen slowly, as if her fingers had cramped around it.

Myrna dropped the brief onto her desk. "Your opinion, Mr. Blackwell?"

"Your Honor, the Blackwell Ranch is a significantly larger operation that is growing and requires more water than the Double T will ever use."

"Perhaps they'll have to buy their water from the Double T," Rachel said slyly, unwittingly revealing her end goal.

If the Blackwell Ranch was truly in financial straits, as Ethan had said, Rachel wouldn't see a dime of Blackwell money.

"Since both arguments have merit, I want you two to hash out an agreement on your own time, as you've suggested, Mr. Blackwell." Myrna tilted her chin up and squinted at her computer screen. "The court will reconvene on this matter in one week at the same time, whereby I expect you to come to terms."

A week? Ben would have preferred she say

by Monday. "And if we come to an agreement sooner?"

"The court docket is full. I'll see you in a week's time regardless." Myrna rapped her gavel. "Next case."

Ben glanced at the middle-aged lawyer in the back of the courtroom. No matter how busy the court seemed, there was still a chance he could broker a deal and get Myrna's sign-off in less than seven days.

"Are you willing to talk compromise?" Ben sauntered out of the courtroom with Rachel, holding the door for her this time.

"My dad died. We sold off land and cattle to stay afloat. *Compromise?*" She walked with a spring in her step, as if she'd already won. "What do you think?"

He lengthened his stride to catch up to her. "You've waited a long time to say that, haven't you?"

"Darn right, I have." Rachel smiled dreamily.

And just like that, she stole his breath. She wasn't a wreck. She wasn't an inexperienced lawyer without skills. She was a beautiful woman turning heads as she passed.

His steps slowed. Since when was he attracted to Rachel Thompson?

Since you decided to "see" her, boy.

Ben shook his head, trying to erase the sputtering feeling that Rachel Thompson was exquisite, confident and a force to be reckoned with. She was a pain in the neck. Specifically, his neck.

He hurried on, trying to stomp out the spark of attraction with every determined step. "Did it feel as good as you imagined? Tossing that in my face?"

"Better." She stopped and faced him. Still grinning. Still radiant. Still annoying in that she was an obstacle to Ben getting on with his life. His shallow, sellout life.

And it was a crime how kissable she looked when she grinned like that. Completely and utterly kissable. When had this woman, his former friend, become so alluring?

Ben cleared his throat, trying to clear his observations of Rachel along with it. "Let's go get coffee and talk about this." Ben was free the rest of the day and ready to leave Myrna's turf and the unwanted appeal of Rachel behind.

"Ms. Thompson?" A harried-looking woman carrying a toddler stopped a few feet away. "I hate to interrupt, but I wanted you to know I'm ready. My mom will be here any minute to watch Alex."

"It's no interruption, Nelly." Rachel showed more warmth to this woman than she'd shown to Ben all morning. "How are you, buddy?" She smiled at the toddler and gave him a high five.

The power lawyer image faded. Rachel became infinitely soft, infinitely huggable, infinitely more kissable. Ben gripped his briefcase with one hand and shoved the other in his pants pocket. He'd stolen her water. There could be no embracing, no pulling her close, no tasting her lips.

Soft is beatable.

That was the sentiment that had driven Ben for years. The sentiment that had advanced his career in New York. Until he'd met one of the plaintiffs in a case. Until softness had a face and was an orphan, like Ben.

He felt ill.

Rachel checked her phone. "We have just enough time to grab a snack for Alex before we're due in court."

Ben was sure Rachel expected him to politely retreat into the background, head back to the ranch and await her call. He'd bet that's how she treated those other Montana lawyers she dealt with.

Ben wasn't polite. He wasn't patient. He

didn't always follow the rules. That's why he got results.

He headed back inside the courthouse.

CHAPTER FIVE

"WHAT ARE YOU doing here?" Rachel spotted her adversary in the courtroom as soon as she walked in.

Ben had taken a seat in the visitors' gallery, behind the table she was assigned to, standing out in his tailored suit like a diamond in a shallow bowl of wooden beads. Broad shoulders, shiny hair, a hint of a grin. Back in high school, she'd been proud to call him *friend*. He was handsome and a Blackwell, one of the most powerful families in the valley. Today, she was itching for a reason to demand the bailiff throw him out of court.

"I'm a courtroom junkie." Ben leaned back in his seat, spreading his arms on top of the adjacent seat backs. "Pay me no mind."

Ben Blackwell had never been ignorable.

Rachel pushed her glasses up her nose, wishing she could punch something else.

Nelly came forward and joined Rachel at the table, looking nervous in her white polyester dress and pleather flats. Her mother sat outside in the hallway with little Alex.

"Go home, Ben." Rachel didn't want him watching her, judging her, holding Rachel up to the standards of a tough litigator and finding her lacking. "You don't belong here."

Ben didn't move. No. That wasn't right. Ben's lips moved. His smile widened, flashing a mouthful of teeth that appeared cavity-free.

A sound came out of Rachel so low and feral, Nelly gasped in the chair beside her.

Ben just laughed.

Nelly's husband entered with his lawyer. Darnell was a big man with a hardheaded attitude and a perpetual scowl, which made him look more ornery than the bull Rachel had tried to rope last night. He tried to catch Nelly's eye, but Rachel had instructed her client to ignore her husband completely.

"Geez, he's big." Ben leaned forward, making his seat groan. "I've got your back, Thompson."

"All rise…" The bailiff began the court proceedings before Rachel could tell Ben to butt out.

Judge Edwards took her seat, sending a questioning look Ben's way before getting down to business. "Counselors, I'm very disappointed that mediation didn't work for the O'Ryans. Especially you, Ms. Thompson, as failed mediation seems to be a habit you're cultivating."

"Your Honor." Rachel stood. "My client was threatened by her husband in mediation. We had no recourse but to appear before you today."

"Lies," Darnell muttered, loud enough for the judge to hear.

"Careful, Mr. O'Ryan, or you'll be found in contempt." Judge Edwards stared at Darnell, her eyes narrowed to hard black dots.

Darnell stared at the ceiling, biceps flexing beneath the chambray sleeves of his shirt.

Judge Edwards turned her attention back to Rachel. "What is your recommendation for child and spousal support, Ms. Thompson?"

"Three—"

Ben coughed thickly, over and over, as if he was dying. He finally choked out, *"Five hundred."*

Rachel glared at Ben. Five hundred was unheard of in these parts.

"What was that, counselor?" Judge Edwards assessed Rachel with a death-sentence stare and then leaned slightly to the side to give Ben his share of disapproval. A thick lock of her white hair fell forward, uncharacteristic of Judge Edwards, who never looked shaken, unlike Rachel. "The court warns that another interruption will result in contempt, just as sure as I've got orthopedic supports in my shoes."

"Your Honor," Rachel began. "We request…" she half glanced at Ben "…five hundred dollars." Why not shoot for the moon?

Nelly paled, looking like she might faint. Darnell huffed like the air had gotten thin on his side of the courtroom.

Judge Edwards made a notation in her file. "That sounds reasonable."

"Reasonable?" Darnell rocketed to his feet and curled his fist in Nelly's direction. "I will not pay for *my wife* to date other men. I will not pay for a house I don't live in. And I will not pay for some kid when I'm not even sure he's mine."

Rachel's knees felt weak. Darnell was a bully and used to backing up his loud claims with force. Nelly had shown Rachel the bruises on her arms where her husband had grabbed her during mediation. Rachel had taken pictures and sent them to the sheriff, who'd told her they couldn't do anything until Nelly filed a complaint, which she hadn't done. Not this time, nor any of the previous times.

Judge Edwards pounded her gavel as if she was driving a nail into a two-by-four. "Order! Order in the court. This is your last warning, Mr. O'Ryan."

The elderly bailiff took a few steps forward, glaring at Darnell, whose attorney got him to quiet down. Everyone in the courtroom took a breath.

"The way I understand it," Ben said into the void. "She won't be your wife after the judge signs those papers."

Standing again, Darnell growled like a race car revving up to charge off the starting line. He shook off his lawyer's hold.

"Order!" the judge warned.

Based on Ben's behavior, he had no idea what that word meant. "And you'll be required *by law* to pay five hundred big ones every month." Ben stood, as if preparing to leave. "Your wife and son deserve a thousand."

Darnell released a war cry and hopped over the rickety wooden railing separating the visitors seats from the courtroom proper. Two strides and he launched himself in the air.

Ben was a dead man.

What happened next seemed to play out in slow motion. Nelly screamed, scrambling as far away from her husband as she could. The viewing gallery gave a collective gasp.

And Rachel? Rachel couldn't breathe.

Darnell's flying tackle was met with a deft swing of Ben's silver briefcase. The crack of skull against metal echoed in the high-ceilinged courtroom louder than the judge's pounding gavel.

And then everything resumed in real time.

Nelly was still screaming. Darnell was flopping on the floor like a hooked fish fighting for air. Several onlookers ran out into the hallway shouting for help. The elderly bailiff proved to be a man of wiry strength, dropping onto Darnell's back like a pro wrestler sensing an opportunity.

When order was finally restored, Darnell was lying face down on the floor being handcuffed, the judge had lost control of another stiff lock of white hair, and Rachel had a sneaking suspicion that she was going to come out ahead on this case.

Turned out Darnell's head wasn't so hard after all. He couldn't get to his feet.

Ben returned to his seat, examined the dent in his briefcase and then straightened his tie.

"Mr. O'Ryan." Anger amplified the judge's

voice. "You are ordered to serve a weekend in jail."

Nelly did the I-want-to-be-invisible slump in her chair, lower lip trembling.

"Objection." Rachel came to her feet. "Two days doesn't seem long enough, Your Honor."

"Overruled, Ms. Thompson." The judge glared at Darnell. "This man will not miss out on work to appease the court, and then use that as an excuse not to pay his five-hundred-dollar-a-month child and spousal support. Based on his behavior here today, if he misses a payment by so much as one day, the court will garnish his wages. I want papers with these divorce terms presented to me on Monday. Do you understand what's going on, Mr. O'Ryan?"

"It's not fair," Darnell slurred. His head swung as if it was too heavy for him to hold up.

"I'll make sure he understands," Darnell's lawyer said.

"Bailiff, please take Mr. O'Ryan downstairs for processing and a medical evaluation. And then return here to escort Ms. Thompson and Mr. Blackwell into my chambers."

What? Rachel had barely sat down when she had to rise again. "Your Honor, I—"

"Will see me in chambers in a few minutes." Judge Edwards stood and disappeared by degrees behind her tall bench.

The bailiff removed a swaying Darnell from the room.

Rachel's mind whirled with the implications of what had just happened. She'd lost control of her case. Unbidden, a new mantra was added to her list.

Win back the water rights.

Set the ranch to rights.

Get a signed custody agreement.

Learn how to be a better rancher.

Learn how to be a better lawyer.

She resented that last one. It brought a bitter taste to her mouth and cast doubt into her soul. She whirled on Ben. "You're incorrigible. You have no limits. No…no…decorum. No *honor*."

Ben ran a hand over his hair but said nothing.

Because that's what good lawyers did. They knew when to speak up and when to stay silent. They knew how to work people and situations and the system to their advantage as intuitively as they knew how to breathe.

And Rachel didn't. What had she gotten herself into?

She wanted to be sick. Preferably all over Ben's expensive shoes.

"I need air," Nelly said in a shaky voice.

Rachel helped her client to the hallway and into the arms of her mother.

"Five hundred dollars a month," Nelly broke down in tears. "I can only dream it's true."

"Five… I was praying she'd get two," Nelly's mother admitted. She was sturdily built with long brown hair and a harried smile that characterized most of Rachel's clients. "You are a miracle worker, Ms. Thompson."

Rachel wasn't the miracle worker, Ben was. She marched back into the empty courtroom and glared at him. "What was that all about?"

"You should be thanking me." Ben straightened his shirt cuffs. "I got your client an extra three hundred a month and by Monday, she'll be divorced."

"You staged that." Rachel shoved her folder into her leather briefcase when she wanted to shove her hands over his mouth and wipe that grin away. "Poking at him on purpose."

"Yes, I did." The unapologetic grin showed no signs of diminishing.

The feral growl she'd made earlier collected in her throat, making it hard to speak with any semblance of decorum. "In what court is goading a man until he tries to kill you acceptable?"

"I do my pro bono work in night court. Provoking a client to show his or her true colors expedites things." Ben patted his briefcase, which she now noticed had several other dings. "I made sure he stayed down so he wouldn't hurt you or your client."

Rachel was too angry to admit how satisfying that had been. "Mr. Blackwell…" Now she sounded as old and stuffy as Judge Edwards, a thought simultaneously empowering and worrying. "There are rules in the courtroom." She tugged her suit jacket smooth. "A code of honor to be upheld."

Ben's smile fell so hard his face seemed to pale.

Heartened, she pressed on. "The courtroom is the last bastion of civility and integrity."

Color returned to his cheeks. "You have no idea what happens in the legal trenches, do you?" Ben looked as if he…as if he *pitied* her.

Rachel shook the feeling off and pointed at the scuffed linoleum between them. "This is where the playing field is leveled."

He leaned into the argument. "This is where things get dirty."

She leaned right along with him. "This is where dirt is revealed."

"Only the dirt the opposing counsel wants you to see." His smile, the one she hated, was back—the one that said Ben knew more than she did about being a lawyer. "Admit it. You learned something today."

The truth rammed Rachel and her insecurities like that bull had rammed the Blackwell gate last night.

The bailiff returned, pausing in the doorway to talk to someone in the hallway.

"You're wrong." Rachel pushed her glasses more firmly in place and lowered her voice. "This is where we're going to be reprimanded."

"Thompson." Ben moved to Rachel's side as if they were on the same team. He smelled of fresh woodsy cologne when she probably smelled like her bitter protein drink. "The judge didn't cite us with contempt. We're fine."

Us? We?

There was danger here, perhaps just as much to her heart as to her career since her courage was bolstered with Ben at her side. "I've never been called back to chambers," she admitted.

"It's not so bad." Ben picked up her briefcase and handed it to her. "Sometimes you need to push the limits to get justice for your client."

Their hands brushed when she claimed the handle of her briefcase.

Rachel's breath caught, slowing her comeback. "Justice? Since when were you interested in justice?"

"Only all the time." He raised his brows. "It's why I went into law."

"Uh…" She didn't remember it that way. She thought that Ben, like herself, had gone into law because it was a classy means to make a lot of money. Or so she'd thought. She hadn't taken into consideration that she'd have a limited client pool in Falcon Creek.

"You don't remember me whining about unfair punishments?" Ben said in mock horror. "I had four brothers and we weren't allowed to bicker. Big E handed out edicts without regard to circumstance. I wanted a future where I won fair and square." This last came out at a considerably lower volume.

Was he doubting his ability to practice law aboveboard? Oh, she had him now. "If you believe in justice, then you should concede to me on the water issue."

Ben smiled down at her in a way that made

her heart stutter. "And give you everything you want? Where's the justice for the Blackwells? For Ferdinand?"

His ability to make fun of himself took some of the wind out of her sails. She glanced at the bailiff, willing herself not to cave. "Your cattle have been getting fat on irrigated pastures while ours forage for dried grass, none of which was necessary."

"Okay," Ben allowed, surprising her. "What we should do is sit down and figure out how much each ranch needs before the water company—"

"Don't try to scare me with your water company boogey man."

Ben's arm swung wide, encompassing the empty courtroom. "You don't see him here, do you?"

He couldn't be right. And yet…the man he'd pointed out in the hall had only watched their proceedings.

"Sir? Ma'am?" The bailiff gestured them closer. "The judge will see you now."

The heat of the unknown made her palms sweat. Rachel hurried to follow the bailiff, unsteady in her heels.

Judge Edwards was turned sideways at her

desk, typing, when they came in. "Sit down. I'll be done in a moment."

Rachel took a calming breath and made the mistake of looking at Ben, who was smiling. *Smiling!* Did nothing throw the man off his game?

Judge Edwards faced them. She'd smoothed her hair into place since the events in the courtroom. "Ms. Thompson, I don't think well of lawyers who allow themselves to be manipulated by the peanut gallery."

Rachel threw herself on the mercy of the judge. "I'm sorry, Your Honor."

Judge Edwards measured Rachel's sincerity before nodding and fixing her gaze on Ben. "You were Day Three, weren't you?"

"Yes, ma'am." For once, Ben's smile seemed forced.

The elderly woman leaned forward, her gaze narrowing to small dots again. "Do you have any idea how much heartache you and your brothers caused with your shenanigans?"

Rachel was at a loss. She looked between the two, trying to figure out what was going on.

"In my defense, Your Honor," Ben said evenly, "I was twelve and grieving."

"What are we talking about?" Rachel blurted.

Ben spared her a glance. "Myrna—"

"Judge Edwards to you." The judge looked down her nose at Ben, no small feat considering how short she was and that they were both sitting.

"Judge Edwards—" Ben corrected with a nod to the older woman "—married my grandfather a month after my parents died."

Rachel knew about Big E's numerous marriages, but had forgotten about this one, perhaps because she'd been so young when it happened.

"And…" Judge Edwards prompted.

"And we facilitated her release." Ben lowered his voice, as if they were in a crowded room, not a judge's chambers. "You know, Your Honor, that marriage of yours wasn't meant to last."

"Grow up!" the judge snapped, gripping the edge of her desk and rocking back in her seat. A lock of white hair fell onto her forehead. "Just because your marriage never got out of the starting gate doesn't mean all marriages fail. I was in my fifties. Of course, *I* wanted to believe it was true love."

Perhaps this had nothing to do with the spectacle associated with the O'Ryan case. Perhaps this was about the bad blood between

Judge Edwards and the Blackwells. In which case, Rachel was at risk of being collateral damage. She tried to make herself invisible.

She shouldn't have worried. Judge Edwards was on a roll. "The five of you boys railroaded me out the door. And then none of you were brave enough to drive me off the land." When Ben opened his mouth to speak, Judge Edwards waved him to silence with more irritation than a traffic cop outside the final night of the annual rodeo in Bozeman. "You think I don't remember you stranding me at the ranch when I had to be in court? You think I've forgotten what it was like to drive a tractor while wearing a suit and heels?"

After a year of balancing a legal life with ranch management, Rachel felt a sudden kinship with Judge Edwards. Driving a tractor in heels would suck.

"A stolen tractor," Ben unwisely pointed out.

Judge Edwards tsk-tsked as if she were exasperated with him.

"The facts are, ma'am, that my parents had just died, it was too soon for me and my brothers to accept another mother figure into the house, and I was a twelve-year-old boy. It's well documented that twelve-year-old boys make at least ten stupid mistakes a day."

If the expression on the judge's face was any indication, she thought a lawyer in his thirties made at least as many mistakes per day as twelve-year-old boys.

Rachel waited for Ben's comeuppance with bated breath.

"Mr. Blackwell." Judge Edwards's words weren't just chilly. They were hard chunks of ice. "You aren't twelve anymore. If you want to continue to practice in my courtroom, there will be no more shenanigans. Understood?"

Rachel sat back in her chair. Stunned.

That's it? A warning?

Rachel's neck twinged. If that was Ben's punishment, no wonder he was so bold in the courtroom.

"Yes, ma'am," Ben said, as contrite as could be. "Thank you, ma'am."

The judge turned her attention back to Rachel. "Ms. Thompson, you have to ask for what your client needs."

"And then some," Ben added.

Judge Edwards frowned at him. "Mr. Blackwell, you are dismissed."

The twinge in Rachel's neck spread into

her right shoulder. Why was she being asked to stay?

Ben stood. "I apologize, Your Honor."

The judge stared at him over the top of her glasses. "For...?"

"For what happened all those years ago." He reached for Rachel's hand and drew her to her feet. "When I mixed your whites with your colors on day three of your marriage."

"You went through my unmentionables." Judge Edwards cleared her throat and smoothed her hair back in place. "No lady should be subjected to that. It's not an honorable thing to do."

Maybe it was Rachel's imagination, but Ben seemed to draw back when his honor was impinged.

"Again, I'm sorry." Ben was like a soldier, unwilling to leave a man behind. He towed Rachel smoothly toward the door. "And I apologize for my behavior today. It was unbecoming of a lawyer in your court."

Stunned by the events of the morning, awed by Ben's diversionary tactic, Rachel allowed herself to be led.

"It's a red letter day." Judge Edwards waved them toward the door. "So many Blackwell apologies. That's more than I got from your grandfather."

"I'm sorry for that, too." Ben gripped the door handle.

Rachel imagined she gripped his hand just as tightly.

"Ease off the sucking-up pedal, Mr. Blackwell." The judge didn't say any more until he opened the door. "Oh, and Mr. Blackwell. Some advice? There'll come a day when that banged-up briefcase is going to fail you. And then you'll have to rely on the law."

Ben had nothing to say to that.

CHAPTER SIX

"I LIKE MY odds in this case," Rachel said to Ben as they stepped out into the bright summer sunshine. She switched her eyeglasses for sunglasses.

Your odds stink.

Ben held the response and his pride in check. Mediation. A summons to judge's chambers. Had he come out ahead? He'd have to say yes. But the game was still in play. He couldn't blatantly rub it in Rachel's face. "We need to meet and hash things out."

"My calendar is filled for the rest of the day," Rachel said.

It was lunchtime. The courthouse parking lot was empty. Rachel headed toward a red-and-white double-cab truck that was so old, it could have been her purchased new by her grandfather.

Thankfully, the spell she'd cast over him earlier with her beauty seemed to have worn off. Gone was the urge to hold, to touch, to kiss.

Well, almost.

He caught her arm. "You think Judge Edwards will be happy next Friday if we haven't made any progress? You think maybe—*just maybe*—she was going to tell you not to blow our court-ordered mediation time like you did on some other case?"

"I didn't say I wouldn't talk about it." Rachel yanked her arm free and kept walking. "I said I was busy *today*. I'll call you."

"You don't have my number." Ben reached for his wallet and his business cards and then stopped. All the contact information except his cell number was outdated. He didn't want Rachel to know he'd been fired. "Give me your card."

Rachel jerked open the truck door, which stuck as much as the door to her office, tossed her briefcase inside and then rooted around her purse for her business card. "I'll call your house when I find time for you."

Which he bet would be never.

She got in and slammed the truck door, started the engine with a roar and backed out, rolling down her window with a hand crank.

Ben walked slowly to his Mercedes. He didn't need to be a stalker to compile information about Rachel. That old truck needed a new starter and lacked air conditioning. Rachel still had an above average level of pride and a lead foot. The trick was to use the information about his opponent to his advantage.

Ben took the time to remove his jacket (Rachel hadn't) and loosen his tie before getting in to the car. He turned on the air conditioner full blast and thought about the case.

Rachel had the ranch's water information. Advantage: Rachel.

Judge Edwards held a grudge against Ben. Advantage: Rachel.

Rachel wasn't willing to risk it all to win. Advantage: Ben.

He needed Katie to verify the water usage figures and he'd have to project out how the guest ranch would impact water use in years to come. The sooner he had data to work with, the sooner he could pin Rachel down to a meeting, negotiate terms and leave.

Thanks to a quick call to Ethan, Ben tracked Katie to Brewster Ranch Supply. The afternoon was warm. Ben removed his tie and rolled up his sleeves.

He jogged up the steps to the long wooden porch that ran the length of the store, planning to dart inside past the old man sitting in front of a chessboard.

"Not so fast." Pops Brewster had looked ancient to Ben twenty years ago. Not much had changed since then. Flyaway white hair. Sun spots and wrinkles. And a grin that welcomed anyone with a buck to spend at the family feed store or a minute to spare over his chessboard. "No one goes inside dressed like that without having to play a chess move."

Ben was used to strategic games of a different kind, but Pops had always been kind to him when he'd come to the feed store. He surveyed the board. "Who's been playing with you?" Usually there were a handful of old coots hanging out with Pops. He was alone today.

"Whippersnappers on school break." The old man scoffed. "They don't know what they're doing. Put you in a bit of trouble, I reckon."

Ben moved the white queen diagonally across the board. "Checkmate."

"What the…?" Pops peered at the board, rubbing a hand over his grizzled chin.

Ben hurried inside, craning his neck to see above the high shelves and between ranchers wearing cowboy hats. The feed store smelled of hay, leather and new clothes. He spotted Katie's red hair in the back. She was at the counter settling up a bill. Her blue-gray heeler sat obediently at her feet. Ben complimented Mrs. Gardner on her tamales, patted Katie's dog on the head and pulled Katie aside, explaining what he needed.

"Ben." Katie looked pained as she brushed flyaway red hair behind her ears. "I've got a gazillion things to do when I get back, including interviewing new ranch hands. Can it wait? I plan to catch up on paperwork this weekend after the Ziglers check out."

"I have to have an agreement on the judge's desk in seven days." At the latest. He wanted an agreement Monday, if possible. His reaction to Rachel unnerved him. He'd been pitted against attractive legal adversaries before, but never ones he wanted to kiss. It only added to his resolve to leave. "Do you want me to negotiate with Rachel blind? Are you willing to accept whatever terms she tosses my way?"

"No." Katie knelt down to stroke her dog's velvety ears, eliciting an enthusiastic tail wag. "I file the meter readings monthly along with the bills. I need time to pull all the information. I suppose we can check the readings on the water pump on Sunday to get an estimate of future use, but it'll only be based on the guest ranch being open a week."

"This needs to be high priority, Katie." Opening the safe hadn't been. "I can sort through your files myself if you need me to."

"No." She got to her feet so fast, her dog stepped out of the way. "I mean, my dad..." She looked uncomfortable. "He doesn't like anyone but me going through the ranch's paperwork."

If Ben was running things, he'd straighten out the situation between Katie and her dad, at least from a ranch management perspective. Katie deserved the title of foreman considering she handled the bulk of the work. And Lochlan... He was like family, but Ben hadn't seen him since he'd arrived. If Lochlan was too old to handle the job... "I can get the pump reading myself, but it'll mean nothing to me without the history."

"Okay." Katie seemed grateful for the concession. When he turned to go, she grabbed his arm. Lines of worry framed her blue eyes. "I'm sorry, Ben. You've come back to a mess."

He patted her hand. "It's okay. I know what to do." His stomach growled. It was long past lunchtime. Maybe it was time to cave to nostalgia and have a pot pie at the Shiny Spur.

As he stepped outside, he spotted Rachel driving by in that red-and-white boxy pickup truck, windows down. She turned right, toward the center of town, rather than heading toward the Double T. Ben knew he should wait before trying to talk to her again, but his feet were moving and he reached for his car keys.

Pops was setting up another game. "Do you have time for a first move?"

"No, I'm playing catch-up today." Ben hurried down the stairs. "But I bet Katie can spare a moment for a turn or two."

Ben knew he couldn't conduct a serious negotiation on the street with Rachel, but he could hopefully get her to commit to a day and time to meet. He pulled around the corner, as she had. There weren't many blocks to drive around downtown. Falcon Creek hadn't changed much. Antiques, secondhand shop, appliance repair. Insurance, coffee shop, sheriff's office.

Just when he was afraid she'd driven to a more remote part of town, he spotted Rachel's truck in front of a beauty parlor and parked next to it.

Jem Salon. Unlike salons in Manhattan, where you couldn't see women with hair in curlers or aluminum foil from the sidewalk, Ben had an easy view of all the stylist stations through the front window. He got out of the car prepared to enter the female den.

Turns out, it wasn't necessary. Rachel held the door for her grandmother, who walked out with carefully placed steps. The older woman wore crisp blue jeans, a blue polka-dot blouse and cowboy boots.

The elder Thompson spared Ben a glance that went from inquisitive to disapproving in a blink.

The expressions of the two Thompson women matched.

Ben decided to face the storm head-on. "Mrs. Thompson, what nice hair you have." That came out wrong.

"The better to blind you with my beauty." Rachel's grandmother laughed, but it was more like a cackle. She patted her neat white curls and said to Rachel, "You should have married this one. He has a brain. Then it might have stuck."

Rachel pressed her lips together, as if used to her grandmother's barbs.

Ben fell back a step, more surprised by the information imparted by Rachel's grandmother than the tone of her delivery. Deep down in his chest, where non-lawyerly feelings he rarely acknowledged dwelled, something tensed, something that felt suspiciously like jealousy. "Rachel is married? But…*Thompson*?" Rachel's maiden name was written on the Double T brief.

Inside the salon, people were turning their way. Someone raised a hair dryer off her head to stare at them.

"Rachel took back the Thompson name when she got divorced." Rachel's grandmother was a fountain of information. "Ted Jackson was a real sour grape. Seems like there are a lot of 'em around Falcon Creek. At least the women who want to get rid of them know where they can find a lawyer with a sympathetic ear." She tilted her white head toward her granddaughter. "They go to Rachel."

"And now we're all caught up." Rachel blushed in a way that did nothing to allay the feeling in Ben's chest. "Thanks, Nana."

"Not quite *all* caught up." Her grandmother nudged Rachel with her bony elbow. "Did you ask if this Blackwell fella was married?"

"She didn't." Ben grinned. "And I'm not."

"Never?" At the shake of Ben's head, Rachel's grandmother kept talking. "I bet that means you never got over Zoe."

Ben took another step back, losing his hold on his smile. Suddenly, the sun felt too hot on the back of his neck. "Oh, I got over her." Quicker than he'd expected.

"Thank heavens for that." Rachel's grandmother fanned her sharp-angled face. "Golly, it's hot. Why are you lurking outside the beauty parlor? Looking for a date?" She shuffled closer and fluttered her eyelashes in Ben's direction.

"Nana," Rachel scolded. "You're embarrassing me."

And amusing Ben, along with the gathering audience in the beauty parlor window.

Ben ignored Rachel, ignored the pin-curled ladies in the salon and played along with the elderly minx on the sidewalk. "Are you free to date, Mrs. Thompson?"

"I'm not free or easy." The old woman chuckled. "And neither is my granddaughter."

Cheeks still aflame, Rachel took her grandmother by the arm. "I'm going to give Nana Nancy a ride home and lock her up where she belongs."

"That's the trouble with you kids nowadays," her grandmother said, trying unsuccessfully to dig in her boot heels.

Kids? Ben mouthed to Rachel, feeling that easy camaraderie they'd had when they were younger. He was tempted to sling his arm over Rachel's shoulder and laugh.

Rachel rolled her big brown eyes.

"You kids," the old woman continued. "You don't come right out and say you're ready to settle down." She moved as slow as a snail.

"I tried settling down." Rachel put more authority in her voice than she'd had in the courtroom.

"And now you're overextending yourself. You should quit that law practice and focus on the ranch."

"I *own* the law practice, Nana."

"I get the feeling that this is a long-standing argument." Ben pointed to Rachel's truck. "Does this old thing have air conditioning?" He knew it didn't. He'd seen inside. Plus, Rachel drove with the windows down.

"It doesn't. All that wind." Nana Nancy stopped on the hot asphalt. "It straightens my curls."

"Why don't I drive you home, Ms. Thompson?" Ben offered on impulse, reaching for the old lady's arm. "I have air conditioning."

"Objection." Rachel swatted his hand away from behind her grandmother's back.

Inside the salon, their audience laughed.

Rachel won the hand war, but glared at him for good measure. "You only want to drive Nana home so you can spy on the Double T."

"I'm hurt." Ben tried to look innocent instead of relieved. "I'm only concerned the money your grandmother spent on her lovely hair will be blown to pieces without air conditioning."

"He's right," her grandmother said, turning toward his car like a windup toy with limited movement. "It's not like Beatrice does my hair every day. Lead on, youngster."

Rachel sputtered. "But…"

Nana Nancy put her palm inches from Rachel's face. "Talk to the hand." She shambled toward Ben's Mercedes, chuckling as she went. "Saw that in a movie the other day." She repeated the phrase under her breath and chortled some more.

Ben opened the passenger door.

"I don't know what you're up to exactly," Rachel said, poking Ben's chest as her grandmother almost fell backward into the low front seat. "But you better be careful with my grandmother."

Ben liked the way Rachel's dark eyes flashed. He liked the way she called his every move as she saw them. He liked how she looked in a suit and those ridiculous overalls she'd worn the other night. "I'll treat your nana as if she was one of my own grandmothers." Probably better, considering he didn't talk to the women his grandfather had married and divorced, including his paternal grandmother, Dorothy. Apart from the birthday and Christmas cards his assistant sent to her.

"If you treat my nana the way you treated Judge Edwards all those years ago…" Rachel left her threat unfinished and leaned down to her grandmother's level. "This is your last warning. Ben is not to be trusted. I can't be responsible for your safety if you let him drive you home."

Nana Nancy reached for the door handle with a petite hand. "I can take care of myself."

"Fine." Rachel watched her grandmother try to close the heavy door. And then she made a grumbly noise deep in her throat and closed it for her. "Blackwell, you'd best behave."

"Always, Thompson." Ben walked around the car, slid behind the wheel, started the engine and pointed the middle air conditioning vents at his passenger. "Nana Nancy, it's my honor to drive you home."

"You can't call me that," Rachel's grandmother snapped. "I don't like you."

"That seems to be going around today," Ben murmured, thinking of Myrna and Darnell. "You liked me well enough to get in the car." And to ask about his marital status.

"I was annoyed with Rachel. She wouldn't let me stay longer at the parlor. I was going to miss all the news about Marilee Inez."

"What news?"

"I don't know." Nancy frowned. "I had to leave just as June was snapping the drape around her neck. Last I heard she was chasing the new principal around town because your brother Jonathon got engaged to that woman on the news."

Ben backed onto the street and pointed the car toward the north end of town, noting that Rachel went in the opposite direction. "We seem to have lost your granddaughter."

"She'll be along." Nancy lowered the visor and opened the mirror. She patted her hair, turning her head from side to side to admire her new 'do. "Rachel used to like you, you know."

Why wouldn't she have liked him? "Well, sure, we were friends."

"But you didn't take friendship into account when you took the Double T to court all those years ago. And then my son died because of you and Big E." The look she gave him was sharp but not hateful. She might say she blamed Ben and his grandfather for her son's death, but she didn't really believe it. "I used to tell my son he needed to learn to like you because someday you'd come to your senses and quit Zoe for Rachel. What a fool I was."

The air left Ben's lungs in a rush. He remembered being dumbstruck by Rachel earlier in the day. She had substance, whereas Zoe did not.

"Let's be honest," Nancy continued, seemingly happy to have the floor. "Zoe has always wanted to be a trophy wife and it didn't much matter to her which wealthy Montana rancher she found for herself."

"That's very insightful." Ben wished he could have recognized that truth when he was eighteen. Or twenty-seven.

"From an early age," Nancy went on, "that girl played with her mama's good china, ordered the most expensive item on the menu and demanded a new wardrobe every season. My friend Janet would *not* be rolling in her grave to hear what her granddaughter is doing today. She'd say, yep, I called it."

"And Rachel?" Ben drove past the turn for the Blackwell Ranch, feeling something suspiciously like relief.

"What about her?" Nancy lifted her chin, which was as sharp as her gaze.

"I meant—" Ben used the conciliatory tone he employed in early negotiations with opposing counsel "—what was Rachel like as a little girl?" He knew, but he was interested in her grandmother's perspective.

"She always tried to be what anybody needed. A good daughter, a good sister, a good friend."

True. "A good lawyer?"

She peered at him. "That remains to be seen, doesn't it? If she beats you?"

"She's been practicing for years and you said she's getting divorce clients."

Nancy waved a thin, leathery hand. "That's small stuff. Her clients can barely afford to pay her fees."

Ben slowed to enter the driveway of the Double T. There was only a simple metal sign marking the property with a cowboy wielding a lariat chasing after a steer, nothing as grand as the Blackwell arch. The land looked dry and thirsty. The driveway extended about a mile before reaching the ranch proper. A row of rusted paint-faded old tractors served as a metal hedge around the main buildings. To a kid, they'd been a jungle gym, but to an adult, they were an eyesore.

He glanced at his passenger. "What's the real reason you accepted my invitation to drive you home?"

"Ha!" She swatted his arm gently with the back of her hand. "Points to Mr. Blackwell for knowing I have enough hairspray on my pin curls to withstand a strong wind." Nancy chuckled. "Fact is, I don't want to see my granddaughter get hurt."

"Successful lawyers have thick skin."

"I'm not talking about your court case." The old woman scoffed. "I'll take those points back now." She shook her head. "And they say you're the smart Blackwell."

Ben was at a loss as to which attack to defend against—her assumption that he and Rachel might be about to be involved or her derision about his intelligence. He decided the safest course of action was to keep silent. Besides, they'd arrived.

He hadn't been to the Double T since almost forever. It looked much more rundown than Ben remembered. The house needed paint. A rain gutter on the house hung lopsided. The gravel between the outbuildings was thin and the road full of potholes. The gate blocking the road between the Thompson and Blackwell properties listed as if the hinges were loose.

Regardless, it would never withstand a blow from Ferdinand.

Is this what his family's ranch would look like if they lost the aquifer and took second position in river water rights?

That's right, boy. Water makes or breaks a spread.

And Ben had helped break the Double T.

Guilt churned in his gut. Ben might not want to live on his family's property, but he didn't want to see it sink into disrepair. An unlikely sense of determination sparked inside him.

Ben parked and got out into the heat, hurrying around to the passenger door to help Nancy.

Nancy grunted as she rose to her feet a bit unsteadily. "Why do they have to make cars lower than they used to? The only people getting shorter are old folk with creaky joints. Does it hurt your knees to squat down to reach that leather?"

"No, ma'am." Ben escorted her to the front door, a process that seemed to take forever given her short, shuffling steps.

"You have manners, I'll give you that." She put her hand on the doorknob. "But I'm not letting you in until Rachel gets here, and she might not let you in. Ever."

Rachel's truck sped over the gravel driveway, fast approaching.

"I can live with that," Ben said, although he didn't budge from the porch.

CHAPTER SEVEN

BEN STOOD ON the Thompsons' front porch, looking as out of place as a crystal ornament on Charlie Brown's Christmas tree.

Rachel didn't know whether to be awed or annoyed.

Seeing Ben over the past few days had been like that. Pulse-jumping annoyance that he'd one-upped her on everything. Energy-draining relief that he'd survived a charging bull and a bullish defendant. And his good looks…

A part of her was peeved that Ben was still waiting for her, pushing up the folded sleeves of his white dress shirt as if he planned to do some work around the property. She wanted to project the image of a bulletproof lawyer, but her suit was wrinkled, her hair was escaping from its bun, and she had Poppy in the back seat. Dear, sweet, adorable Poppy. She wouldn't trade her for anything, but Rachel knew how a man like Ben viewed moms. He'd think she was a softhearted pushover.

Rachel wanted to be viewed more like Judge Edwards—powerful and respected, if a little less cranky.

Rachel hadn't suffered postpartum depression, but she was struggling with her own identity. Princess? Lawyer? Rancher? Mommy? How could all those things exist inside her? And how was she supposed to present herself confidently in each role?

"Ga-ga-ga-gahhh!"

Rachel parked and moved quickly to the back seat, unbuckling a pink-cheeked Poppy and lifting her into her arms.

"Why are you hanging out here, Blackwell?" Scowling, Rachel turned to face her adversary.

Ben stared at Poppy. "Is that...*yours*?"

"I was married," she huffed, grabbing Poppy's diaper bag and marching toward the house.

Her mother and grandmother had their noses pressed to the front window. They scurried back at Rachel's approach.

He matched her step for step. "I'm sorry." It might have been her imagination, but he'd never looked at her in that way before. With compassion. "Really sorry."

"*You're* sorry?" Rachel captured his blue

gaze and stopped walking to face him. "You're *sorry*?"

He nodded and his gaze drifted to Poppy.

"You were sorry to hear about my dad's passing and now you're sorry to hear that I have a baby?"

"Yes… No…" His blue eyes scanned the horizon before meeting her gaze squarely. "I'm sorry your marriage didn't work out. I'm sorry the guy you thought would love you forever wasn't strong enough to stick around for her." He gestured to Poppy.

Rachel's breath stuck in her throat.

It was a nice thing to say and completely unexpected coming from the heartless, egotistical Ben Blackwell. Only…it wasn't so unexpected coming from a man who'd been jilted by his first love. It wasn't just nice. It was honest and conveyed how he'd felt when Zoe left him.

If Rachel had learned anything from her marriage and subsequent divorce, it was that marriage wasn't just about love. It was about trust. And with Ben's words, with his apologies, Rachel trusted him a little bit more.

At least as far as an adult Thompson could trust an adult Blackwell.

Poppy stared at Ben with wide eyes and then reached for him. "Bye-bye."

"I think she's confused." Ben grinned. No. It was more than that. He twinkled in a way that heartless, egotistical Ben Blackwell wasn't supposed to.

"I think she has the right idea." Rachel stepped around him, almost at the front door. "Good-bye, Blackwell."

Her grandmother and mother were fogging up the front window. Rachel waved them away. Poppy began to wail, reaching her hands toward Ben over Rachel's shoulders. *"Bye-bye! Bye-bye!"*

Ted's mother had mentioned she'd been unsettled today, probably because Rachel hadn't gotten her to bed at her regular time last night. She'd been out rescuing a lawyer from a bull.

Rachel struggled to hold on to her squirming baby and the diaper bag. Why didn't her mother or grandmother open the door and help?

She knew the answer to that question. They were engrossed in the unfolding drama in front of them.

The diaper bag fell to the porch. Poppy wailed louder. *"Bye-byeee!"*

Rachel bent to pick up the bag in an ungainly high-heeled bend just as Poppy was plucked from her arms.

"Hey, pumpkin." Ben's voice was sugary sweet and kid-friendly. "I bet you didn't get your nap today."

Mom and Nana Nancy's eyes widened.

Rachel supposed hers did, too. Ben was talking to Poppy as if he had experience with babies.

Rachel stood and pinned him with her gaze. "Explain your Mrs. Doubtfire skill there, cowboy."

"I'm rather good with babies," Ben said, jiggling Poppy and holding her hand.

"Since when?" Did he have kids of his own? Had he been married? Rachel felt hotter than the heat index.

"Sometimes my assistant has to bring her kids to work. And sometimes she needs help." He swayed back and forth as if dancing with Poppy, who giggled. "Babies like me."

"Of course they do." Because the universe had to make things that much easier on Ben and that much harder on Rachel. She reached for Poppy, nearly toppling over the diaper bag she'd neglected to pick up.

Poppy put a chubby arm up to her wet cheek and shrank deeper into Ben's embrace.

"I've got her." Ben walked past Rachel, scooped up the diaper bag and opened the door. "Come inside. It's hot out here."

Rachel followed them on sulky heels.

"Ben Blackwell." Mom sat in Dad's brown recliner, which still rocked slightly from how quickly she'd leaped into it. "This is unexpected." She studied Rachel's face, mostly likely to see if she should be angry or welcoming.

"Hi, Mrs. Thompson." Ben set the diaper bag down on the floor by the door, in the same spot that Rachel usually dropped it. "I gave Ms. Nancy a ride home."

From the couch, Nana sniffed and patted her hair but said nothing, perhaps also waiting for Rachel's cue. Sitting next to her, Fanny was curled in a fluffy white ball. She stared at Ben but didn't so much as growl.

What was wrong with everyone? There should be shouts of trespassing and growls of boundaries breached.

"Ga-gah," Poppy murmured in a tired-out voice.

"There's my girl." Mom reached into the covered Cheerios bowl and then reached for Poppy.

Poppy didn't lunge out of Ben's arms for her

grandmother, not even for her favorite cereal. She tucked her head in the crook of Ben's neck and sucked on her fingers.

Unwilling to give up, Mom waved the small treat back and forth like a hypnotist. "Don't you want one of these, sweetie?"

"No." Rachel's daughter waved her hand with more fervor than Mom had.

"Ted's mom probably fed her early," Rachel said, taking pity on her mother.

Ben sat on the arm of the couch and rubbed Poppy's back. "It smells as if dinner is in the oven. I'm guessing it's not chicken casserole since you had that last night."

Mom gasped. "How did you—?"

"Rachel told me." At their blank stares, Ben added, "I was out running by the river and was surprised by a bull, who wasn't supposed to be in the pasture. Rachel rescued me. Didn't she tell you?"

"No." Nana gave Rachel a speculative look and crossed her arms over her chest.

Couldn't Ben keep a secret? Rachel wished she could call on attorney-attorney privilege, not that such a thing existed.

"Rachel had to listen to me reminisce about the wonders of your chicken casserole." How did Ben's smile look so sincere when he was such a horrible suck-up? "I remember it would always be gone first at the school potlucks."

"That's true." Mom preened, finger-combing her short blond hair forward.

First, Ben had sweet-talked Judge Edwards, Nana Nancy and Rachel's baby girl. And now her mother? Rachel stood in the center of the room but felt as if she was outside the window, peering in and fogging up the glass.

"What was a bull doing in the lower pasture?" her grandmother asked. "He should be up in the high country with the heifers making hay."

Ben kept rubbing Poppy's back and added rocking side to side. "He slipped away from Katie Montgomery."

Nana snorted, startling Poppy out of near-sleep. "Everyone knows that girl is better with horses than cattle."

"We have a stray down here, too," Rachel felt compelled to point out. "A heifer who likes our vegetable garden." She hadn't seen the picket fence repaired when she'd driven up. She needed to check on Henry and his list of things that needed attention.

Ben frowned. "If your heifer is in season, Ferdinand will charge through every fence to get to her."

Rachel hadn't thought about that. Had Henry caught her today? Is that why the fence wasn't fixed? Did everything around here require her supervision in order for it to get done?

Rachel caved in to mommy fatigue and removed her heels, putting them next to the diaper bag. For a moment, she froze by the door, struck by the thought that she'd removed a piece of her feminine armor too soon.

"The last thing we need is Blackwell blood in our herd," Mom said, seemingly recovered from Ben's praise of her cooking, perhaps because he'd temporarily usurped her role as Poppy's favorite person. "You have Black Angus and we have Herefords."

Rachel nodded. Black Angus and Herefords were like apples and oranges.

"Not always," Nana said in an unusually sage voice. "Everyone knows inbreeding means low numbers at calving time. Used to be the ranches in the valley would trade bulls for the summer to strengthen the lines."

Apparently, Rachel wasn't everyone. She hadn't known that fact. Add reading up on cattle-breeding practices to the list of things she needed to do, along with comparing calving numbers over the years by digging in her father's dusty file cabinet. Had she updated the file last year? Her neck twinged with the weight of self-doubt.

Did she have time tonight to flip through file folders? She'd much rather flip through a magazine with fall fashions, like the one her mother had on the coffee table.

Speaking of fashionable... Holding a baby while wearing a dress shirt and trousers, Ben looked like the kind of guy some women might dream of.

Not that Rachel was one of those women or even admiring him in any way.

Ben's deep voice cut into her thoughts. "My older brother Jonathon is experimenting with crossbreeding."

Should I have known that?

Sadly, Rachel assumed the answer was yes. Jon's property bumped up against the Double T in spots. She needed to up her game where ranch management was concerned.

"Oh, Rachel. Before I forget, the doctor's office called today to remind you Poppy's shots were due last week." Mom stroked Poppy's sock-covered foot, unwittingly triggering Rachel's growing set of mantras.

Win back the water rights.

Set the ranch to rights.

Get a signed custody agreement.

Learn how to be a better rancher.
Learn how to be a better lawyer.
Try to be a better mother.

Rachel wanted to get out of her court clothes, crawl into bed and forget about all her mismanaged responsibilities and her unachievable list of mantras. At the very least, the universe should align, and Ben should leave so she could tackle the ranch's long to-do list.

As if reading her mind, Ben stood. "This little one is asleep. Do you have a place I can put her down?"

The answer was a resounding, whispered yes.

Rachel led him down the hall to her old bedroom, where she kept a portable crib set up. Ben transferred Poppy to the crib with ease. Her daughter sighed and rolled over. Rachel covered her with a light blanket and then straightened, cheeks heating from the embarrassment of Ben in her childhood room.

"There's a shrine to our high school days," Ben whispered, peering at Rachel's bulletin board. He didn't seem to notice her discomfort. "Look at the three of us." He pointed to a photograph of him, Zoe and Rachel on graduation day. Ben's arm was slung across each girl. "We were like the three musketeers."

Past tense. Rachel was a team of one now. Zoe was either busy with the Blackwell ranch or traveling with her husband.

Ben took in her bright leopard-print bedspread, blue cheerleading pom-poms in the corner and her debate team trophies. "You don't live here, do you?"

"I haven't lived here since I went away to college." Before Zoe's marriage, she and Zoe had shared a small house in town, one Rachel still rented. She edged between him and the bulletin board where a pinned picture of Tommy Whitehall had a heart sticker in the corner. "Every once in a while, I stop and look at those photos and wonder why you put up with me back then. I was always the third wheel."

"Zoe didn't want you to be sitting home alone on Friday nights and I didn't mind." He frowned. "I suppose that should tell me something about the depth of my feelings for Zoe."

Rachel hid her surprise by inching closer to the door. "It wasn't until you asked Zoe to marry you that I realized I wouldn't be going to New York with the two of you." She'd been torn. Happy for her friends, but sad to be left behind. And then she'd been alone in that little house after Zoe had eloped, and eventually she'd met and married Ted.

Ben was still frowning. "Zoe chose to stay in Falcon Creek. She chose you."

"She chose your grandfather, not me."

Poppy murmured and shifted positions.

Rachel hustled Ben out before he woke Poppy.

He stopped her in the hall after she closed the door, and repeated, "Zoe chose your friendship and Falcon Creek over me."

"You say that like it makes you feel better about her marriage to your grandfather. I told you they love each other. It's true." She tried to get past Ben, but he stopped her with a light touch on her arm.

"Think about it." His voice was low and husky. Most of the curtains in the house were drawn to keep the house cool. They stood in intimate shadow in the hall—the two of them and his husky bedroom voice. "You told me on my wedding day that there was no way Zoe would have moved away from her family and friends to be with me. You were right."

"I don't know why I said that," she admitted with a twinge of that old guilt. "I was angry about the court decision."

"I suppose I don't regret Zoe changing her

mind. Without having a wife in New York, I devoted all my energy to my career and it soared." His hand dropped away. "And Zoe was here when you needed a friend to lean on through your father's death and your divorce."

In a way, Ben was right. Zoe had been there when Rachel needed her most.

During those early days when Rachel had taken a beating in court, she'd gone straight to the Blackwell Ranch to vent to her best friend. Before Rachel got pregnant, she and Zoe had spent weekends shopping in Bozeman or Missoula, collecting design samples and firming up plans for the guest ranch. In the days after Dad died, Zoe hadn't left Rachel's side as Rachel dealt with grief, a failing marriage and the burgeoning realization that Mom and Nana Nancy couldn't run the ranch without her.

Rachel lifted her gaze to Ben's handsome face. "You're right." Her voice sounded young and wondrous, more like the girl she'd once been, sitting next to Ben, thinking parents never died and friendships lasted forever.

Ben had a faraway look in his eyes. "Our marriage wouldn't have lasted. I work long hours and Zoe always had to come first, even when other things were important, too." And then those sharp blue eyes came to rest on Rachel and didn't seem so sharp.

They stood close enough to touch. She could smell a hint of his woodsy cologne. She could imagine his arms coming around her—supportive, comforting, energizing. And instead of jumping back to the friendship zone and rejecting images of his warm embrace, every cell in her body seemed to be pressing forward...toward Ben.

What was going on here?

I'm sleep deprived and stressed. Get over it.

"Blackwell." Rachel swallowed and put more oomph in her words. "This is one big overshare." She tried to slip past him, flattening herself against the wall.

He turned, too, so they faced each other. This time when he reached for her, he claimed both arms. "Things have changed. I know that now."

Things? What things?

His hold was tender. His hands moved upward, toward her shoulders. His gaze dropped to her lips.

He's going to kiss me.

Thoughts of Zoe and friendship boundaries flitted through her short-circuiting brain. She should give him a gentle push, make a crack about things staying the same and show him the door.

His touch was so light she might have been dreaming it had she not been looking at him. Or had those blue eyes of his not been staring into hers.

He's going to kiss me.

Curiosity, loneliness, longing. Rachel couldn't move.

"Dinner!" Mom called from the kitchen.

Ben leaned back, but his hands remained on her shoulders. They traced along her neck. His fingers were warm on her skin.

Is he going to kiss me?

Her knees felt weak with uncertainty.

Ben cleared his throat and straightened the collar of her jacket. "This has been flipped up since you came in."

He'd held her like that to correct a wardrobe malfunction?

Her single-lady sensors were on the fritz.

Rachel darted down the hall on legs that threatened to buckle. There was no way he could have misread the signals she'd been sending about being open to a kiss. To his kiss.

He had her on the run. She only hoped that wouldn't extend to their battle in the courtroom.

"Dinner? So early?" Ben was behind her,

but Rachel could tell he was grinning, she could hear the amusement in his voice. "It sure smells good."

She forced herself to meet his gaze and tried to seem unaffected by his presence. "Are you trying to mooch food off my mom?" *Are you trying to stupefy me with the promise of sweet kisses?*

"Yep." That grin.

Rachel's heart beat faster. She was in trouble. Big, big trouble.

And she couldn't think of another mantra to guide her to safe waters where Ben was concerned.

Truth be told, she wasn't sure she wanted to be safe. Ben made her feel alive, mentally stimulated and pretty. Ted had had no patience for her talk of legal strategy. Zoe's eyes glazed over when she tried to discuss a case. Her mother and grandmother didn't care to hear much beyond whether she won or lost.

Ben was infuriating and invigorating. Handsome and tricky, and yes, sexy.

And Rachel was going to beat him in court. She was going to beat him and he wasn't going to hate her for it. He was going to look at her with more than speculation in those blue eyes. He was going to look at her with respect.

Right before he kissed her.

Rachel sucked in a breath and moved toward the kitchen. Clearly, her mother and grandmother weren't the only Thompsons who watched too many romantic movies.

"Set another plate, dearie," Nana said, shuffling into view. "The Blackwell is staying for dinner."

CHAPTER EIGHT

I ALMOST KISSED RACHEL.

What right did Ben have to kiss her after he'd taken her water?

Ben sat in his car in front of the Blackwell ranch house and rubbed his hands over his hair. The contact didn't wipe away the shame he felt for not doing the right thing all those years ago.

Rachel was making do with the hand she'd been dealt—a ranch with a limited water supply, a legal practice without an experienced senior partner, a family who depended on her, including a sweet little baby.

Her situation wouldn't have been near as bad if Ben had lived up to the ethical oaths he'd taken as an attorney. Now he wanted nothing more than to make things right for her.

What good would giving them the aquifer land do now, boy?

Ben shut out his grandfather's voice in his head. He didn't—couldn't—agree with him.

The damage was done. And state water boards showed no mercy or do-overs. The truth for Rachel was grim and upheld by several cases settled within the past few years in Montana. Agricultural water rights were based on the most recent years of use. The Double T wasn't using water to irrigate its pastures now, therefore the ranch wouldn't be granted the right to irrigate it. Ever. It wouldn't matter if the Double T won first position river rights. Rachel would still be water poor. All Ben had to do was present the previous cases to the judge and her case would be dismissed.

Still, the nagging feeling that justice hadn't been served persisted.

Ben got out of the car.

"Where've you been?" Ethan sat on a bench on the porch. "You didn't answer your phone. You said you'd tell me more about what happened in court when you got home."

Home? Ben bristled. Home was New York and an absence of Big E's problems. "I was at the Double T."

"Working out a deal?" Ethan hurried down the steps. "I knew you'd get results right away. What should I tell Jon?"

"Nothing." Ben hated to disappoint his twin. Ben's conscience was getting in the way, just like it had on his last case at his old firm. And look where that had gotten him. Fired.

"So…" Ethan stopped. "No deal?"

"I've got six more days to hammer one out." Ben explained how he was waiting on Katie to give him the detailed information on the ranch's water use so they could calculate future projections. "Did you know Myrna—as in Big E's ex-wife—is the judge in this case?"

"Yeah." Ethan shivered dramatically. "She made me suffer when I requested upping my signature limit on the Blackwell accounts and when I asked for more time for you to get here. Payback is the worst."

"You might have warned me." Ben climbed the steps, hoping there was still beer in the fridge.

"I thought you knew. Wasn't it in the documents Rachel provided?"

"No." Ben brushed past his twin, pausing when the untraditional ranch furnishings pummeled his senses once more.

"Sorry about that." Ethan crowded him out of the way to get inside. "How are you feeling about our chances?"

"It's…" *clear-cut* "…complicated."

"You're not going to tell me the details, are

you?" Ethan pressed his lips together, as if trying to hold back judgment.

"No." Ben clapped a hand on his brother's shoulder. "The less you know, the better." The easier for Ben to work all the angles without his brother second-guessing Ben's decisions or criticizing his actions, especially the ones from the past.

Ethan settled his ball cap more securely on his dark hair. "This conversation is beginning to sound like the ones I used to have with Big E."

Ben felt the blood drain from his face. "On that note, I'll say good night." He was nothing like his shortcutting, manipulative grandfather.

Think again, boy.

"Okay, but Jon invited us to his house for dinner Saturday night." Ethan held Ben's gaze. "He wants to talk about selling." Ethan didn't have to add that he wanted Ben on the side of keeping the ranch. The plea was there in his eyes.

Ben went in search of that beer.

What was the point of keeping the ranch if Big E held the reins? Maybe he and his brothers could vote their grandfather out of power, but that would mean someone would have to run the place. Jon was busy with his own ranch. Could Ethan be a good husband, a good father and establish a veterinary practice here on the ranch?

And what about Ben's sudden awareness of Rachel? She'd always been just a friend. At least, until they'd become frenemies. Why did he want to kiss her now?

The house was quiet and offered no answers.

Ben didn't normally mind quiet. He lived alone in a high-rise apartment in Manhattan. But he thought about the noise and laughter at the Double T and Rachel's smile, and the silence here felt as uncomfortable as being at a cocktail party where he didn't know anyone.

A thick brown file folder on the kitchen table caught his eye. There was a yellow sticky note on top with Ben's name scribbled in bold letters. It was the water usage for the ranch for the past decade. Katie may have been a no-show regarding the safe, but she'd come through with this information.

Ben sat down and began to sort things out.

The more he knew for certain, the more certain he'd be about his interest in the Blackwell Ranch and the next steps in the fight for water with the Double T.

But no amount of meter readings would help him figure out his feelings toward Rachel.

"WHAT WAS THAT all about?" Mom may have asked the question, but a second pair of Thompson eyes stared Rachel down. "I thought we didn't like Ben Blackwell?"

Rachel sighed and went to the kitchen sink to wash her hands. She'd closed up the barn and made the nightly rounds after Ben left. It was time to get the paperwork done. "He offered Nana a ride home from the salon. The judge says we have to *try* to come up with an agreement on water rights by next Friday."

"He wasn't here for water rights." Mom's eyes sparkled with mischief.

"He couldn't keep his eyes off you." Nana's frown brimmed with displeasure.

The pair of women had followed Rachel into the kitchen, flanking her at the sink as she washed her hands.

"While I'm negotiating, there will be no shenanigans." Rachel had best heed her own advice. "And don't be fooled by Ben. He has a way of looking at people when they speak is all."

"Oh, honey." Her mother smiled knowingly. "He looked at you even when I was speaking."

"Doesn't matter how infatuated he is with you," Nana said knowingly. "He's a Blackwell. For all we know he could be trying to romance those water rights from you."

"I doubt that." Mom finger-combed her short blond hair behind her ears, all the while giving Nana a challenging look. "Poppy likes him."

"Poppy likes everyone." Rachel dried her hands. "Ben wants one thing and one thing only."

Her mother and grandmother exchanged glances but didn't say anything.

"He wants to block our water rights." Rachel chopped out the words.

"That wasn't the one thing I was thinking of," Mom murmured, calling Rachel's bluff.

"I watch TV, you know." Nana nodded at Rachel. "This lawyering thing involves presentation of the facts and manipulation of the emotions."

Rachel agreed with Nana. "Ben is really good at both." Hence Darnell's villainous swan dive.

"So you have to be better." Nana took Rachel's hands and squeezed. "For all our sakes."

"You want her to string him along?" Mom sounded aghast.

Nana smiled. "Of course. Don't you?"

"It sounds like you've been watching too much television." Rachel pulled her hands free.

"That boy may be hot stuff in New York City, but he's got a soft spot for you and Poppy." Nana kicked her voice up a notch and shuffled toward the living room. "He'd exploit that if your situations were reversed. That's all I'm saying."

"Nonsense." Mom hugged Rachel. "Stick to your plan, sweetie."

Plan? Rachel didn't have a plan other than to hope Judge Edwards saw things her way.

CHAPTER NINE

SOMEONE WAS IN the house.

Ben rolled out of bed and tripped over the mountain of pink pillows in the dark, trying to place the sound that had woken him.

The click of a door latching? Footsteps downstairs?

Ben switched on the bedside lamp and squinted against all that pink.

Outside, in the gray light of dawn, a heifer mooed as if in pain. Or maybe it was a cat in heat. Or...

No one was in the house. Someone was outside yodeling. At four o'clock in the morning. On a Saturday, no less.

Ben groaned.

They should have charged the Ziglers double to hold their family reunion on Blackwell property.

One floor below him, something bumped into a wall.

Ben waded through the sea of pillows and

came out of his bedroom onto the landing, peering below. A light was on in the foyer. Ben hadn't left it on last night.

"Come out with your hands up," Ben called, grimacing. He didn't have a gun.

And then Ben recognized a slender redhead and a blue-gray dog.

"Oh, sorry." Katie called back. "I thought I could sneak in and out without waking you. I wanted to get the accounts balanced. I need the check register Ethan's been using."

The yodeling continued.

"Can you open the safe?"

"I can. I brought the combination."

"I'll be right down." There'd be no going back to sleep, not with that yowling. Ben retreated to his bedroom to exchange his T-shirt and sleep pants for a fresh shirt and pants, before hurrying downstairs. "Who's making all that racket?" he asked Katie when he caught up with her in the study. "He's up earlier than the roosters."

"The guests had a bet and Arthur lost." Katie waited for him, wearing faded blue jeans and a red T-shirt with the Blackwell brand on it.

Her dog sat at her booted feet, staring at the door. Growing up, she'd always had a dog.

Katie, whatever dog she had, and her sister, Maura, were as thick as Ben and Ethan or Chance and Tyler. At least they had been until Maura had married Chance, and the couple had left Falcon Creek to pursue Chance's singing career.

Katie noticed Ben staring at her dog. "This is Hip, short for Hippolyta."

"Hippolyta?" Ben rubbed his forehead, trying to place the reference. "Greek?"

"Hippolyta was an Amazon warrior."

Of course, she was. Katie would never name her dog something simple like Trout or Spot. Words carried weight with her just as they did with Chance, a skilled songwriter.

"Why can't you just say he loves the color of her eyes?" Ben had asked Chance once, after hearing him sing two lines about the sparkling green of a girl's eyes a dozen different ways while Ben had been working on his geometry homework.

Chance was supposed to be writing a history paper. Instead, he'd been strumming his guitar on the front porch and writing a song. "Anybody can say a girl has beautiful eyes. The words a guy chooses to describe them tells a girl a lot about how he feels."

Fifteen-year-old Ben had laughed. "I think

Zoe knows I'm saying I love her when I say I love her eyes, or I love her in that dress."

Chance had given Ben a private smile, one that seemed older than his thirteen years. "But if I tell a girl her green eyes take me back to shamrocks—"

"She better be Irish," Ben said.

"—or reflect the depths of the ocean—"

"Which you haven't seen," Ben pointed out.

Chance's little smile turned into a big frown and he'd raised his voice to drown out Ben. "She'll remember me and not some boring schmuck, okay? She'll remember me and buy my album and stare at the ceiling every night wondering why she didn't say yes when I'd asked her to the promotion dance." His fingers closed around the frets of the guitar and he stomped off the porch, heading toward the backyard.

"Not that he's writing a song about anyone in particular," Ben had murmured, chuckling to himself. Nope. There was nothing like coming out on top against his brothers.

The caterwauling at the guest ranch stopped. Shouted jibes and laughter echoed across the plain.

Hip's ears swiveled, but the dog was otherwise still, staring at Katie with loving eyes.

"Well, Hip, doggy warrior..." Ben leaned down to scratch her ears. "The joke's on us, up too early on a Saturday."

"You used to get up early every day and be in jeans and boots in no time." Katie slanted a gaze toward his trousers. "My dad used to call you the horse whisperer. Why don't you change and go for a ride?"

"I didn't bring jeans or boots." And his trail horse had been turned out to pasture long ago. Rodrigo was probably an old swayback by now, if he was still alive.

"Some of Ethan's clothes are in the laundry room." Katie disappeared into Big E's study, followed closely by Hip. "I only know this because I've had to take on the role of house-keeper the past few weeks as well."

Ben didn't care about ranch clothes. He cared about what was inside the safe. He followed Katie down the hall, barefoot. "I don't remember the ranch ever being strapped for cash."

"Luxury guest ranches don't come cheap, I suppose." Katie stood at Big E's desk, flipping through a check register. "What are you looking for in the safe?"

"Big E put the court documents from the last Double T go-round in there. I want to review them." Ben lingered in the doorway, trying not to seem overly eager.

Katie moved to the fireplace and pulled the leather chair on the right side away from the hearth. Just as Ben was about to tell her she was on the wrong side, she lifted a board out of the floor and revealed a safe.

That wily old coot.

There were two floor safes?

Katie opened the safe and removed two passports, a small pearl-handled gun and a sheaf of papers with blue backing, the kind lawyers prepared for wills and trusts. "Was this what you were expecting to see?"

"No." Ben walked in a tight circle around Katie. He was cautious by nature and if Katie didn't know about the safe to the left, he didn't want to clue her in. "Can you write down that combination in case I need it?" In case it was the same sequence that would open the other safe.

"Sure." Katie set the items on the floor, scribbled the numbers on a scrap of paper from the desk, and then picked up the check register. "If you change your mind about a ride, you know where the barn is. We've got a lot of good stock."

"Tame nags, you mean?"

"Not all of them." Katie smiled conspiratorially. She'd always loved working with the horses. "Speaking of nags, it's been kind of nice to have you boys back."

"Don't get used to it. I've got to leave in a week." But he said this with less conviction, seeing Rachel's smiling face in his mind's eye.

Katie backed out of the room. "It's kind of nice to have you visiting then." When she left, the house was quiet once more.

The legal document she'd handed to him was the Elias Blackwell Family Trust that outlined the shares and management of the ranch, both before and after Big E's death. It had been signed by Big E and witnessed by Jon. The boys and Big E each owned a similar share in the ranch. Ethan wouldn't just need Ben's vote to keep the ranch. He'd need Tyler or Chance's vote as well.

Assuming Big E's was a vote to keep the place, which was hard to believe, considering he'd left the ranch in financial trouble and wasn't answering his phone.

Ben returned the items to the safe, replaced the boards and then uncovered the second safe to the left of the fireplace. "What are you hiding, old man?" Not much, it seemed. The combination worked. The yellowed sheet of paper documenting the land trade was the only thing inside.

Ben sat and stared at the words.

I, Mathias Blackwell, hereby trade the land in the northeastern parcel currently used by the Blackwells and the Thompsons to reach the river for Seth Thompson's prize bull. September 7, 1919.

The right thing to do was to initiate a title search. Property transfers weren't legal until recorded with the county. A title search would protect the Blackwells from being blindsided if Rachel had indeed found out about the bull-for-land trade.

Ben wanted to believe that he'd do the right thing if it turned out the land over the aquifer belonged to Rachel. But there was Ethan to consider. And Ben's own financial interest... With money from the sale, Ben could start his own practice, be choosey about his clients, afford to have principles.

Ben hung his head. When had he gotten so far off track? He'd had honor when he lived here, hadn't he?

"Why would you tell Tyler that I said he couldn't ride Butterscotch?" Dad had crouched in front of Ben, who sat in the corner of Rodrigo's stall, hands clasping his knees. "Why would you tell him you were Ethan?" His twin.

"Tyler *loves* Ethan," ten-year-old Ben had said mulishly.

"Maybe that's because Ben used Tyler's army men for BB gun practice," Dad said gently, talking about Ben in the third person. "Or because Ben told Tyler he'd play hide-and-seek if Tyler hid first, and then didn't go to find him."

"I'd say that shows the initiative of a true leader," Big E said, leaning on the stall door.

Back then, there had been something appealing about his grandfather's clever comments and comebacks. Big E had a killer instinct and seemed to respect those who also had it.

Dad had ignored Big E. "I'd say it shows a lack of honor. You want to make me and your mother proud, don't you?"

Ben had nodded, perhaps not as quickly as Dad might have liked.

"It's easy to take advantage of the weak, Ben." Dad ran a hand over the top of Ben's hair, letting his palm come to rest on Ben's shoulder. "It shows honor and strength of character to protect them, even when it's not popular, even when it's a sacrifice to do so."

Laughter drifted from the guest ranch once more, pulling Ben back to the present.

He ran a hand over his hair, a gesture Dad had often used to show his boys forgiveness, to express his love. Ben's head hurt. He didn't feel absolved. He didn't feel redeemed or loved.

He needed fresh air. Maybe Katie was right. Maybe he needed a ride.

Ben went into the laundry room. He grabbed a folded pair of his twin's blue jeans and a red sweatshirt from the top of the dryer and a pair of scuffed boots from the corner. He changed and made himself a cup of coffee.

Only after he'd had his morning caffeine did he set off for the barn. The sun was not yet up. The sky was in that long lingering gray before dawn.

The first few stalls were occupied by plump trail horses who paid Ben no mind. A couple of ponies shared the next stall, eyeing him warily. Two stalls were occupied by mares and their foals, the ones he'd seen on display in the enclosure built near the guest ranch's backyard. One of the mares was Butterscotch, his mother's tan-and-white paint. Ben paused to greet her, rubbing a hand beneath the fall of her white mane the way Mom used to. Her foal watched Ben from the corner.

"Do you have a recommendation as to who I should take for a ride?" Ben figured he'd choose one of the aged trail horses. It wasn't like he was going to run hell-for-leather toward the hills.

Instead of answering, Butterscotch tried to nibble Ben's hair, her long white whiskers tickling his face.

"I'm sure Katie will be by to feed you soon," Ben reassured her with a final pat. He moved down the line.

In the last stall near the tack room, a big, proud black stallion gave Ben a regal once-over. He wasn't a horse built for a casual trail ride or rounding up cattle. He had the form of a racehorse or a jumper.

Ben went in the tack room and after poking around, he found his old saddle. It was in the back and hung from a post set in the wall. He scooped it onto his arm and turned, looking for a bridle. A tan leather bridle with silver trimmings hung high on the wall.

An unexpected wave of sadness struck.

"It's beautiful," Mom had said on the morning of her birthday. She'd held the blond leather headstall up with her thumb and forefinger where a horse's ears would go. The silver buckles and trim had glinted in the sunlight streaming through the windows. "Much too fancy for Clara Bell." The old mare she'd been riding for as long as Ben could remember.

On the floor at her feet, Chance was quietly singing "Happy Birthday," putting his own distinct stamp on the melody.

"We had a different horse in mind when we bought that for you, honey," Dad had said, pointing out the front window where Big E stood with a tan-and-white paint mare.

"Is that... Is she for me?" Mom had whispered. All five boys and Dad had assured her it was. "She's beautiful." Tears welled in Mom's eyes as she hugged the leather to her chest. "Her tan patches are the same color as the bridle."

"She's the same color as butterscotch," Tyler piped up, unwrapping a butterscotch candy in his hand. His dark hair stuck up from the cowlick at the back of his head like untamable brown weeds ringing a fence post.

Mom had never asked for much. She'd been more the sentimental type, holding on to things that she loved. She'd worn a faded green sweatshirt with her high school's leaping tiger mascot on the chest around the barn on chilly mornings as she fed the horses. She'd worn both a wedding ring and the promise ring Dad had given her, even though the promise ring had a diamond chip in it you could barely see. And she used to keep a pair of boots from each of her five boys in a row against the wall in her bedroom. They hadn't taken up much space given they were toddler-size.

Ben couldn't remember what had happened to those boots after Mom and Dad died.

Impulsively, Ben pulled a stepladder over, climbed up and took his mother's bridle off the short post it hung from. He couldn't ride Butterscotch, given her age and that she had a foal, but he could use Mom's fancy bridle. Though he didn't want Jon or Ethan to see him doing so. Ethan would think he'd won Ben's vote to keep the place.

Being sentimental about your mom doesn't mean you've gone soft, boy.

Ben was afraid he was going soft on too many things in Falcon Creek.

The stallion nuzzled Ben's shoulder as he came closer, saddle over one arm and bridle in the other. The horse was like a sleepy kitten demanding some attention. Or maybe, like Butterscotch, he wanted breakfast.

"Hey." Ben stopped. "You don't really want

to go for a ride. You wouldn't look macho with a pretty blond bridle on you, fella."

The stallion shoved Ben's shoulder again. He was extremely tall, black as night and clearly built for speed with a long graceful neck and lofty elegant legs. Someone had probably traced his bloodlines back a hundred years. A brass engraved plaque on the stall stated his name. Devil's Thunder.

"That's an off-putting name." Ben set the tack down on the ground and took hold of the stallion's bridle, looking him in the eye. "They should just call you Blackie." He was as tame as the plump trail horses a few stalls over.

The stallion nibbled his sweatshirt.

"Okay, I get it. You're bored. You want to go for a ride?" Ben set the saddle and bridle down on the floor, entered the stall and ran his hands over the horse's neck and withers. He picked up each hoof in turn, checking to make sure the stallion was shod and his shoes firmly set. "Because who knows when anyone had you out last."

Blackie put up with Ben's inspection better than most ponies. If he'd been skittish in any way, Ben would have moved along. Since the stallion was calm, Ben saddled him up and led him out of the barn, checking the girth strap one more time before standing back and realizing just how tall Blackie was. His withers came up to Ben's nose.

"I don't want to be a greenhorn, Blackie, but I could use a mounting block." Ben may have adopted running tights, but he didn't do yoga. The stirrup was above his waist and it would be a struggle to bring his foot up that high, much less use it to lever himself into the saddle.

Thankfully, someone had put a mounting block near the paddock fence, probably for the "dudes" staying at the guest ranch. Ben had no qualms using it since his brothers weren't watching.

The day was dawning golden and bright. As soon as he settled in the saddle, Ben had to hold the stallion back. He wanted to run.

"Blackie, even athletes take it slow at first and warm up. We'll run when we get on the road to the river." The one separating Blackwell land from the Thompson's property.

Blackie pranced sideways, fighting Ben for control. And then he bucked.

"And here I thought you were a cream puff." Ben used his legs and the reins to bring the horse back in line.

Given his even temperament, Blackie was

probably very well behaved but had a little spring fever from being cooped up. His small stall had a paddock of its own, but this horse had been bred to be an athlete. He needed room to move.

From the saddle, Ben opened the gate onto the road he and Rachel had ridden on the other night. "Let's see what you can do, fella." He eased the tension off the reins.

The stallion leaped forward. He had a choppy trot as he tried to break into a run.

And then Ben gave him free rein. Suddenly they were flying down the road faster than Ben had ever gone before. That long stride ate up the mile to the river. The stallion galloped like a Thoroughbred racehorse in a dead heat.

Whoever had bought this magnificent animal, Ben was going to tell them it was worth every penny. He and the horse moved as one.

There was no court case. There was no wrestling match with what was right or wrong regarding water rights or what his father would have done. There was only the wind in Ben's face and the feel of a powerful horse beneath him.

And then disaster struck.

Out of nowhere, the bull that hated Ben appeared on the other side of the fence. He slammed into a fence post as they passed. Midstride, Blackie leaped sideways, away from the bull. He tossed his head, snapping the old leather rein free on one side, which meant Ben was no longer in control and Blackie could run.

And run he did. Toward the riverbank, Zoe's observation platform and the fifteen-foot drop down to the rocky river. The horse's flight instinct had been triggered and he wasn't thinking about safety ahead. He was thinking about threats behind.

"Whoa!" Ben shouted, hoping the horse had been trained in emergency stops. He moved his heels forward, interfering with the stallion's stride.

Blackie slowed, but didn't stop. Why would he? Ferdinand was running alongside the fence, snorting like a steam engine about to jump the track.

Ben pulled the remaining connected rein steadily, bringing Blackie's head around. That got the horse to slow down until he was trotting sideways like one of those Lipizzaners.

Ferdinand took advantage of the slower pace and rammed another fence post, cracking the wood.

Without warning, Blackie bucked and spun

better than any rodeo bronc. Taken by surprise, Ben went flying. The world spun by in slow motion—dirt, fence, sky.

Thud.

Ben stared at the blue-gray sky above him and willed his lungs to fill with air.

They didn't.

A black, velvety nose nuzzled Ben's head, shoved his shoulder, snorted in his face. The horse's version of CPR didn't open Ben's lungs. He was reaching for the horse's dangling rein just as Ferdinand rammed the next fence post. This one right beside Ben.

Blackie jerked back, neighing like he was part donkey, braying at Ben's bad luck. And then he made a run for it. Returning the way they'd come. The long leather rein flying behind him like a kite's tail.

Ben flopped in the ditch with enough impact to open his airways. He sucked in oxygen, belatedly wondering why the breeze on his face was warm and smelly.

Ferdinand pawed the ground next to the fence, glaring at Ben and covering him in a shower of dirt.

Ben wiped his face free of earth and bull snot.

"I'd like to tell you I landed on this side of the fence on purpose, Ferdinand." Ben rolled to all fours, realizing he was once again wearing red. Ethan's *red* sweatshirt this time. "But that would be a lie. I've been lucky twice with you."

The third round, if there was one, was due to the bull.

In the distance, someone shouted.

Ben looked up. A horse and rider approached, Blackie in tow. At first, Ben thought it was Katie.

It wasn't.

It was Rachel. Her blond hair caught the sun's early rays.

Ben was happy to see her, if only because she'd saved him the embarrassment of explaining to Katie and Ethan why he'd taken out such a fine piece of horseflesh and why he hadn't used newer tack.

Rachel trotted up, leading the stallion by the broken rein and grinning like she'd just found a way to win their impending court case. "Geez, Blackwell. You need a keeper."

"Apparently, you're the designated warden." Ben stood, every muscle in his body protesting. He claimed the thin strip of leather from her and leaned on Blackie's chest, riding out the sharp pain of a back-and-neck spasm. When his muscles settled into a dull burn,

Ben examined the broken rein. "The stitching on the buckle is rotted." Explaining why it'd given way.

"What's a lawyer doing taking a ride on half a million dollars of horseflesh?" Rachel directed her big-boned strawberry roan away from Ferdinand. She rode along the Double T's fence line, scanning her pasture. She wore blue jeans today and a blue plaid button-down beneath a sleeveless jacket.

The bull huffed behind Ben, making the stallion dance.

"Easy, boy." Ben rolled his head, trying to loosen up his muscles. "You're overstating things, Thompson. My grandfather would never invest that much in a horse."

"Zoe's starting a breeding program." Rachel stood in her stirrups and scanned her pasture. "You didn't happen to see a heifer running loose, did you? She ransacked the vegetable garden again last night and I can't figure out where she's hiding."

"I'll help you look." But Ben clung to the saddle horn, and not just out of shock that his tight-fisted grandfather had agreed to spend a fortune on an animal. Was this why Ethan was talking financial ruin? Expensive stock wouldn't help them sell the ranch. And speaking of help... "Hey, um, Rachel?"

"Yeah." She turned her horse around so she could see him squarely.

"I...uh..." He massaged the back of his neck. "I need a boost."

Rachel's mouth worked, as if she was testing out different responses before deciding on one. "Do you want me to put your horse on a lead for you, too?"

"We'll be fine." Ben should be able to control Blackie if they didn't run into any other surprises. "If you don't find that cow, Ferdinand is going to find her and then we'll both be needing to fix a fence."

Rachel swung to the ground. "I wish I could take a picture of this. No one is going to believe me." She came to stand at Blackie's shoulder, laced her fingers and braced herself to take Ben's weight.

Ben placed the ball of his boot in her hands and swung into the saddle. "Thanks."

"Code of the west, Blackwell." She wiped her hands on her jeans and got back on her horse. "Can't leave a man behind. Let's start in the midlands pasture. The gate is back a ways."

Rachel had honor. She'd disclose a document regarding land ownership and water rights.

Guilt came galloping back in Ben's gut, wreaking havoc with the coffee he'd had for breakfast.

That did it. First thing Monday, Ben was initiating a title search. If the aquifer belonged to the Double T, so be it.

They headed back along the road, riding in silence. Ben hurt from his hips to his ears.

"Who's that?" Rachel pointed ahead. "That's not a Double T truck. Is it one of yours?"

A big white truck drove toward them, kicking up dust. Ferdinand snorted and charged ahead, prepared to defend his turf.

"Is that…" Ben squinted. "It looks like a utility truck."

"We're not in court. You can stop trying to put one over on me." Oh, the sarcasm in her tone. She was about to be schooled.

Ben pointed at the fast-approaching truck. "You're going to owe me dinner if that's a water company vehicle. And during dinner, we're going to hammer out a water agreement."

"Blackwell…" She didn't finish her sentence.

The vehicle slowed down as it approached. It was indeed a Falcon County Water Company truck.

Ben and Rachel moved their horses to the Double T side of the road to let the driver get past. Without speaking, they turned their horses around and followed the truck to its destination. Ferdinand came, too.

"Morning," Ben said to the driver. "What brings you all the way out here on a Saturday?"

"The boss said I've got to get some water readings." The man was in his twenties with shaggy brown hair and a pair of work boots that had seen more than one muddy pasture. He was old enough to have some experience on the job and young enough to be intimidated by someone who spoke with authority. He surveyed the Double T's pasture and then proceeded to open the gate without permission.

"Is it normal for you to collect readings out here?" Using his legs and the single rein, Ben directed Blackie to follow.

"Normal? Nope. Not out here." He carried a small tablet. "My supervisor was saying this morning that he couldn't remember the last time we'd come out this way."

Ben frowned deeply at Rachel, trying to

say, *See? I told you so.* He hated that he'd been right. Maybe Mr. Middle-Age had been a water company attorney after all. "Are you scheduled to get readings off the Blackwell pump, too? Because we've been having trouble with that bull."

The meter reader glanced over at Ferdinand, who was pacing back and forth behind the gate. "I'm not supposed to come back without them. You'll need to move the bull to another enclosure."

"No can do." Ben held up his single rein. "I have equipment failure. He's not the kind of animal you go in to get half-cocked."

"Were you given a reason to collect a reading?" Rachel was trying to ask casually, but she fiddled with a lock of her blond hair, a sure tell.

"I just do what I'm told." The meter reader opened the door to the Double T's water pump shed and disappeared inside.

"Ben," Rachel whispered.

"Not now," Ben whispered back.

They waited for the meter reader to reappear. Blackie channeled Ben's frustration, pawing the ground and shifting on his feet.

"Easy, boy." Ben patted his neck.

The meter reader emerged, shut the door behind him and then walked past Ben and Rachel, pausing at the gate to turn and face them. "If you can't move the bull, I'm going to have to report this as a refusal to allow a reading. I can get written up for this."

"I'm sorry," Ben said, trying to sound sincere. "You can tell your supervisor to call Katie Montgomery." Ben leaned on the saddle horn, schooling his smile to be as friendly as little Poppy's. "Katie's the acting ranch manager for the Blackwells. She'll tell you what a problem that bull is."

"We wanted to help," Rachel added with faux sincerity. "We really did."

"Uh-huh." The meter reader wasn't buying it. He climbed behind the wheel of his truck, executed a three-point turn that had barbed wire scraping fenders in the tight space and left them in a cloud of dust.

Without getting off her horse, Rachel closed the gate, shutting them on Double T property. "You weren't kidding about the water company lawyer, were you?"

Ben had been, so he said nothing. But he was thinking. He was thinking his father would be frowning down on him from heaven.

The water company was going to take the extra water Rachel was banking on.

Ben's empty stomach clenched. He headed northwest, toward Jon's property. They still had a heifer to find. "I can't remember you ever growing crops this far from the homestead."

She brought her much shorter horse even with his. "We never have. This has always been fall and winter grazing pasture. Why do you ask?"

Ben hesitated, but they were in this together now. "River water can't be owned by any one property. It flows downriver and there needs to be enough to provide for those users downstream."

"We have an allotment, Blackwell. And since you aren't using your allotment, we can take it."

"No, you can't." He caught her gaze. "There've been legal cases resolved as recently as this spring regarding river water rights in Montana."

"What kinds of cases?" The emotion in her big brown eyes turned from annoyance to worry.

"Land owners and water companies downriver challenging property owners upriver. Cease and desist orders for upriver water use being upheld in court." He tried to soften the news, but facts were facts. "The losers have been property owners upriver who own water rights they haven't used in the past. There was a man in the next county who bought land bordering his existing ranch. The additional property came with lots of untapped water rights. He wanted to expand his crop production to grow his herd. But the land hadn't been farmed in twenty years and the downriver users blocked him from using the water rights that came with the land."

"That's not fair." Those brown eyes sought reassurance Ben couldn't give. "Is that why you get a funny look on your face every time I talk about growing feed crops in this pasture?"

Ben gave a curt nod. "I don't think you can do it. I bet the water company is going to make a legal play for the unused river water from both our properties."

I could protect her and the Double T.

"But that's just a guess," he said.

Don't veer out of your lane, boy.

"An educated one," he added, talking louder, as if he could drown out his grandfather's voice. "Unless we can stop their legal moves before they start or Montana state policy changes, the court will rule based on precedent."

"I need this water, Blackwell. I need this water like…" Rachel stood in her stirrups "…like I need to capture that heifer." She sat back down and kicked her horse into a gallop.

CHAPTER TEN

"FINALLY, THAT TROUBLEMAKER is where she belongs." Rachel sat back in Utah's saddle and heaved a sigh of relief.

Not that she had anything to be relieved about after what Ben had told her. He'd been right about the water company's interest in her lawsuit—in her *water*. Why wouldn't he be right about the legal precedent?

Which she hadn't researched.

Oh, she'd thought about researching case law that had to do with water rights issues, but other things had seemed a higher priority— keeping the stock fed, balancing the ranch books, playing with Poppy and, occasionally, sleeping. And now, it seemed as if her case was nothing but a waste of time. She wouldn't even score a moral victory if she beat Ben.

The heifer finished wading across Falcon Creek and scaled the steep bank on the other side with mountain-goat agility. They hadn't needed to rope her, or more accurately, Rachel hadn't had to embarrass herself in front of Ben by trying. The heifer had been defeated, but she didn't act like it. She acted as if she was in control of her own destiny.

Rachel could take a lesson from her.

"When did this bank crumble?" Ben rode the perimeter of what had once been a tall riverbank but now resembled a sloping dirt-beach. "It looks like the trees died—" there were two uprooted elms that had fallen into the creek "—and their roots stopped holding the bank together."

"I don't know when this happened." It hurt to admit, because it felt as if she'd failed. Her list of shortcomings related to her responsibilities was getting distressingly large. "Someone should have known. Henry or Tony or…" *Me.*

Rachel felt weary, as if the reins of her life were slipping through her fingers.

The wind gathered, puffed and swirled, the way it often did at full sunrise before it settled into a more predictable flow from the Rockies. Rachel's hair whipped over her eyes. By contrast, apropos of her life lately, the wind only ruffled Ben's short dark hair, teased the ends of the stallion's long black tail and did absolutely nothing to the heifer across Falcon Creek.

Ben continued to ride along the bank, looking for she didn't know what. "If you're using the banks as a natural barrier, like we do, you'll need to put up fencing here or she'll come back."

Sound advice. "I thought you were a lawyer, not a rancher."

"Lawyers are always full of potential solutions." Ben guided the beautiful black Thoroughbred toward her, competent despite the broken reins, in his element on horseback and on the range.

More than the wind tugged at her, more than jealousy at his skill at handling whatever was thrown at him or the frustration at the way life sometimes seemed to stack the deck against her. Rachel had to look away before his gaze caught hers and put a word to the emotion she was feeling. Because it swelled inside of her until she was certain it shone from her eyes. Rachel wanted someone beside her who was strong and competent and beautiful, like Ben. Except she didn't just want someone like Ben.

I want Ben.

Her gut clenched in denial. *Not Ben. Not a Blackwell.*

The tug of longing persisted, despite it being

a betrayal to the Double T, to her father and to the many Thompsons who'd come before her.

Ben came along beside her. He'd been the last to speak. Rachel needed to say something.

"In my experience—" she twisted her hair into a makeshift ponytail and tucked the long ends into her bra strap "—lawyers are always full of something."

"Options, mostly," he said calmly, not taking the bait.

She'd expected Ben to fire off a clever reply. She'd expected him to keep things light between them. But no. He was serious and compassionate. Did he know she was in above her head on just about everything? Did he know she needed someone like him in her corner?

Rachel had to look at him then. But she avoided his eyes. She looked at his perfect form in the saddle, at strong legs that shifted subtly to control his horse, at wide shoulders that seemed as if they could bear any load and finally, at his face.

Understanding shone in his blue eyes. "It's hard, isn't it? To be in charge? To have the authority to make decisions but to second guess your every move."

Ben knew what Rachel was going through. Perhaps he always had.

A memory surfaced, long buried beneath resentment toward the man she credited with stealing her family's water supply.

It'd been the first year she'd gone to the state debate championships. Rachel was the only student representing their county. Nana, Mom and Stephanie had been in Boise on a long-planned visit to family. No one had expected Rachel to final. But Dad said he could take her. Dad didn't take vacations. Ever.

The morning of the competition, there'd been some kind of emergency on the ranch— heifers missing or bulls on the loose. Rachel couldn't remember. She'd called Zoe in a panic and her friend had suggested Rachel call Ben. He was a few months older than the girls and had his driver's license. Ben had agreed to drive Rachel because that's the kind of guy he was. Zoe had stayed in town. She had a hair appointment she refused to miss because that's the kind of girl she was.

"I suppose this is going to take all day," Ben had said when they arrived at the university where the competition was to be held.

Rachel looked up from the notes she'd made on the topics that had been posted for the competition. "Why would you say that?"

"Because you always win."

Rachel had smiled. She'd smiled from head to toe. She held Ben's compliment to her chest as tightly as the binder with her many factual references. Under the umbrella of his praise, she'd practically floated into the auditorium.

Rachel lost in the semifinal round. She walked into the stage wings in shock. Even though she was only a sophomore, she'd never lost a debate at their school or in their district.

"It was only a matter of time before that small town girl got knocked out." A young voice reached Rachel from the shadows backstage.

"It's kind of pathetic how they let these little schools like Falcon Creek in." Another young voice, impossible to place in the gloom. "We outclass them."

Mortified, Rachel looked around. No one met her gaze. She didn't know any of the students clustered about. But they knew her. They knew she'd lost. They'd known it was inevitable.

How had they known when Rachel hadn't? She glanced down at her stylish blouse, blue jeans and city boots. How had they seen that she had limitations when Rachel had naively felt she had none?

A sob had climbed Rachel's throat. She ran.

Out the backstage exit. Down a long flight of stairs. Across a stretch of lawn between university buildings. She ran until she couldn't hold the sob in her throat any longer. And then she collapsed on a bench near a small pond and let the crying come.

"Rachel." A familiar voice. A sturdy body. Ben wrapped his arms around her. She'd buried her face in the crook of Ben's neck, unable to stop the stream of tears.

He'd let her cry for what seemed like forever. He'd wiped her tears away with a fast-food napkin he'd had in his pocket. Only then had he said, "Don't let anyone judge what you know is true, Thompson. You're good at this. You'll get them next time. You'll win this thing."

The demoralized dreamer in her memorized those words, vowing to make them a reality. The cynic in her noted that athletes like Ben had heard more locker room pep talks after a loss by age sixteen than she'd ever hear in a lifetime.

Those words, the cynic said, meant nothing.

Those words, the dreamer countered, meant everything.

He'd bundled up the demoralized dreamer and taken her home. He'd never said anything about her breakdown. Not to anyone at school. Not even to Zoe.

All those years later, Rachel felt a similar sob build in her throat. She held both Utah and the sob in check as Ben came up beside her. "What am I going to do, Ben?"

Ben, not Blackwell.

If he realized the significance of her using his given name, he ignored it. "I think metal stakes and barbed wire will work." Ben took her question out of context. "A one-day job for anybody around here."

"No." She could let it go at that. She could swallow that sob and ride home without saying more. He'd let her get away with silence. But Rachel had reached a dead end in terms of ideas. She needed advice. "What am I going to do about the water? About…the Double T?" Her throat was thick with doubt and that darn sob. "I was banking on the water to keep us afloat." To put more cattle in their pastures. To pay off Mom's credit card bill.

"Rachel, you shouldn't ask me that." Ben's voice was as deep as the roots of their ranches, as soft as the river gurgling as it rounded the bend. The soothing quality of his voice made Rachel tremble. She clenched her fingers around the reins.

"I'm opposing counsel," Ben continued matter-of-factly.

Opposing counsel. Her enemy.

There was no going back to the boy who'd comforted her. There was no moving beyond the court case that divided them. If Rachel ever discovered who'd sent her the Blackwell Ranch's water information, she'd give them a piece of her angry mind.

"Forget the lawsuit for a minute and think about…" Rachel closed her eyes, willing herself to hold everything inside the way her father used to. Except she wasn't her father and every day she felt more and more out of her element. "I'm not equipped to run the ranch. Things are slipping away from me. Ask me what shoes to wear with a midlength cocktail dress and I could tell you in my sleep." She opened her eyes, finding Ben's face with its chiseled planes that were as solid as the Rockies. By contrast, she felt as insubstantial as the collapsed riverbank. "But this… It's been over a year since Dad died and all I do is play catch-up. I need to do better. The family needs me to do better."

"You could sell."

His words numbed her. The sob escaped. She wheeled Utah around and kicked the gelding into a gallop, needing to get away, needing to get home, to hold Poppy. Because holding her daughter was the only time lately when she felt hope.

Utah's hooves thundered on the plain, eating up distance.

But getting away from Ben was impossible. His horse was magnificent, catching up to Rachel and Utah as if they'd been standing still.

Ben was magnificent, too, controlling the horse with his legs and one rein, as confident in the saddle when the chips were down as he was in the courtroom.

"Rachel," he shouted. "Listen to me."

She shook her head and leaned over Utah's neck, letting the wind whisk away unwanted tears and tug her hair free of its makeshift ponytail. She should never have asked Ben for advice. She should never have voiced her insecurities. She was stronger when she held everything inside and pretended she had it all under control.

"Rachel." Ben wasn't one to waste words. He guided his horse closer to Utah, who was forced to adjust his stride and slow down to avoid a collision. "You asked me a question. Let me explain."

For Utah's sake, Rachel slowed the roan

to a trot and then a walk, refusing to look at Ben. "Fine. Say your piece and then get off my land."

"You have options."

"I'm not selling." Her shout was lost in the wind.

"If you're going to run the Double T—" Ben's voice cut with the sharp edge of truth "—you're going to have to make hard choices. Not all of them are going to be agreeable to every Thompson, including you."

"I'm not selling." That was nonnegotiable. The only point she wouldn't compromise on.

"Rachel, listen to me like I was your lawyer." There was no give in his voice. He thought what he thought, and he thought she had to listen to him.

The urge to flee made her hands tremble once more. This conversation was a mistake, one in a long string she'd made. "You're not—"

"You asked me for advice." Ben reached over and gave Utah's reins a slow, steady pull. "Whoa." It was a long reach. In the saddle, he was a good foot taller than she was.

Both horses stopped and swiveled their ears back, perhaps wondering what they were doing standing still in the middle of the high plains with no cows in sight.

Ben released the reins and settled his hand on Rachel's shoulder. It was tempting to lean into his touch, to rely on Ben's strength. But there was another sob, waiting like a big dry pill stuck in her throat. And there was her pride, forcing her shoulders to rise and straighten.

Ben sighed and let his hand drop to his thigh. "The good news is you have options. Several options. Let's start with the worst case, at least emotionally, which is selling."

Selling would gut her and Nana Nancy. Her sister Stephanie and Mom wouldn't care.

"Everyone would get a big enough nest egg that they could start somewhere new if they wanted." He didn't try to persuade—she would've slugged him if he tried to wheedle her to sell. "You could open a practice in a bigger city. Your mom could get a place in town. Your grandmother could move to a retirement home. You know—" his tone lightened, softened "—the larger retirement communities have their own beauty salons, coffee shops and movie theaters."

"Nana would hate it." But Rachel wasn't entirely sure that was true. Nana would hate the fact that no Thompson was on the Double T, but she'd enjoy a movie theater and people to talk to. And the frailer her grandmother became, the more appealing a retirement home appeared. It would be a safer environment and give Nana more immediate medical care.

"All right, then." Ben didn't seem put out by her rejection. "Let's consider option two. You could lease your land to someone."

Rachel gave him a sideways glare. "Not the Blackwells." Was he trying to push her in that direction? She reached for her reins.

He leaned down and covered her hand with his. His warmth seeped into her cold fingers. "Okay, not the Blackwells. Although, as your lawyer—"

"Which you most definitely are *not*." She shoved his hand away.

"—I'd advise you to consider leasing to those owning surrounding land, as they'd be the most likely parties interested."

The wind settled into a mild breeze. Rachel hated that Ben's ideas made sense almost as much as she hated the Double T being surrounded by Blackwell land. "Moving along..." She forced herself to meet his gaze, which was as blue as the brightening sky.

"Option three." Ben's lips might have twitched upward. "You could marry a rancher."

Rachel nearly fell out of her saddle. "You did not just say that as if it was a serious option."

"I did." And Ben didn't look a bit remorseful. "A week ago, I would have said Jonathon was the best candidate, but he's engaged. Have you met Lydia? I'm having dinner with them tonight."

Rachel knew better than to grind her teeth, but her jaw was clenched when she said, "And the advantage to marrying another rancher would be…"

"Pooling resources, including water." Ben gestured to the river at their backs. "Especially water."

"The nearest unmarried rancher is Hugh Bellacobble. He's ninety." If he was still alive, that is. Rachel was slightly appalled that she couldn't remember. Mommy brain was wreaking havoc with her ability to retain facts.

"If Hugh has no other heirs, he might be open to a young woman's charms." Ben was definitely grinning now. At Rachel's glare, he held up his hands in surrender. "And of course, there's option four—legal courses of action to protect your river water rights before the water company comes gunning for you. Contact your congressman. Contact the state water board. Work the backside of the situation."

She didn't have time to work the backside of any situation. "Alone? No one's going to listen to me."

"Not alone." His gentle voice soothed.

Did he know her aversion to handling everything alone? Did he realize how intimate his offer sounded? How tempting it was for this little lady to set her cares on his sturdy shoulders?

"You should combine forces with landowners who might be in the same predicament as you." He tapped his swelling chest and shattered the image that he was offering anything other than a business deal.

"Join up with you?" A shout of laughter shot out of her throat, clearing it of pitiful sobs. "That'd be like the Hatfields joining up with the McCoys."

He crooked a brow. "You seem to forget we were friends once."

"Once." And once, they'd stood in a shadowy hallway and she'd seriously considered what it would be like to kiss him. Had that been last night? It seemed like a lifetime ago. "I need to get back."

Because Poppy liked to get up at 4:00 a.m., which made it easy to come out to the ranch before sunrise and get the day started. Poppy had likely worn Rachel's mother out by now. Both Mom and Poppy would be ready for a nap, and Nana Nancy would need her morning medication.

"You asked me for my opinion," Ben said with more patience than Rachel might have, had their situations been reversed. "A rancher would deliberate on the options their lawyer presented."

"I don't like any of your options, Blackwell. I—"

Before she knew what was happening, he leaned across the distance between the two horses, slid his hand to the back of her neck and pulled her mouth up to meet his.

Rachel sucked in air and the taste of Ben, of coffee and warmth.

She'd wondered what it would be like to kiss him when she'd asked him to the Sadie Hawkins dance in the seventh grade. And then last night… She'd thought about Ben as she contemplated the crack in her bedroom ceiling, sometime between worrying about refilling Nana's medication and getting Poppy to the doctor for her booster shots and wondering about ranch gates that miraculously opened. With a kiss under her belt, she'd be able to at least put thoughts of Ben out of her head.

Ben was a good kisser. Better than Ted, who'd kissed her sloppily on her wedding day, having kissed a whiskey bottle first. Better than Andy, who'd given Rachel her first kiss on the Fourth of July and kissed her goodbye at prom.

And just the fact that Rachel was thinking of other males she'd locked lips with instead of enjoying Ben's kiss said something about the chemistry between them. As in, there was none.

What a relief. Finally, something was going right.

Ben released Rachel, tilted his head and peered into her eyes. With the subtlest of leg movements, he urged his horse's hindquarters to swivel away from Utah's. He hopped to the ground and pulled Rachel out of the saddle, almost before she knew what was happening.

"What are you doing, Blackwell?" Oh, she knew what he was doing. She was just so very certain that whatever he was trying to prove wasn't going to prove anything. "This is ridiculous. That kiss only goes to show we're destined to remain frenemies."

"Now see…" Those blue eyes sparked. "That's the problem with you. You're too quick to judge."

"Ben, I—"

"Obviously, this is the only way to win this argument." And then Ben placed his hands on Rachel's hips, drew her close and kissed her.

This time, Rachel didn't think about coffee or the seventh grade or another male.

This time, Rachel was drawn into Ben's kiss like a kid to a pillowcase full of Halloween candy.

This time, Rachel didn't think about being a mommy or a family caretaker or a ranch manager. She thought about nights that were too cold and beds that were too big and how none of that had to be her future.

All too soon, Ben released her, grabbed his horse's broken rein and led the stallion toward the gate that separated their properties.

"What?" she said in a daze. Rachel's boots didn't budge. "Where are you going?" They'd kissed. They had to talk about it.

He led his horse through the Double T's gate, closed it and crossed the road. He opened the Blackwell gate on the other side and went through that one. All without a word. All without looking back.

As if their kiss meant nothing.

CHAPTER ELEVEN

THAT KISS MEANT NOTHING.

Ben had been trying to tell himself that all the way back to the ranch.

It was like telling himself that keeping the bull-for-land trade a secret from Rachel was the right thing to do. He could say the words as often as he liked, but he couldn't escape the nagging feeling that it wasn't true.

There was truth in their kiss.

Well, at least the second kiss. The first had been more like a dress rehearsal of an opening argument that struck all the wrong notes. But the second kiss...the one where his feet had been firmly planted on the ground? His wide stance hadn't stopped the emotional turf from shifting inside of him. He wanted to tuck Rachel under his arm and lift any burden she faced.

Unfortunately, he and his family were part of her many problems.

And yet, option four. They'd be fools not

to partner together to face a powerful water corporation.

Ben led Blackie to the barn. The stallion had a manner of walking that was more like an athlete's strut after a spectacular score. He kept outpacing Ben and bumping him in the shoulder with his broad chest.

"Dude," Ben said the third time it happened. "I'm not sure you have anything to strut about." Ben certainly had nothing to be proud of. What right did he have to kiss Rachel?

Correction. What right did he have to kiss her twice? Because now that he'd kissed her, he felt the strongest urge to be by her side and to make life easier for her, which would be difficult given she didn't trust him.

"What do you think you're doing?" Katie and Hip ran up to Ben from the main barn with a white billy goat trotting behind them. "Nobody takes that devil of a horse out. If anything were to happen to him, Big E would kill me. He cost the ranch a fortune."

"Blackie was fine." Ben handed over the broken rein, appreciative of Katie's offer to brush the horse down and clean his hooves. He had another case to prepare for. The one against the Falcon Creek Water Company. "He needed a little airing out."

Hip sat on her haunches and stared off

at the pasture, ears pitching toward a prairie dog poking his head above ground. The goat reached them and bleated, as if chastising Katie and Hip for leaving him behind.

"Blackie?" Katie's slender red brows lowered. "You don't call a horse like this Blackie. Blackie is a swaybacked trail horse that's so old he refuses to die. This—" she pointed at the stallion with both hands "—this horse is royalty. The monthly insurance on him alone is more than most house payments."

"Calm down. *Blackie* is fine." Ben gave the horse a pat and received a nose nudge in return.

"Fine?" Katie latched on to the bridle and examined Blackie's head, gasping when she noticed the rein had snapped off. She stared at Ben harder than any opposing attorney ever had. "He broke free?"

"No. Ferdinand startled him." At her confused look, Ben added, "Maybe you should gather some hands and escort that bull across the river to higher ground with the herd."

"I would if I had the extra help. Hiring new hands isn't that easy." Katie checked over Blackie's legs for injuries. "You know, this bridle is for show. The guests get a kick out of seeing something so fancy hanging on a wall. I didn't take you for a showboater, Ben, but I guess I should revise that impression."

"That bridle was my mom's," Ben said in a husky voice that probably revealed he still missed her, if his taking the bridle did not.

Katie stopped examining Blackie and straightened, searching Ben's face. "I'm sorry. I'd... I'd forgotten."

He didn't want to think about Mom, or worse, Mom and the ranch. "I hope the other tack is in better shape than that bridle. I don't suppose I need to warn you about liability."

"Please don't." She went back to examining the horse, looking uncomfortable.

"The horse is fine, by the way." Ben reached up to tug his hat brim down and was suddenly surprised he didn't have a Stetson on. The ride had been a mistake. Just like those kisses. He needed to shut himself in the study and be a heartless lawyer.

"I know that tone." Katie confiscated Blackie's reins. "You're thinking you're going to take him out again. Don't do it." She led the stallion toward the barn, followed by the dog and the goat.

Don't do it.

Good advice. Especially when applied to kissing Rachel.

But when was the last time Ben had heeded good advice?

"You're just in time," Mom called from the kitchen when Rachel walked in the door still reeling from Ben's kisses. Poppy sat at Mom's feet banging on pots with a wooden spoon. "We're making hash for breakfast and we need a tiebreaker. Who is sexier in *Bridget Jones's Diary*? Colin Firth or Hugh Grant?"

All Rachel could think of to say was Ben Blackwell, despite him not being one of the choices offered.

"Choose Colin and I'll crotchet Poppy a flowery headband." Nana Nancy sat at the kitchen table dicing potatoes. Her coveted beauty salon curls were squashed over her ears, making her hair look like a white mushroom. "A pink one would look real cute with that flowery dress she's wearing."

"Ma-ma-ma-mahh." Poppy banged the pots harder.

It was only seven thirty and a Saturday, but Mom already had on a pretty lime-green sundress, delicate white sandals and makeup. Just went to prove you could take the girl out of the city but not the city out of the girl.

Rachel realized she'd gone looking for the rogue heifer this morning without makeup. And she'd been kissed. The world worked in mysterious ways.

"Oh, Nancy." Mom sliced tomatoes on the cutting board and slid them into a bowl next to the skillet. "Why do you always try to bribe Rachel to your side?"

Nana harrumphed.

Poppy stopped banging on the pots and pans and crawled toward Rachel. "Ma-ma-ma-mahhh."

Fanny emerged from her dog bed in the corner, stretched and then checked the baby for crumbs.

"If you insist upon playing dirty…" Mom fixed Rachel with a hard look. "Rachel, you'll be doing the dishes this week if you don't vote for Hugh."

The little white poodle noticed Rachel and gave an obligatory growl before sniffing her boots.

"Shush, Fanny." Rachel picked Poppy up, relishing the familiar comforting weight of her little girl in her arms. Nothing about her morning had been familiar or comforting.

Except…maybe…that second kiss.

Poppy's eyes drooped, her head dropped to Rachel's shoulder and she yawned.

"Why the sudden fascination with movies and heroes?" Rachel asked.

Her mother and grandmother went suspiciously silent. Nana ducked her head, as if the potatoes she was dicing required all her attention, and Mom moved to the refrigerator.

This wasn't good. "Have you been sneaking off to the bargain matinee in Livingston every afternoon?"

"No," Mom said too quickly, practically burying her head in the vegetable crisper. "Don't dillydally. Colin or Hugh. Choose."

Sadly, Rachel's vote would still be cast for Ben Blackwell. If only she knew if his interest in her went beyond a few kisses.

Not that it mattered at the moment. She had other loose ends to tie up. Two to be exact. "I'm going to put Poppy down for her morning nap. Better come clean when I get back." Rachel was in no mood for secrets… At least, not ones Mom and Nana kept from her. "If they know what's good for them, your grandmas will confess," she said to Poppy on their way down the hall.

When she returned to the kitchen, the pair of Thompson matriarchs stood side by side.

"It was her idea," Nana blurted, pointing at her daughter-in-law.

"Tattletale." Mom huffed and put her nose in the air. "If you must know, we were bored one day, and I called the cable company to complain about how few channels we had."

"You were bored?" Rachel wanted to be sick. "There are so many other things you could be doing besides watching TV." Any of the little things that Dad used to do, like sort Nana's prescriptions into the little box so she knew what to take and when or pay the ranch bills and balance the accounts every month.

"And they told me—" Mom raised her voice to drown out Rachel's upset "—about all these other channels we could watch." She spoke in an accusatory voice.

"You didn't," Rachel squeaked out.

"Four hundred channels." Nana nodded, a grin working through the wrinkles on her thin face. "We've been having a field day." Her expression turned dreamy. "Movies without commercials and we're not even at the theater. Can you imagine?"

"Call them back." Rachel jabbed her finger toward the living room and the offending cable box. The one she hadn't noticed was new.

"Why?" Mom wouldn't meet Rachel's gaze.

"Because we can't afford luxuries like that." Rachel gripped a chair to steady herself. "*I* don't have luxuries like that."

"Luxuries?" With a wave of her hand, Mom

brought Rachel's attention to the dilapidated state of the kitchen. "What luxuries? We have no luxuries."

"She means like going out to dinner every week," Nana said softly, not quite on Rachel's side and not quite on her daughter-in-law's either. "Or buying a new pair of shoes that isn't on sale."

"Or signing up for four hundred channels." Rachel flexed her hands on the wooden kitchen chair. "Call them back and cancel."

"No." Mom crossed her arms over her chest. "We've scrimped long enough. We can't scrimp forever."

When had Rachel become the parent in the house? Tears pressed at the back of her eyes. "You can have those channels if you give up something else."

"Like what?" Mom's high-pitched challenge bounced off the ceiling. "The electric oven? Seeds for your grandmother's vegetable garden?" Mom had momentum and wasn't backing down. "Tell me how else we can cut back."

Sell the ranch. Ben's words echoed in Rachel's head.

Don't say it. Don't say it. Don't—

"We could sell the ranch," Rachel blurted.

"No." Nana's head shook faster than a bobble-head on a dashboard on a bumpy road. "Never."

Mom sputtered, "And where would we live?"

Again, Rachel tried to keep her mouth shut. It was important to keep the peace, to bite her lip, to make new cable boxes from a sow's ear. But she couldn't be like her father. She couldn't carry everyone's load by working herself into the grave. "Nana could move into one of those fancy retirement homes and, Mom, you could move in with Stephanie, although you might have to get a *job*." They were nasty words and Rachel regretted them the moment she gave them voice.

"You'd lock me up in one of those old folks prisons?" Nana demanded in a strangled voice.

"I am *not* getting a job outside the house!" Mom looked horrified. "Being a housewife is what I do. Can't you move home? That would save us some money."

And drive Rachel crazy. "No." Thankfully, that hadn't been on the list of Ben's options. "You could…you could…get married again."

Her mother clutched her throat. "Your father is barely cold in his grave."

Rachel somehow managed not to point out that Dad had passed nearly two years ago.

Nana's gaze turned speculative. "Married to who?"

"I hear Hugh Bellacobble is available." The ninety-year-old rancher down the road.

"That old timer." Nana cackled. "He hasn't got all his teeth and he snores like the dickens."

Rachel held up a hand. "I don't want to know how you know he snores."

"What's happened to you, Rachel?" Mom had tears in her eyes. "We used to shop together and have lunch in town. We used to laugh."

Rachel remembered those moments, but they seemed a long, long time ago. "I had to fill Dad's shoes to keep a roof over your heads." It had to be said. Rachel had babied her mother long enough. She couldn't do it anymore. Not if what Ben said about their water was true.

Down the hall, Poppy began to wail, winding out the sound like a fire truck being called to put out the flames of this argument.

"You want to stay here?" Rachel started to leave. "Then don't spend money we don't have."

"We're going to have plenty when you win our water back from that Blackwell boy," Nana said, making Rachel stop in her tracks.

"That's right." Mom wiped away a tear.

"More water. More cattle. You promised. Your father always kept his promises."

"Yes, he did," Nana added, rubbing Mom's back. "He never let us worry about a thing. And Rachel, you were so confident that everything would go back to normal that we were confident, too."

Poppy wailed louder. Rachel wanted to wail along with her.

"I'm sorry." Rachel walked out of the kitchen and down the hall. "But I'm not Dad. I can't shoulder this alone."

Ben Blackwell had kissed her. The Double T's water dreams were slipping away. She wasn't confident about anything anymore.

CHAPTER TWELVE

IF THE DOUBLE T looked in need of love, the JB Bar Ranch, Jonathon's spread, looked well loved.

The fencing and outbuildings were straight and tall. Not a gate listed. Not a plank of siding was warped or out of place. The sprawling pale gray white-trimmed home had been built in the last decade and it had bright red and yellow blooms lining the front porch.

"Those flowers look cheerful," Grace, Ethan's fiancée, said, as she led Ethan and Ben up the walk. She had blond hair, gentle hazel eyes and the ability to negotiate the tightrope that spanned the distance between Ethan and Ben. She'd carried the conversation on the car ride over from the Blackwell Ranch.

"You can have as many flowers as you want at our place," Ethan said magnanimously, if with a fair dose of mush.

Ben supposed Ethan was entitled to being

mushy since Grace was carrying his child, not that she was showing much of a baby bump.

"Flowers? Easy for you to say." Grace reached the porch with Ethan just a few steps behind her. Once he was next to her, she slipped an arm around his waist. "We haven't even decided where we're going to live. A small apartment over an office isn't the best location to raise a baby."

"I'll build you a house wherever you want one." Ethan hooked his arm around Grace's waist and swept her in the front door. "Someday."

Someday would come a lot sooner if Ethan voted to sell the ranch. Ben shook his head. Sometimes his twin didn't know what was good for him.

Ben followed the couple inside the house and found himself in the kitchen. The space was grand, modern and sophisticated. Granite counters, stainless steel appliances, a big island and a formal dining room beyond that.

Jon's twin girls, who looked to be five or six, were shouting, "Uncle Ethan!" and hugging him as if they hadn't seen him in years.

Jon and a woman Ben assumed was his brother's fiancée were talking to Grace and hugging her.

Jon's dog, Trout, came to sit in front of Ben. They exchanged glances. It was the second time he'd seen the black-and-white shaggy dog. After a moment or two of inspection, Trout wagged his tail. It wasn't exactly the greeting Ethan had received from the rest of the family, but at least some poor soul was offering Ben welcome. He gave the dog a pat and came forward to be introduced to Jon's fiancée.

Ben had assumed Lydia would be stylish with a bit of an attitude, like Jon's first wife. Instead, Lydia was warm and welcoming. She had beer and wineglasses on the counter and appetizers on china plates. In short, Lydia was way too classy for Jon, and on impulse, Ben said so.

Jon chewed on that for a second, and then he laughed and hugged Ben, an air-stealing, backslapping affair. "You've finally forgiven me."

Ben didn't think that, but in a flurry of hugs that came his way from the two energetic little girls and Lydia, and finally Ethan and Grace, he had no time to belabor the point. Before he knew it, he was seated at the dining room table, listening to a recorded country music song by his little brother Chance and being served a slab of prime rib.

The beef was delicious, as were the risotto and homemade rolls Lydia had prepared. She won Ben over. Not that it mattered. Jon and his daughters, Gen and Abby, had already accepted their former nanny as one of the family. Watching the girls and Lydia interact, it was clear to Ben Lydia's love and affection for his nieces was genuine and vice versa.

When the meal was over and the Blackwell boys had done the dishes, Jon led Ben and Ethan out to the porch. Ben explained about the meter reader and the threat of the water company.

Jon took the grim news with a sigh and a change of subject. "It hasn't rained for a few weeks. Hope it does soon."

Ben stared up at the cloudless blue sky. "Are any of the riverbanks eroding on your ranch, Jon?"

"I saw one spot go in the spring. Erosion is a natural process. The exact flow of the river is constantly changing." He paused and then said, "Why do you ask?"

"There was a collapse over at the Double T." Ben sat down on the top step. "A heifer came back across. I was just wondering if you'd had similar problems."

"Hang on." Ethan came to sit opposite Ben on the step. "When were you on the Double T?"

"This morning. I was out for a ride on Blackie—"

"Blackie?" both his brothers said in unison.

"The big black stallion in Big E's barn?"

"Nobody rides him." Ethan grabbed Ben's arm and lifted it. "Are you sure you don't have any broken bones?"

"Blackie is a kitten." Ben resisted admitting he'd been thrown, even as he yanked his unbroken appendage back with enough intensity to send his sore muscles twinging.

"I thought you said you didn't bring any boots or blue jeans." Jon crossed his arms over his chest and gave Ben his I'm-dead-serious look, the one he'd used when he'd tried to keep Ben and Ethan or their younger brothers, Tyler and Chance, in line.

"I borrowed Ethan's." At their incredulous expressions, he added, "You know he's always leaving his clothes lying around. I found some in the laundry room."

"Let me get this straight," Ethan said. "You rode a half-million-dollar horse without permission onto Double T land, also without permission."

"I had permission to go on Double T land."

"No." Ethan shook his head like he wasn't going to quit shaking it.

"I'm confused." Jon's expression hadn't softened. "The Thompsons are suing us for water. Rachel will barely talk to me when I see her in town. When you say you had permission, is this lawyer doublespeak?"

"I came across Rachel on my ride and we spotted the heifer she was looking for. We joined forces to put the heifer back where she belonged." That wasn't all they were joining forces on.

Rachel may not have agreed yet, but she would.

Ethan and Jon exchanged glances, and then they started to laugh.

"What's so funny?" Ben demanded.

"You didn't just happen to stumble upon Rachel out in the midst of acres and acres of grassland." Jon grinned.

"You knew she'd be there and you took out the most expensive horse, hoping to impress her." Ethan was grinning, too.

"You two are so wrong." Ben stood, subtly rolling the kinks out of his stiff back.

"You always wanted the best, even as a kid," Jon said. "To be above the rest."

"It's why you went out with Zoe." Ethan leaned lazily against a post and folded his arms over his chest as if the case was closed.

"And now you're going to romance those water rights out from under Rachel. It's not what I would do, but desperate times call for desperate measures."

"I don't need desperate measures." Ben ran a hand over his hair, thinking about the bull-for-land trade, their father and the compulsion to do what was right.

"Little brother, Big E would be proud." Jon nodded knowingly.

Ben took the steps down to the front walk. He felt sick to his stomach. The prime rib had been too rich. "There's nothing...*underhanded* going on."

The Rockies towered in the distance. There was nothing dishonest about those mountains. They were hard, but they were fair, treating everyone equally. His parents had been honest and fair. But somewhere along the line, Big E had bumped Ben's sense of right and wrong out of the black and white, and into the land of the gray.

He sucked in a breath, knowing it was true. *I have to tell them the truth.*

Ben turned, facing his brothers, prepared to admit the truth and accept the consequences. "All the underhanded dealings went on five years ago. Big E has a scrap of paper that says the land over the aquifer was traded to the Double T in 1919."

"But that means…" Ethan looked like the prime rib had been too rich for him, too. "What does that mean?"

"Big E seemed to think it meant nothing." Ben couldn't look at his brothers, especially Jon. "He argued that there'd been a trade that had either gone wrong or been fulfilled another way with lost documentation or no documentation."

"Big E argued," Jon said solemnly. "Did you argue with him, Ben?"

"Yes, of course." Ben nodded. "I wanted to know if we owned the land free and clear."

"If we owned the water, you mean." Jon's mouth twisted, as if he'd tasted something bitter.

Ben nodded again. He was used to cases where his clients hadn't been the most honorable, but he couldn't muster the passion to defend Big E. Or himself.

"But…" Ethan was still trying to wrap his head around Ben's news. "All this time…you said nothing."

"I'm sorry." It seemed like he'd been saying that a lot since his return to Falcon Creek.

"You lied," Ethan surmised. "You lied to protect Big E."

"To protect water that didn't belong to us." The bitterness was in Jon's voice now. He'd never have stooped so low.

"I lied to protect *you*." Ben's composure cracked and the long-held resentment broke free. "I lied to protect the Blackwell heritage that everyone seems so proud of. I *lied*. *I* lied." He had to say it twice.

That was the *when* Ben had been looking for, the moment he'd crossed the line from honorable to dishonorable. That was where he stopped questioning fairness and began keeping tallies of courtroom wins. It had all started here, in Falcon Creek, with a man who was more interested in power than in principle, the man who'd made sure Ben had to do the same.

"And then the next day…" Anger was choking Ben, wrapping strong fingers around his windpipe as if trying to reduce his words to monosyllabic cries of frustration. That anger. It lashed at his pride, at his soul, at his self-image, until the world blurred and darkened around him.

He'd made a choice. Just one. And look what he'd become.

Ben cleared his throat, because this needed

to be on record. His brothers had to know the role they'd played. "The very next day…" his vision cleared, focused "…the very next day, the people I lied for… They all betrayed me."

Jon and Ethan drew back, knowing exactly which day Ben was talking about. His wedding day.

"That's right," Ben said as he saw recognition dawn in their eyes. "Big E left with my bride and you two—" Ben's voice filled the air like rolling thunder "—put me on display like some bull destined for slaughter at the county fair. Yes, I lied. By omission. By my silence. But don't you ever think that it came easy. That I'm like our grandfather. That I'm proud of who I am."

Ben had to look away, back to the mountains. Deep down he knew the truth. For five years, he'd been exactly like his grandfather and it had taken a stranger, a tiny orphaned baby his former law firm had wanted to short-change, to make that likeness unbearable.

"I'm going to make this right," Ben said softly. "The truth may not help the Blackwell Ranch. It may hurt Ethan's plans to establish a practice and get out of debt." An image of Grace and the baby she carried flashed before his eyes, followed by a quick stab of remorse.

Her glowing face was replaced by Rachel's worried one. Remorse deepened to guilt. "But I have to tell the truth. For both the Blackwells' sake and the Thompsons'."

His brothers said nothing. They didn't sustain his arguments. They didn't object.

That did it.

"I vote we sell," Ben whispered.

Selling would mean someone else would have to stand up in court and admit the aquifer wasn't owned by the Blackwells and hadn't been for nearly a century. Someone else would have to deal with the Falcon Creek Water Company and fight to use water that was ranch-owned. Someone else would have to watch Rachel say goodbye to her heritage and cast aside her dreams for Poppy. But Ben's involvement... Ben's involvement would end here.

Ben faced his brothers and repeated, "I vote we sell."

Rachel would land on her feet, hurt but wiser. Jon would be able to focus on his ranch and growing family. Ethan would take his share of the sales proceeds, get out of debt and buy a veterinary practice somewhere. He'd probably have enough money to buy Grace a house and those flowers she longed for.

His brothers were silent.

Ethan had paled.

And then Jon gave a little whoop.

Ben should have felt relief. He'd told the truth. But he couldn't shake the feeling that there was one other person who needed to hear the story from him.

Rachel.

CHAPTER THIRTEEN

"WHAT'S A MAN like you carrying a bridle like that for?" Pops Brewster greeted Ben as he came up the Brewster Ranch Supply steps on Sunday afternoon. The old man cocked a bushy white brow. "You gonna hang it on the wall of your fancy place in New York City?"

Ben glanced at his mother's silver-studded bridle. He supposed he deserved the ribbing, given he was wearing black slacks, leather loafers and a white dress shirt at a feed store. "The reins broke. I'm here to get them fixed." His mother would want nothing less.

Pops snatched the dangling reins in one age-spotted hand. "Go ahead and make your move, city boy. You won't be calling checkmate today."

Ben studied the board. Whoever had been playing with Pops had moved a lot of pieces. "What's in it for me?"

"Ten percent off your repair." The old man was cagey.

"Pops, stop with the unauthorized discounts." Mrs. Gardner, Grace's mom, she of the tasty tamales, stood in the doorway, smiling at Ben and her misbehaving father. "I'll give a discount to you, of course, Ben. You're going to be family when Ethan marries Grace. But this old man needs another incentive to get people to play with him."

Ben moved a black bishop diagonally across the board. "Check."

"No." Pops leaned forward, scratching the white stubble on his chin. "That can't be."

"You might try checkers," Ben recommended as he entered the feed store.

It was Sunday, but the place was busy, filled with cowboys and ranchers of all shapes and sizes. Young ones stumbling around in their boots and too big hats. Older ones walking with more finesse, if slightly bowed legs from too many hours spent in the saddle.

Ben supposed he should pick up a pair of jeans while he was here. He'd bet anything Ethan was going to raid the house for the rest of his clothes. He couldn't ride Blackie in dress pants. Ben poked around the stacks of blue jeans on a display table, but he really didn't want to buy any.

"Ba-ba-ba-bahhh."

Ben turned as a woman wearing a base-ball cap, a yellow-checked shirt and blue jeans passed him carrying a baby. "Poppy?"

"Ba-ba-ba! *Ba-bahhh*!" Poppy reached for Ben. She'd been calling to him all along.

"Hey, Rachel," Ben said when opposing counsel stuttered to a halt. Clearly, she'd seen him and was trying to sneak past. He almost wished she had. And yet, he gathered Poppy from Rachel's arms without thinking. "I didn't expect to see you here."

Her cheeks a deep pink, Rachel held her arms out to take the baby back. "I need fence posts and barbed wire."

"You're not going to set the fence alone, are you?" Ben frowned. "Barbed wire can be tricky." It came in coils and if you weren't careful, it could snap back and gouge you.

"You think I can't do it?" Rachel's hands fell to her side. Her brown eyes turned colder than the morning chill that had nipped at Ben during his and Blackie's ride.

Ben hedged. "It's a job for your foreman."

"Henry is semiretired." The way she said it, Ben felt Henry was more like fully retired.

"Don't you have other ranch hands?"

Don't you see where this is going, boy? It's not your problem.

Ben was afraid that when he'd kissed Rachel yesterday, he'd taken on her problems as his own.

"No more full-time help other than Henry. Not anymore." She held out her hands to Poppy and tried to smile, although that smile looked more like a grimace.

The impulse to come to her aid was strong. The kind of strong that called to a soul deep down. The kind of strong that made a man lean down in the saddle and kiss a woman.

"Ma-ma-ma-mahh." Poppy practically leaped from Ben's arms to Rachel's, saving Ben from making a fool of himself by saying he'd help her. But only temporarily. Somehow, his lips started moving of their own accord. "I can babysit while you build that fence."

Immediately, Ben wanted to issue a retraction, to make a formal apology and admit his offer had been made in error.

"I have plenty of babysitters," Rachel said coolly.

"Ba-ba-ba-bahhh." Poppy did her swan dive back toward Ben.

Ben chaperoned her transfer and fit her on his hip. "This is a game for her?"

"Yes. When she's rested." It was an unwelcome game if Rachel's tone was any indication. She gave him a disapproving once-over. "Why are you wearing court clothes on a Sunday? You don't go to church."

"I'm wearing court clothes because I'm a lawyer." He lifted a dark pair of new blue jeans. "But I'm willing to morph into a ranch hand temporarily to help you build a fence. You can watch Poppy while I work. Don't argue." He hesitated, half hoping she would. He didn't want to help her, but apparently the values his parents had instilled in him about being a good neighbor were resurfacing. Which was just another reason he needed to get out of Falcon Creek soon.

Rachel stared at the blue jeans and said nothing, which was confirmation that her building that fence was possibly a mistake in her mind as well. But just in case she formulated an argument, he cut her off early. "Have you ever built a fence before? One with barbed wire?"

That pert nose went in the air, which was where she tossed her gaze, too. "It's not rocket science."

She hadn't. "I have." And Ben had a scar on his shoulder to prove it. "We can talk about water company strategy while we work." Ben checked the label to make sure the jeans in his hand were the right size. "And about the terms of the water agreement for Judge Edwards."

"Assuming I let you help me..." She glared at him. "I will not let you talk about water."

They were practically standing toe-to-toe, like prizefighters promoting a fight.

They'd stood like that on his wedding day. Her, shocked by his refusal to talk water terms. Him, shocked by the revelation that his bride had eloped with someone else. An impasse. One where they both lost. This time, he'd try for an outcome that would be mutually beneficial.

His gaze grazed her lips. If only he hadn't kissed her.

If only I could kiss her again.

Ben sent that thought down the spiraling drain with his other bad ideas. "I was out of line yesterday morning when we... When I..." Ben wouldn't admit much more than that. "You must hate me."

Her eyes widened. She fidgeted. Scuffing her boots, crossing her arms, looking away. And finally saying quietly, "I don't hate you, Blackwell."

"Ma-ma-ma-mahhh!" Poppy tilted toward her mother.

"I'm glad to hear it," he said gruffly, relinquishing the baby.

"I hate what you did to my family," Rachel said in a hard voice bringing her gaze back to his face, showing him the depth of pain in her eyes.

Those eyes... He swallowed and forced himself not to waver.

Rachel didn't notice she was probing his weakness like a doctor examining infected cells under a microscope. She kept right on talking. "I hate that my dad worried night and day about how to water our cattle until he worried himself into his grave. I hate that I wasn't a good enough lawyer back then to make you eat your lunch."

Now it was Ben who fidgeted, readjusting his stance until his feet felt firmly grounded. "You know the irony of being a lawyer?"

She shook her head, eyes still on him, big brown pools of liquid emotion.

He swallowed and stared at the toes of his loafers. "You have a reputation as not caring, when it's exactly the opposite. You care very much." He forced himself to look her in the eye. "You care so much it keeps your brain working when it should be turned off and sleeping. You go to work thinking you can't get into the office fast enough. You need extra time to research precedent. An extra thirty minutes to polish that opening argument. An extra twenty to review points you need to object to. That's all you need to beat someone and to protect your client. It has almost nothing to do with getting paid a sick amount of money an hour. It's about shielding those who need it and fighting for justice."

That's how it should have been. Except it felt more like Ben had become a hired gun, one who fought on the wrong side of the law.

Would Dad be proud of me?

Ben thought not.

"Ba-ba-ba-bahhh!" Poppy lunged toward Ben with a drooly grin. She didn't care about past mistakes or that Ben could be bought. She cared about the here and now, the joy in the moment, the joy she could bring.

Ben hoped another baby with big brown eyes, a little girl living in Long Island, was as carefree as this one.

"Is that what you do in New York? Fight for justice?"

"No." Ben couldn't afford to break her gaze. If he did, she'd know he was more interested in winning than in justice.

And yet, the deep brown of her eyes seemed

to see deeper inside him than anyone had looked before, down to the level where he stored things like guilt and regret.

Poppy swan dove to her mother.

Ben blinked, and his gaze dropped to Rachel's lips. She licked them.

Ben's gaze flew back to hers, looking for a hint of welcome awareness, a sign that whatever was happening in his chest when he looked at her was happening to her when she looked at him. And all the while, he tried to appear like a ranch hand who was ready to do the boss's bidding, one who wore broken-in blue jeans and boots.

Crud. If he was going to help Rachel, he needed a pair of boots, too.

Rachel blinked, looking confused.

He couldn't blame her. Ben felt confused. Why was he feeling something for Rachel when he hadn't felt much of anything for years? He'd been happy once, working settlements where victims of negligence were just names and numbers on a list. Why did things have to unravel? Why had he rediscovered his conscience and a near-burning need to restore his honor?

Ben needed space. "I'll meet you at the gate on the road to the river." He went back toward the boot display. It would take Rachel several minutes to pay for her order and get it loaded in her truck. In the meantime, he needed guilt-free air. He wasn't in Falcon Creek to start something with Rachel. He was here to protect Blackwell interests for Ethan's kid, even if that meant protecting the ranch's interests so they could sell their legacy for more money.

Selling legacies is almost as distasteful as selling your soul.

Ben paused. That voice hadn't sounded like his grandfather's. That voice had sounded like his own.

BEN WALKED OUT to the metal gate in Ethan's old jeans and boots. The new blue jeans and boots had felt too odd, like the impulse to kiss Rachel. They fit, but not comfortably.

In the pasture just east of him, Ferdinand was pulling up tufts of brown grass and ignoring Ben.

He didn't have to wait long for her red-and-white truck to approach. He crossed the road and opened the Double T's gate so Rachel could pull through.

The afternoon sun was heating things up. The truck windows were down. He greeted the friendlier Thompson first. "Hey, Poppy."

"Ba-ba-ba-bahhh!" Little Poppy released the clear plastic dry cleaning bag hanging nearby, kicked out her feet and extended her sturdy little arms his way, fingers opening and closing as if she wanted to latch on to him.

"That's right, Poppy." Ben handed her a sugar cookie he'd swiped from the guesthouse on the way over. "Ba-ba is here."

Rachel groaned.

Poppy smashed the cookie into her face, cooing with pleasure.

Ben could remember laughing with Ethan in the backyard at Tyler and Chance doing the same thing, pressing food in their mouth with the flat of their hand and wiping it all over their chubby little faces.

Warmth spread in his chest.

That warmth... It would disappear the moment he told Rachel about the land deed. The need to tell the truth pressed on him harder than it had the night before with his brothers.

"Get in." Rachel pulled the brim of her baseball cap lower. "And before you ask, my mother and grandmother went to see my sister today. And my former mother-in-law went into Livingston to watch a movie. I'm not only short ranch hands, I'm short on babysitters."

"Glad I could help, then." He was grateful for the small talk. They could navigate the tricky legal waters between them tomorrow in their court attire. Blue jeans and boots seemed too intimate for that. "Before we start, I need to get this out of the way." He reached for Rachel's dry cleaning in the back. Poppy had been playing with the plastic covering, and he didn't want her to choke.

Ben ripped the plastic bag off the suit Rachel had worn to court the other day and stuffed it far away from inquisitive Poppy and potential suffocation. Satisfied the little tyke couldn't get into more trouble, he climbed into the passenger seat.

They set off. The pasture was bumpy and Rachel's shocks were too old. The truck creaked, groaned and bounced like an unsafe ride at the fair.

In the back seat, Poppy gagged.

Ben turned. "Are you okay?"

Her little face was red and her big brown eyes watery. She wheezed and choked.

"Poppy?" Rachel stepped on the brake and rammed the truck into Park as Ben twisted around, reaching for the baby.

Poppy shook her head, strained against the straps of her car seat, and then turned sideways, projectile vomiting right on Rachel's suit.

"THIS CAN'T BE my fault," Ben said for the umpteenth time.

"You took the protective bag off my dry cleaning." Rachel was down to one suit. At this rate, she'd be showing up to court in her mother's poodle-embroidered overalls. "You gave Poppy the cookie she choked on."

"Your daughter's fine, by the way." Ben leaned out the truck window. "If it upsets you so much, I'll buy you a new suit."

Rachel twisted the steering wheel the way anger twisted her insides. "I can buy my own suit, thank you." In a year. If she won the water rights, she could plant feed crops in the far pasture and buy pregnant heifers this summer.

"I'm just saying, given that you said you were on the brink of ruin."

She hated that he was right. She hated that she'd been unable to think of little else but Ben since yesterday. It was easier to declare Ben off-limits—repeatedly—than to deal with increased cable bills and collapsed riverbanks.

Setting aside the fact that he'd just built forty feet of fence for her and was offering to help defend the Double T's water rights, Ben wasn't the man she should be interested in. Ben's kiss had been a wow. But she couldn't trust Ben even if he was helpful, so she needed to keep him at a distance.

They reached the gate to the road separating their family properties. Ben got out and opened the gate so Rachel could drive through.

She was tempted to keep driving, but he'd been nice the entire day. He hadn't mentioned that kiss other than to apologize. Nor had he suggested another.

She suspected his friend-zoning was part of the reason she was cranky.

You can't have it both ways, remember?

After he latched the gate, Ben approached her window. "Why don't we meet at your office tomorrow? Say noon? We'll hash through a water deal for Judge Edwards and we'll review our options to defend against any water company challenges."

Rachel had to say yes. She had no other choice. "Sounds good." Ted was scheduled to come by around eleven to sign the custody papers. He'd be long gone before Ben got there.

Ben glanced at Poppy in the back seat—maybe wanting to say his goodbyes?—but she was asleep. "See you tomorrow."

Rachel nodded and drove on to the Double T, reciting her long list of mantras.

Win back the water rights.

Set the ranch to rights.
Get a signed custody agreement.
Learn how to be a better lawyer.
Learn how to be a better rancher.
Try to be a better mother.
And then she added a new one.
Find a new man who isn't Ben Blackwell.

CHAPTER FOURTEEN

RACHEL STOOD IN the open doorway of her law office, waiting for Ted to arrive. She was wearing her last court suit and her hands shook.

Par for the course.

She hoped to get the custody agreement signed today, crossing a mantra off her list.

Poppy was awake, playing with her blocks on a little carpet in Rachel's office.

Ted pulled up with a squeal of tires. He was thirty minutes into his lunch hour, which meant they had thirty minutes to conduct their business before Ben was due to arrive at noon.

Rachel stepped inside, letting in her ex-husband, who did his best not to look at their daughter. Was that a good sign?

Rachel squeezed the door shut, no thanks to the warped frame, and hurried to put the custody agreement in front of Ted. "I added the clause about raising Poppy in Falcon Creek. We won't move."

Ted's smile was slow coming, but he did

smile, and took a seat in the chair opposite her desk. "I knew you'd see it my way."

Poppy began babbling happily at Ted, offering him a block, which he ignored.

The jerk.

"Ted, you've got everything you wanted," Rachel said evenly. "It's time to sign."

Outside, a car door slammed. Rachel didn't get much foot traffic, probably because she didn't keep reliable office hours. That would have been impossible, what with her responsibilities at the Double T. Was the feed store parking lot full?

Poppy crawled to the edge of the desk and babbled some more, holding out the block to her father.

"What about support?" Ted reclined in his chair.

"I didn't ask you for any child support." Were those steps outside?

The front door was shoved open. Ben stood there, looking up at the offending door frame. He wore a dark suit and carried his dented briefcase, but her mind took liberties and pictured him in his blue jeans and chambray shirt, riding that big black stallion to her rescue.

Which was ridiculous. Nobody ever rescued Rachel. It was why she had so many mantras.

Poppy spotted Ben. "Bahhh!" She crawled toward him, carrying the block in her fist.

"I meant, what about support for *me*?" Ted laced his fingers over his chest, not bothering to look around to see who might have come in or who his daughter was beelining toward. "I should be kept in a style I'm accustomed to."

Rachel couldn't afford to pay Ted a penny. She couldn't afford a new suit for court. "Ted, you signed a divorce agreement that did *not* include spousal support. We're talking custody *only*." There was no reason this argument should make her hands shake harder. On this point, she had the upper hand.

She didn't need to dwell on Ben, to spot the worry shadowing his blue eyes, or watch him pick up Poppy with one arm and marvel at the red block she offered him. She did not need to call in reinforcements. Rachel had Ted right where she wanted him. She held the pen out to her ex.

But just like a sidewinder, Ted came at Rachel broadside. "How badly do you want custody of that kid?"

"That kid?" If Rachel had been a man, she'd have gotten up, grabbed Ted by the neck of his T-shirt and tossed him out the door. As it was, she threw the pen on the desk and said,

"Do you mean that adorable, loving little girl you can't bring yourself to look at? If I had my way, you'd never see her again."

Ted's eyes narrowed and he drummed his fingers on his chest. "You're getting upset. You know what I want."

"Well, I don't." Ben set his dented silver briefcase on the desk and handed Poppy to Rachel.

Her ex-husband sat up and scowled. "Who are you?"

"I'm Rachel's divorce attorney." Ben didn't say his name. He smoothed his expensive red power tie and returned Ted's scowl. "Given the custody agreement hasn't been finalized in a timely manner, Montana law allows Rachel to bring you back to court and sue you for alimony *and* child support. If she wins—which she will, because Montana is a mommy-friendly state—she can have your wages garnished going back in time to the date of separation."

"Is that…?" Ted perched on the edge of his seat and looked from Rachel to Ben and then back again. "Is that true? I mean, how can that be true?"

It wasn't true. Even saying it was unethical. But Rachel kept her mouth closed.

"Would I be here if it wasn't true?" Ben drummed his fingers over the top of his silver briefcase, an earnest look on his face so unvarnished it would have won him a best actor award. "I bill by the hour, my friend. And every hour I bill Rachel gets added onto your tab."

Ted laughed uncomfortably, his gaze swinging around the room but not quite finding a target. "So…" He cleared his throat. "I should sign?"

"Consider this your last chance. Rachel's been kind to you, handling the proceedings herself." Ben took the pen and placed it in front of Ted. "Or don't sign. In which case, I won't quit until I've found every spare penny you have and obtained legal permission to take it all. That means you won't have a dime to spend in the bar you like to hang out in. You won't have a nickel to bet on football. You get the point." With every statement, Ben's expression darkened and his words sharpened, until even Rachel believed him. "Now sign."

Ted gulped and scribbled his name on every red-flagged line. All three copies.

Just like that, Rachel had a signed custody agreement and one less mantra to remember.

BEN ESCORTED TED OUT, nearly slamming the door after him.

Ben had arrived early for his meeting with Rachel after having spent most of the morning at the county recorder's office doing title searches on both the Double T and the Blackwell Ranch. The clerk had only managed to pull information back to the 1950s. Ben was going back again tomorrow.

He'd walked in, managing to get by the sticking door, ruing the fact that he'd forgotten to bring a planer to fix it, regretting he couldn't fix more for Rachel when he heard a man's voice. He'd seen the concern on Rachel's face, the strand of blond hair that hadn't been captured in her hair clip and the gummy smile of Poppy as she motored his way at a fast crawl. And then he'd listened to Rachel's ex-husband try to blackmail her into a bigger settlement. This, he could help her with.

The custody agreement had been signed and the ex was driving away. Now was the time for truth.

Ben's blood was still pounding when he approached Rachel, swept Poppy up high in his arms and tried to calm down.

"Thank you." Rachel had been standing front and center in her office, arms crossed over her chest as if that alone was holding her together. She wore a cream-colored suit and a teal blouse that matched the color of her high heels.

"Anybody would have stepped in." Emotion made Ben's words suddenly thick.

"Not anybody." Rachel hurried across the room, past the receptionist's desk, past Ben's briefcase on the floor. By the time Rachel reached Ben, she was practically running. She crashed into him, put one hand on his shoulder and reached up on her toes to kiss him. Just a peck on the lips.

Except...somehow...when she pulled back to look in his eyes, her arm wound around his neck and his free arm circled her waist, and they weren't exchanging a friendly thank-you kiss anymore. They were kissing like it was Saturday night and he'd walked her to her door after the most fantastic date in the history of dates.

A large truck—sounded like a semi—downshifted somewhere outside, brakes squealing in protest. The feed store across the street was probably getting a delivery.

Rachel eased back but kept her arm around Ben's neck. Color blossomed in her cheeks. *"Hi."*

"Hi." Ben straightened but kept his hand at her waist.

Poppy chuckled from her perch on his chest.

Ben drew the baby closer. He wanted to kiss Rachel again. He wanted to talk openly about her water options. He wanted to apologize for withholding information five years ago. He wanted to admit he was falling in love with her. But mostly, he wanted to kiss her again.

"Bye-bye," Poppy said, falling into what little space was between them.

Rachel nestled her daughter in her arms, the weight bringing her hand from around Ben's neck.

A door slammed outside, metal on metal, a semitruck door, for sure.

"Thanks for nothing," a woman shouted.

Cradling Poppy, Rachel moved to the window. Ben followed her.

A reedlike woman stared at Ben's Mercedes. She had limp blond hair and wore a frilly, wrinkled white dress with purple and orange polka dots. She carried a thin yellow bag and a large, white floppy hat, the kind women wore at royal weddings and the Kentucky Derby. It was accented with purple and orange feathers reminiscent of the chandelier back at the ranch. She turned to the offices of Calder & Associates.

"Zoe?" Ben breathed.

This woman looked nothing like his former fiancée. She was too thin, too hard, too rumpled.

The semitruck that had dropped her off jerked into first gear and drove away.

Rachel's gaze darted to Ben's face, dropping briefly to his lips. The softness in her eyes disappeared. She squared her shoulders and walked around Ben, yanking the door open so hard she almost flung it against the wall. "Zoe." Rachel's gaze slid Ben's way one more time before she added, "You're back."

"Bye-bye." Poppy waved to Ben.

Zoe hobbled up the steps. One of the high heels on her bright pink shoes had snapped off. She crossed the threshold without hugging Rachel. "I'm back. No thanks to that idiot husband of mine." Ignoring the baby, she tossed her bag and hat on the receptionist's desk, put one hand on Rachel's shoulder and slid off her shoes one at a time. "I just want a long soak in a hot bath and my own bed."

Zoe was so lost in her own universe, she didn't see Ben.

This was not how he'd envisioned their first

meeting after she dumped him. "Where's Big E?" Ben asked gruffly.

Only then did his former fiancée, now step-grandmother, notice Ben's existence. She scowled. "Of all the… Big E couldn't even wait until I got home? I only stopped here because I couldn't convince the truck driver to take me to the ranch. You Blackwells. Heartless, the lot of you." She picked up her broken shoe and threw it at Ben.

"Hey." Ben swatted the shoe harmlessly aside.

Zoe was livid. Cursing, she threw her other shoe at him.

Ben dodged another pink leather bullet. "Knock it off. Where is my grandfather?"

Zoe pressed her lips together and glared at him.

Rachel set Poppy down on her blanket, in the midst of her blocks, and handed her a bottle. Poppy accepted the distraction, taking a drink and banging one block against another.

A Blackwell Family Ranch truck came to a halt out front. The truck bed was full of pink suitcases and brown cardboard boxes. Katie got out and went to the tailgate, wisps of red hair floating around her head.

"No." Zoe marched outside. "You take all

that back, Katie Montgomery. You take it back right now."

"Sorry, Zoe." Katie hefted a suitcase to the sidewalk. Then another. And another. She climbed into the truck bed to reach more.

"It's *Mrs. Blackwell* to you," Zoe shrieked.

"Not anymore." Katie sounded almost gleeful. She hopped out of the truck bed and reached in the open window for a sheaf of legal-size papers. "Consider yourself served."

"Served with what?" Rachel asked, looking as perplexed as Ben felt.

"He wouldn't dare divorce me." Zoe whirled to face Ben. "He's lost his mind. He left me at a roadside shop in Dutch country after he swiped my wallet from my bag. I had to hitch-hike all the way here."

Ben supposed there was some justice in that.

"It's your prenup. In case you'd forgotten the terms." Katie came far enough up the walk to toss papers onto the front step. Then she returned to the truck and the job of unloading Zoe's stuff. "And divorce papers."

Zoe's eyes narrowed, and she swept the assembled with a chilly glare. When she noticed the crowd across the street in front of the feed store, she glared at them, too. Even

Pops Brewster had stopped playing chess with a pigtailed girl wearing a cowboy hat to witness the action.

Rachel plucked up the paperwork.

Zoe leaped toward Ben. "Is that why you're here? To serve my divorce papers?"

"No." Ben held his ground. "That was all Katie." But he might have enjoyed doing the honors. Witnessing Zoe's comeuppance was the next best thing.

Zoe poked Ben in the chest. "You can tell your grandfather that I'm not giving up that easily."

Ben wanted to grab the papers Rachel was perusing. But the prenup and impending divorce were only the short game. Ben had to think beyond this immediate fiasco. "You know where my grandfather is." It wasn't a question.

"You aren't going to trick me into talking." Zoe backed away and leaned against the receptionist's desk. "You know every secret I spill costs me money."

Ben had no idea what Zoe was babbling about.

"She's right." Rachel set the documents down. "Zoe gets money for every year they were married and subtracts money for every secret about Big E and the Blackwell Ranch she divulges."

Ben was so shocked by the terms of the pre-nup and so worried about his grandfather, that he didn't take time to relish his grandfather's savvy. After all, Ben hadn't drawn up a pre-nup for his own marriage to Zoe. "My brothers and I have been looking for Big E." Jon and Ethan thought the ranch was near bankruptcy. If that was true, Zoe wasn't getting anything. "I repeat, where is he?"

Zoe laughed. "You've got your villains all wrong, Ben."

"You should go." Rachel laid a hand on Ben's shoulder. "Let's meet at four at the Misty Whistle."

The last time Rachel had touched his shoulder, she'd brought him close for a kiss. It didn't look like she was going to send him off with one now that Zoe was here.

"We'll talk later." Ben grabbed his briefcase, said goodbye to Poppy and left.

"What happened?" Rachel demanded of Zoe when Ben had driven off. "You took off out of Falcon Creek happily married."

Zoe's normally creamy complexion was pink and her arms peeling as if they'd recently suffered sunburn. Her shoulder-length blond hair lacked volume and bounce, just like the rest of her.

"What happened? One minute we were having a good time at the…" Zoe's gaze turned calculating and she shook her finger at Rachel. "And the next minute Big E was speeding off in the motorhome."

"Zoe, I'm your lawyer." Rachel held up Zoe's prenup. "I'm bound by attorney-client privilege. You can tell me everything."

"Can I?" There was enough suspicion in Zoe's voice to accuse Rachel of murder. Clearly, she didn't trust anyone, not even her best friend. "What were you doing with Ben?"

What was I doing with Ben? I was kissing him!

A twinge of guilt swirled in Rachel's belly, along with a dash of regret and a hint of rebellion. "Ben and I—"

Hearing one of her favorite people's names, Poppy chimed in. "Ba-ba-ba-bahhh!" She crawled toward Rachel, a block in one fist and her bottle in the other.

Rachel walked over and scooped her darling and her bottle up. Poppy glanced around, as if she were searching for Ben. Rachel looked as well, missing his steady, butt-into-your-business presence, too.

"Rachel." Her friend pinned Rachel with a stare that was hard, even for Zoe. "What were you doing with my fiancé?"

"*Ex*-fiancé." A correction was definitely in order. Zoe had a tendency to get overdramatic. And no matter what had happened to her on the road, Rachel wasn't going to be baited into an argument. She rubbed Poppy's back, more to settle herself than her baby.

"Ex… That's just semantics." Zoe rolled her eyes, fluttering lashes that were thin and entirely her own. "What could Ben be doing here?"

The truth seemed the best course of action. "I'm suing him."

Zoe sat on the metal desk, a slow smile creeping across her face. "Tell me."

"Well…" Rachel suddenly felt like she was being stalked by her friend, chased into a dead end. She shook the impression off. Of course, Zoe would be curious. They hadn't talked in over two months. "I'm suing the Blackwells for water rights. Jon and Ethan asked Ben to come home."

Jon and Ethan asked Ben to come home.
But Ben wasn't here to stay.

Rachel moved to the couch and sank into the worn cushions. Poppy sprawled across her chest and drank from the bottle, eyes turning drowsy. Rachel was anything but relaxed. Her pulse was racing and her temples throbbed because…because…

Because I love Ben.

Rachel's heart seemed to swell. The sun streaming through the window and onto her shoulders was warmer and brighter. Poppy was the most beloved and beautiful baby in the world. All because Rachel was in love.

In love! Her heart trilled like an opera singer only Rachel could hear.

It was true. Rachel loved Ben's cocky attitude and his chutzpah. She loved his sharp wit and quick repartee. She loved his kindness. She loved the way he snuggled with Poppy and the way he snuggled with Rachel.

But…

She hated that she'd fallen in love with a man who wouldn't be living in Falcon Creek, who probably looked at her less-than-perfect clothes and her junker truck and compared her to the successful women he saw in New York, the ones who shopped on Fifth Avenue and could afford an expensive nanny. Women who were without mommy stains and mommy brains.

Suddenly, instead of a trilling heart, Rachel had a heart-heavy list of doubts.

"Do you think you'll win the case?" Zoe was saying, staring at a crack in the ceiling, oblivious to Rachel's meltdown.

"Yes." It wasn't a boast. Rachel believed in her chances. She already had Ben on the ropes. "Yes," she said again, because she refused to doubt herself when it came to this one case. All she had to do was find a workaround for the water board's use restrictions. Contact her state congressman or whoever it would take. She could set a new precedent. If Ben was correct, the reversion of water rights from the Blackwells would only be a moral victory without the ability to use the water. If she won the case *and* the right to use the water, maybe he'd stay, maybe they'd build a life together.

Maybe pigs could fly.

Rachel had no right to dream of a future with Ben just because of a few kisses.

"I like your confidence." Atop the desk, Zoe crossed her ankles and swung her bare feet. "I need you to challenge my prenup. I want a bigger divorce settlement."

Rachel gathered Poppy closer. Taking on the Blackwells for water with proof to back her claim was one thing. Battling Big E when there was a valid prenup was another.

"I *need* a bigger divorce settlement," Zoe insisted. "After all, he made me go without a cell phone or my laptop for two months. Two months! And then, when he finally left me, it was like salt in the wound."

Divorces. Rachel's bread and butter. Granted, it was more like store-bought white bread and margarine, but it was an area she had more experience in than water rights and property law. "You could try marriage counseling."

"You think I'd forgive Big E for bugging out on me in Pennsylvania? He left me with nothing but an empty purse and the clothes I was wearing." She plucked at a wilted orange polka-dot flounce on her dress. "I had to make it all the way home in the dress I wore to the Preakness. I had no makeup, no makeup remover, no concealer, no lipstick, no lotion, no sunscreen." She paused to draw breath as if she could go on.

"I get the idea." Rachel held up a hand. "You had nothing, and yet you made it across at least five states by yourself." Big E had probably known Zoe was savvy enough to get home safely. Still, it wasn't like Big E to strand Zoe anywhere or to want radio silence in terms of their cell phones. "Are you sure you didn't argue before this happened?"

"No." Zoe kept her gaze carefully on Rachel's face without acknowledging Poppy. She'd never held the baby or offered to help with her. "There has to be a way to break that prenup. I was a child when I signed it."

Rachel groaned softly. The drama train had officially pulled into the station. "You were twenty-seven, Zoe."

"I don't care! I deserve more than what's in those suitcases." Zoe stood and went to look out the window at her possessions. "I want my jewelry. I want alimony until he *dies*." This last word came out strangled. Her voice dropped to a tremulous thread. "Which will be soon without me to take care of him. He won't eat vegetables willingly. He'll smoke too many cigars, and—"

"Before that happens, he'll find another wife." Rachel tried to say the words soothingly, but it was time her friend faced the truth. "Remember, that's what Big E does. He moves on."

"That's what he *did*." Zoe wiped her nose

with the back of her hand. "We were a team. I stood by Big E when his grandchildren abandoned him. That ought to count for something."

"You were the reason Ben left," Rachel said in a voice meant to gently jolt her friend back to reality.

"When his four other grandchildren abandoned him," Zoe allowed, bitterness keeping her in wonderland.

"Technically, Jon was still around." At Zoe's cross look, Rachel amended her statement. "Three of his five grandchildren cut off communication with Big E around the time of your marriage. Big E could say you were the cause of the rift."

Zoe's jaw dropped. "How can you say that?" The words echoed into the silence.

Poppy was asleep in Rachel's arms. The street outside was quiet. But nothing was settled. Not with Zoe's heart and not with Rachel's.

"I'm your lawyer, Zoe. I'm supposed to be one step ahead of the opposition." Just as Ben always was. "I'm supposed to give you options." And what options did Rachel have in loving Ben?

None presented themselves.

"Options?" Zoe, deflated, dropped her gaze along with her thin shoulders. "Loan me your shoes so I can put my stuff in your truck."

"Okay." Balancing Poppy, Rachel slid out of her pumps and pushed them over with her feet. "I can drive you to your parents' house in Livingston after Poppy's nap."

"No. I can't run away from Falcon Creek, Rachel. That'd be like giving up." Zoe picked up the teal pumps, shaking her head as if the shoes, not her situation, were to blame for her unhappiness. "Katie is going to make sure I don't get onto the Blackwell property, but I can't leave town. What if Big E comes back? Until he does, I can stay with you… Can't I?"

That vulnerability.

A casual observer would take one look at Zoe and assume she was the calculating type. They couldn't see past Zoe's outer, protective layer to her soft inner shell.

Zoe had always been enamored with the dream of a good life, one filled with luxuries and a disregard for price tags. She had always been quick to rile over perceived slights. That made her seem like a prima donna.

But she was also the first to offer aid to her friends, few though they may be, and loyal to a fault. She loved animals and fairy tales and

Christmas. Zoe and Big E had more in common than most people realized.

"Of course you can stay with me." Rachel stood, trying not to rouse her little girl. "You'll have to sleep on the couch, though, because I turned your bedroom into a nursery." She carried Poppy into the second office and put her in the crib. Taking a moment to stare at all that cherubic innocence, hoping her daughter would be better at love than she was.

A spark was flickering in Zoe's blue eyes when Rachel returned. "We can use this time together to plan our attack on Big E and the Blackwells."

"Or a graceful acceptance of the end of a good run." Rachel skimmed Zoe's divorce paperwork.

"It's not fair." Zoe paced. "Big E must have had the divorce papers drafted for months."

"Actually, the paperwork looks boilerplate." Rachel flipped through the pages once more. "It's fill-in-the-blank stuff filed in the state of Nevada." Which was where Zoe and Big E had gotten married. Rachel recalled from her law school days that marriages conducted in Nevada could result in uncontested divorces if filed in Nevada, regardless of which state the parties legally resided in. "When it comes to matrimony, Big E knows what he's doing."

"He makes me so mad." Zoe took off one of Rachel's shoes and threw it at the wall.

"Hey, those are my good court shoes." Rachel went to rescue her pump. "Why don't you just take the money and start somewhere new?"

"Because I want to run the guest ranch." The blurted admission seemed to take some of the bluster out of her. "It was my idea. Please, Rachel. I'm not just losing my marriage, I'm losing my livelihood and my passion."

"You'll have to find a new livelihood." A new passion and a new husband. If Big E had driven from Pennsylvania to Nevada to get a divorce, he meant to get a divorce. Rachel pointed at the prenup. "There's also a clause in here about financial ventures. You get nothing but what you agreed to on your wedding day. Are you sure you don't want to try to reconcile?" Rachel had to suggest it, even though she knew it was hopeless.

"Big E filed for divorce." Zoe's blue eyes welled with tears. She knew it was hopeless, too. "When have you ever known him to change his mind?"

"Never."

"You've always been honest with me." Zoe took back Rachel's shoe, put it on and opened the tricky front door with two hands. "You'll tell me when I should give up and move on. Until then, I'm not."

Big E had been married six times. Rachel was afraid the time to give up was now. But she couldn't bring herself to tell Zoe that. Not when she'd hit rock bottom.

Or maybe it was because Rachel wanted to believe in love more than the law.

CHAPTER FIFTEEN

"ETHAN!" BEN BURST into his brother's exam room across town.

Ethan wasn't doctoring an animal. He was kissing Grace, who squeaked like a mouse, slid off the table and hurriedly straightened her mussed blond hair.

"Don't you ever knock?" Ethan scowled. He clearly hadn't forgiven Ben for keeping the bull-for-land trade under wraps for years, or more likely for siding with Jon to sell the ranch.

"Sorry, Grace," Ben said to Ethan's blushing fiancée. "But my news can't wait. Big E dumped Zoe with the Amish." After dropping that bombshell, which wiped the scowl from Ethan's face, Ben brought his twin up to date on their grandfather's impending divorce and the return of their soon-to-be ex-step-grandmother.

If there was one thing that could unite the brothers, it was Big E jettisoning Zoe.

"Maybe the old man is finally coming to his senses." Ethan clapped Ben on the back. Ben hoped it was a sign of a truce. "Congratulations. That must be a weight off your shoulders."

"I don't care about Zoe anymore." Ben pulled out his cell phone. "It's just now dawning on me that Katie had all Zoe's things packed up in a ranch truck. She must have talked to Big E. Where is she?"

"This time of day?" Grace put on her glasses and tried to look as if Ben hadn't walked in and witnessed an exam of a different kind. "She's probably at the guest ranch. The Ziglers checked out yesterday and she finally managed to hire a part-time housekeeper."

Ben and Ethan each drove their own vehicles to the ranch, stopping at the main house. Katie's truck was there, but she wasn't. They traipsed over to the guest lodge.

"Big E could be on his way back from Nevada right now." Ethan sounded hopeful. That was the thing about Ethan, he often seemed to look at the bright side.

"If he comes back, he'll fight you for control of the ranch," Ben pointed out. "Are you prepared to be an employee of his?"

Ethan's face set in hard lines. "That will never happen."

"At the very least, he'd want you to pay rent on that space in the barn you want for your practice." Ben glanced down at the dust lining his Italian loafers.

Rachel would give him grief if she saw his shoes. She'd call him Blackwell and take a jab at big city lawyers and their impractical attire. He'd give her guff for making fun of his shoes and his running tights, smile his way into her arms and kiss her.

Kiss her...

The dynamics of kissing Rachel had changed with Zoe's return. Not that Ben cared if Zoe knew he found Rachel attractive and loveable. But Rachel cared. He could tell by the stilted way she'd treated him once Zoe entered the law office.

Now wasn't the time to be thinking of Rachel. Ben cleared his throat, focused on the problem ahead of him and offered Ethan more insight into the mind of their grandfather. "Big E might want a percentage of your billings. Worst case, he'd ask you to vacate."

"Were you always this negative?" Ethan lengthened his stride, trying to pull away from

Ben. "Or is this pessimism you developed in New York?"

"This is your lawyer watching your back," Ben snapped, easily keeping up with his twin.

Anyone spotting them would do a double take—two men with the same long-legged stride, similar scowling faces and the same dark walnut hair marching across the plain, one wearing cowboy boots, worn jeans and a baseball cap, the other wearing dress slacks, a crisply pressed shirt and tie. All they needed to be meme-worthy was another oddity—a black bull and a tall black stallion walking docilely beside them. Or a Thompson, holding a Blackwell's hand, and a baby.

That's your dream, boy.

And dreams, by Ben's recollection, didn't come true.

"I would have watched your back five years ago if you'd have told me," Ethan said stubbornly. "You can't blame me for a choice you made on your own. I didn't ask you to lie for me."

The truth of his brother's words left a bitter taste in Ben's throat, one he had to swallow because he wasn't willing to let that grudge go just yet. "Ethan, you need to draw up a contract with terms of operation. You need every brother to sign it. And you need it done before Big E comes back."

"I hope he takes the long road home from Nevada," Ethan mumbled, settling his ball cap lower on his head. "You'll help me draft something?"

"Of course." It was easier to help his brother than to forgive him.

They found Katie and the part-time housekeeper tossing used bed linens over the second-floor railing. The pile was growing near where Ben and Ethan had come in. Hip was frolicking in the sheets and pillow cases as if it was fresh snow.

"Can someone find me another able body to clean this place?" Katie called out. "I should be riding out to the eastern pasture to check on the herd. But no. There are twelve guests checking in tomorrow and—"

"Grace and I could help by making beds again," Ethan interrupted, swiping a hand through the air as if indicating a clean slate. "But I draw the line at cleaning showers and toilets."

Katie frowned.

"Where did the divorce papers come from, Katie?" Ben demanded, uninterested in the guest ranch business. He darted around the laundry and climbed the grand staircase. "And who told you to deliver them today?"

"I got a text midmorning telling me to pack her things and that there was a packet of paperwork waiting at the post office." Katie brushed stray strands of red hair behind her ears. "And I was more than happy to do so. I've spent years with Zoe's designer boots pressing on my throat." Katie tugged at the neck of her tan Blackwell Guest Ranch polo shirt.

"Big E texted you?" Ben reached the second-floor landing, Ethan hot on his heels.

"Yes." Katie produced a cell phone from the back pocket of her jeans.

Ben peered over Katie's shoulder. There was just one message in the thread:

Revoke Zoe's rights as a Blackwell. Pack her personal belongings. Pick up legal docs at the post office. Deliver everything to her attorney. Carry on.

"That isn't Big E's phone number." Ethan had been reading over Katie's other shoulder. "It's a Texas area code."

"And it's not signed," Ben pointed out. "How do you know it's from Big E?"

"Carry on." Katie toggled to another text

thread and showed them her screen. "Granted, these are from over two months ago, but that's how Big E signs off on his texts."

"I wish you would have told us first thing." Ethan poked his head into an empty room, gathered an armload of towels embroidered with the ranch's brand and tossed them over the railing opposite to where the dog was.

"Telling you was on my list of things to do today." Katie glanced below. Hip was still rolling on her back in the dirty linens, feet in the air. "Just as soon as we got all the laundry started."

It was hard to find fault in what Katie did when she was overseeing the bulk of the ranch.

"At least we know Big E isn't in danger." The feeling of elation Ben had enjoyed on the drive from town was fading. "The text proves that. He's probably celebrating his bachelorhood."

Ethan gave Ben a wry grin. "Reality is, Big E is probably picking out a wedding ring for the next Mrs. Elias Blackwell."

"This solves nothing." Ben stared at the pile of linens on the ground floor. There was still the water rights to contend with, not to mention the lack of funds and staff.

"It doesn't," Ethan agreed. "But admit it, you're happy Zoe got dumped."

Ben was. He just wished he'd had more time with Rachel before his ex-fiancée had come back to town.

"WHAT'S THAT NOISE?" Nana Nancy cocked her head and lowered her knitting needles.

Rachel had come out to the ranch in the late afternoon, avoiding the planned meeting with Ben and giving Zoe time alone at the house. Rachel needed distance from him, even if it was only distance for a day.

Rachel's mother glanced up from the quilt pieces she was sewing together. "It sounds like pounding."

Even Poppy stopped what she was doing, pulling the teething ring from her mouth and rolling from her back to her belly.

Rachel scribbled the tally she was making of the number of calves born last year and looked out the window. "That's odd. Henry's truck is gone." And Tony wasn't due back at the ranch until Thursday.

The pounding stopped.

"Hmm." Mom went back to her quilting.

"Huh." Nana went back to her knitting.

"Gah." Poppy rolled onto her back and gnawed on her teething ring.

Outside, there was a clank of metal on metal.

Rachel got up and went into the mudroom to don her mother's pink-and-gold trimmed boots. Somebody had to investigate. What if it was the water company?

In her cream suit and teal blouse, Rachel scanned the horizon, looking for an unfamiliar vehicle. There was none. She searched the barn. The ranch's half dozen horses greeted her. She walked out the back door and found an intruder. "Ben? What are you doing?"

He stood at the entrance to the road, oiling the latch on the gate, which hung straight on securely fastened hinges. There were tools on the ground and the big black stallion was tied to a fence post a few feet away.

Ben gave her a wave and a half smile. "I didn't want the heifer to come back and eat what's left of Nana Nancy's vegetables."

Rachel didn't want to admit there were no more vegetables to be eaten. The heifer had demolished the entire garden, much to her grandmother's chagrin. Rachel didn't want to admit that his small act of kindness brought tears to her eyes. No one had offered to do anything extra around the ranch to help her. No one.

Ben bent his head, testing the latch until it moved smoothly. He was wearing blue jeans and boots and a soft blue chambray shirt. He looked like a ranch hand, not a lawyer. He looked like he'd never seen Times Square and didn't care if he ever did.

He looks like he'll stay.

Rachel was in desperate need of air. She wanted to head back into the barn, shut the door and forget she'd ever seen Ben.

In that moment, Ben straightened, closed the gate and lifted his gaze to hers. "I think I owe you an apology."

"Don't you dare apologize for fixing that gate." She marched forward before she realized what she was doing. "Don't you dare." She stopped five feet away from him and crossed her arms over her chest. What was wrong with the man?

Ben rested his forearms on the top bar and took his time about replying. "I'm not going to apologize for that." His mouth curled into a slow smile. "I think…what happened at the office—"

"Was completely my fault." Rachel's arms

pressed tighter into her chest. "I was out of line."

He grinned. "Feel free to step over that line anytime."

Rachel felt as limp as a noodle. But there was Zoe and Poppy and all her other responsibilities, and a heart she had no time to have broken. "Ben…"

"I understand why you stood me up today. I scared you." His words hung in the air between them for a second, as if he needed to take them in as well. "That's what I was going to apologize for. Truth be told, I think I scared myself a little, too."

"It's weird, isn't it? I mean, we were friends for so long and this…" She gestured between the two of them "There was nothing before."

"There was the debate competition." His gaze drank her in. "There was the morning after prom when Andy broke up with you."

She cherished the comfort he'd offered her on both days. Had he done the same? "And there was the day after your parents died."

"In some ways, you were my rock." He nodded slowly. "Guys are stupid when they're young."

"When they're older than twelve?" Rachel

gently teased. Somehow, she'd moved closer to the gate. Closer to him.

"When they're teenagers and they go for looks, not substance. Certainly not inner beauty."

Rachel knew she should argue that statement. Defend Zoe. Take offense to the fact that she wasn't as good-looking as her best friend. But she knew the truth. Zoe was lovely. And Zoe knew she was lovely. And when they were teenagers, Zoe had capitalized on that fact.

"Now, men…" Ben ran the back of his hand over her cheek and it was all Rachel could do not to lean into his touch "…men can see the inner strength that enhances the outer beauty." His hand settled at the curve of her neck and his voice turned husky. "I can see your strength, Thompson. I'm old enough to appreciate it now."

Standing in her mother's ridiculous boots and wearing a court suit, Rachel should have felt like Henry's little lady. She didn't. She couldn't. Not when Ben had captured her gaze and her heart, and convinced her that love was scary the second time around, but it didn't have to be. Not if they fell together.

She climbed on the bottom rung of the gate and tilted her face up for a kiss.

He smiled down at her, amusement in his blue eyes. "I could get used to you being around all the time, Thompson."

"Shut up and kiss me, Blackwell."

CHAPTER SIXTEEN

TUESDAY AFTERNOON, RACHEL walked into the county courthouse, carrying the custody papers and Poppy.

Zoe trailed behind Rachel, having claimed she was too tense to sit at home alone and the day was too hot to wait in the truck, even in the shade. She wore bright yellow capris and a purple blouse. She'd pulled her hair into a bouncy high ponytail and applied a careful coat of makeup. After a bath and a good night's sleep, she looked much more like herself, although it had taken her all morning to do so.

Rachel felt out of sorts. Her hair felt windblown and dirty from the ride with the windows down. She couldn't find her lipstick anywhere in her purse. And Poppy lay limp as a rag doll, drooling on her shoulder. Her daughter had woken up stuffy and fussy. Ted's mother was busy today and Rachel's mother was taking Nana to a doctor's appointment in

Livingston. Having Zoe stay home and watch her baby wasn't an option.

She should be floating on cloud nine. Ben had kissed her. Several times. He'd said he could get used to kissing her more often. But kisses—although quite nice—hadn't answered any of Rachel's questions, the utmost being, could she rely on Ben?

Edith Frankel looked up from the counter. She had gold crowns that flashed when she smiled and thick glasses that sometimes caught the light, making it seem as if she had blank, alien eyes. "Look at that sweet baby. She's all tuckered out."

"Yes," Rachel agreed. "She's fighting a cold."

Edith smiled. "I was wondering when you might drop by."

Rachel wondered if Edith was a mind reader. More likely, Ted had told someone he'd signed custody papers, and that person had told someone they knew in the legal system, who'd told Edith. Falcon County was large in land mass, but small in body count. News traveled fast. "I want to file these signed custody papers."

"Oh." Edith seemed surprised. But she checked the document thoroughly, stamped it with the date and time and proceeded to enter it into the computer system.

"Is this where divorces happen?" Zoe stared at the plain, dated office. "I thought it'd be grander." Much of the anger had drained from Rachel's best friend. She'd been quiet during the ride to the courthouse.

"Divorces don't have any pomp and ceremony," Rachel said kindly, rubbing Poppy's back. "Not like weddings."

"We were married in Las Vegas." Zoe's gaze turned distant. "At a beautiful chapel overlooking the fountains at the Bellagio."

"My sister was married in Vegas at an Elvis-themed wedding chapel." Edith looked up at them. The light caught her lenses, making them milky white. "She filed for divorce there, too, after her husband left her." Her gaze dropped to her computer screen, and her green eyes came back into view. "Boy, was that divorce quick. And it only required my sister's signature, since that deadbeat Paul was AWOL. You know, in Nevada, you only have a couple of weeks to respond. Doesn't matter if you do or don't, though. If someone wants a divorce there, they get it."

All Rachel's talk to Zoe about reconciliation… It didn't matter. Big E had gone to Nevada. He wanted a no-contest divorce.

"When was the Preakness?" The question tumbled out of Rachel quicker than the hair rising up on the back of her neck. How much time did Zoe have to challenge the prenup?

"A week…" Wide-eyed, Zoe had that deer-in-the-headlights look, the one Rachel assumed was mirrored on her face. "No, ten days ago…" And then anger, Zoe's most ready defense, surfaced. She narrowed her eyes, tightened her lips. "That coward. He couldn't even say it to my face."

Edith handed over Rachel's receipt. "On to the next matter."

Balancing Poppy, Rachel hesitated. Had she forgotten a document from another case?

The clerk put her stamp beneath the counter and slipped her pen into a large blue coffee mug that said Court Clerk Rock Star. "He didn't file anything."

If Edith was referring to Ted… Rachel drew Poppy closer.

"Who?" Zoe asked before Rachel could. "Big E?"

"No. Oh, no." Edith brushed imaginary dust off the counter with one thin hand. "His lawyer. Ben Blackwell."

Rachel's neck twinged, and her mind whirled. "Edith, why would you expect Ben to file any documents here?"

"I had lunch with Mona today and she said he was at her office *again* this morning doing a title search on the Blackwell property—" she eyed Rachel over her thick lenses "—and the Double T. And I hear he was searching for records at the county library as well. I expected there to be some kind of suit filed."

Yesterday, Ben had kissed her. He'd held her. He'd been so kind she'd fallen in love with him.

And he was going to take her to court.

Rachel sagged against the counter. The linoleum beneath her feet seemed as insubstantial as quicksand.

"Rachel." Zoe's voice sounded muffled. *"Rachel?"*

Rachel held up a hand, needing a moment. The events of the past few days were a blur. Rachel had it all wrong. *She'd* kissed Ben. *She'd* hugged Ben. All he'd done was trick her into falling in love with him.

They hadn't spoken about water rights. *She* hadn't wanted to. He'd played her as deftly as he'd played Darnell. She wasn't thinking about legal issues, personal or professional. She'd been thinking about Ben and a pair of sturdy shoulders to lean on.

Rachel's blood was boiling, making her cheeks heat and her body sweat. She'd been a fool.

As soon as she could trust her legs to hold, Rachel thanked Edith, hitched a sleeping Poppy higher on her shoulder and headed for the exit. Despite the sun, despite the heat inside and out, Rachel felt like she was in a haze. Nothing was clear. Nothing was certain. Not her footsteps. Not her feelings. Not her future.

"Are you okay?" Zoe trotted next to her. "What's going on? What did she mean?"

Rachel shook her head. "I don't know." Even that short reply took effort.

"But…it sounded like Ben—"

"Don't make this more than it is, Zoe."

Zoe flinched. "More than what it is? I thought it was only a court case."

Now it was Rachel who flinched. "He kissed me." She omitted the number of times. "I mean, I kissed him. But it doesn't matter." Not to Ben anyway.

"Have you learned nothing from my experience with the Blackwells?" Zoe's question bordered on hysteria. Her blue eyes darted about the parking lot. "You'll be tossed aside."

"*I'll* be tossed aside." As if Rachel hadn't been already? "I'll be tossed aside the way you tossed Ben aside."

Zoe gasped, and her petite features crumpled. "I'm just trying to protect you."

"I'm sorry." Now she was sounding like Ben. "I didn't see any of this coming." Not the attraction, the kisses or the backstabbing.

Well, the backstabbing was something she'd thought she'd avoid.

"That's why they say love is blind." Zoe scurried ahead in her heeled sandals to open the truck door for Rachel so she could return Poppy to her car seat. Once the baby was strapped in, Zoe held out her hand, palm up. "Give me your phone."

"Why?" Rachel clutched the door handle, feeling as if one misstep, one tiny shove, and she'd fall over an emotional ledge, lose control and wail louder and longer than she had when the heifer had ruined her best court suit. One more misstep, and she'd be the woman she'd tried so hard not to be. The woman Ben Blackwell saw as an easy mark.

"I need your phone, Rachel," Zoe said again, leaning close to peer at her face. "Because I don't have mine, and because a man like Ben Blackwell leaves disaster in his wake. We need to know what kind of man he is."

We.

There was no *we*, as in Rachel and Zoe. Nor was there *we*, as in Rachel and Ben.

"This isn't like a divorce." Rachel rubbed her chest, willing herself to think, to breathe, to be the lawyer that Ben would respect, even if she wasn't the woman he loved. "Why did Big E leave you in Pennsylvania? Did you cheat on him?"

Zoe rolled her eyes. "That'd be like cheating on the ingredients of your mother's double Dutch chocolate cookies. It's just not done when you love someone."

Her friend was right. "I'm sorry, honey." Rachel hugged her. "You two had something special." Whereas Rachel and Ben had only shared reminisces and random kisses.

"We had something…" Zoe sniffed. "Maybe not something as special as I thought it was." She took the first good look Rachel had seen her take at Poppy. "Big E said he wouldn't give me kids. Or adopt a baby. Or…"

Rachel hugged her once more. "We'll figure this out."

"I'm the worst friend." Zoe held Rachel at

arm's length. "I couldn't bring myself to be happy for you." A tear slipped down her cheek. "I was so jealous."

"Of me and my divorce," Rachel deadpanned.

"Of you being a mother." Zoe wiped away her tears, checking her reflection in the sideview mirror. "No one can take away mama status, but a marriage…"

"I know," Rachel said morosely. "I see relationships crumble all the time. Maybe this is for the best. You'll find someone else, someone better—" *and younger* "—who'll want lots of babies with you."

"Can we not talk about that right now?" Zoe's expression threatened to crumple again. "Can I just…for once…take care of you? If only because it'll keep my mind off how much my heart is breaking." She gave Rachel a watery smile and then drew a deep breath. "We need to find out what kind of man Ben has become. Give me your phone."

After a moment's hesitation, Rachel handed it over. They got in the truck and drove toward Falcon Creek while Zoe searched online. She was silent for a long time, making Rachel's nerves jangle.

"I can't stand it any more, Zoe. What did you find?"

"Gold." Zoe set the phone on the bench seat between them. "Ben was fired just a few weeks ago for an ethics violation. He's a rat, just like his grandfather."

Rachel's heart sank. Ethics violations weren't filed lightly.

Ben, what have you done?

Needing to know, Rachel pulled over and snatched up her phone. Zoe's search was still live. She scrolled through a press release, finding none of the answers she was looking for. "That's all it says. His firm filed an ethics violation against him and let him go."

"It says enough." Zoe turned her thumb down. "Ben got caught doing something inappropriate, something bad enough his employer fired him. What do you think it was? Embezzlement? Sexual harassment?"

Rachel shook her head. Before Ben came back, she would have believed anything bad about him. But now…

Zoe was bursting with enthusiasm. "You need to confront Ben about his misconduct and use it to your advantage."

"I'm not that kind of lawyer."

Zoe leaned across the seat toward Rachel

until she had to meet her gaze. "You need to be that kind of lawyer if you want to beat Ben at his own game."

Rachel felt ill. But she also felt Zoe was right.

Let's meet at four at the Shiny Spur for coffee.

Ben's text message was so casual. Was there something in there Rachel should be interpreting differently?

She dropped Zoe at the house and took Poppy to the grocery store. She had twenty minutes to buy children's cough medicine and chicken broth because Poppy's congestion always seemed to go straight for her lungs and steal her appetite.

Poppy had passed fussy somewhere between waking up when Zoe got out of the truck and being taken to the Sack and Save. She was so tired and congested, she was angry. Rachel should have stayed home this afternoon to let her rest.

Then I wouldn't have learned about those title searches.

It was closing in on four o'clock—time for Rachel to meet Ben. She should have changed out of work clothes and put on her mommy combat gear—armor that protected the body from a child's tantrum with flailing legs and arms. A shield for her heart, too, which was bruised from being Poppy's target and potentially Ben's.

The balls of her feet hurt in her heels as she pushed a shopping cart around the Sack and Save, trying to remember if the cold medicine was across from the cereal or the paper goods. She was about to enter the cereal aisle when she noticed Ben standing in the middle of it, holding a blue basket. She backed up, right into Zeldeen Whitecloud's cart.

Poppy began to cry, big hearty sobs that probably carried to the front of the store.

"Watch it," Zeldeen said sharply, frowning so deeply her white brows connected. She'd taught science at the high school, a subject Rachel had struggled to pass, which hadn't endeared her to the woman. "Rachel, do be careful. I've got eggs in here." As if a cart fender bender would break any eggshells.

Try protecting a heart from breaking.

Rachel muttered an apology, making direct eye contact with Zeldeen as she did so. Which meant she took her eyes off her daughter, who lunged for a display of Cap'n Crunch boxes and swiped them to the ground. The avalanche silenced the grocery store.

And then a sound arose, like an emergency vehicle's siren. Poppy's war cry.

"It'll be okay, baby." Rachel's cheeks heated. She bent and scurried around her cart to pick up boxes.

"What happened?" Ben's voice. So compassionate. Was he a good actor? He had been when he'd baited Darnell into lunging for him in court.

"Rachel?" He moved closer.

Rachel grimaced and held out a hand to keep him away. "It was an accident." Just like those kisses.

"You shouldn't leave a child in a cart unattended," Zeldeen said, wheeling hers past Rachel.

She was right. Rachel stood and held on to Poppy's jumper at the back, which only made her daughter madder. And louder.

Rachel stood at the side of the cart. Ben stood near the front. Neither one moved. Surrounded by cereal boxes, they just stared at Poppy as other shoppers hurried past. What a pair they made, looking like the statues in front of the courthouse of Lewis and Clark studying a map between them.

Ben cleared his throat. "Is everything okay?"

"Yes," Rachel said, when what she wanted to say was, *What were you doing researching the title to my land?* She tried to extricate Poppy from the cart, but her daughter kicked her sturdy legs angrily. Rachel had to raise her voice to be heard. "She's tired and battling a cold."

He moved around the cart, picking his way through boxes. He was probably going to leave her here to deal with Poppy by herself. She probably wouldn't see him until they were due in court on Friday. And then he'd take her water—and maybe her land—and she and her heart would be shattered.

The thought nearly gutted her.

But she couldn't fall apart. Not now. Not in the middle of the Sack and Save. "Poppy. Come on, baby. Shhh." She stroked her darling's hair, only to have her hand swatted away. On any other day, Rachel wouldn't have taken it personally. But today…on top of whatever Ben was cooking up…

"Hey, now." Ben put his basket in Rachel's cart and removed Poppy from her seat as easily as if he'd done so a thousand times. "There's no need to cry."

Poppy drew a shuddering breath and stared

at Ben. "Ba-Ba." She dropped her head on his shoulder, still crying but not nearly as loud.

Rachel wanted to cry, too. Her feet hurt. The band of her control-top pantyhose was cutting into her waist. Some time during the day she'd gotten baby snot on her blouse. And now there was an ache in her chest when she looked at Ben holding her daughter.

"I bet you want something like this, Poppy." Ben plucked a pacifier from a nearby rack, tore open the plastic, popped it in and out of his mouth and then offered it to Poppy.

Who took it with a small sob and quieted.

Rachel's fingers curled around the handle of the cart. "I made a conscious decision *not* to use a pacifier." And like everything else in her life, that decision was now a moot point.

"She likes it," Ben said simply, as if the argument should sway her.

A teenage store clerk appeared, frowning at the mess and at Rachel.

She knelt and gathered boxes, stacking them on the endcap as quickly as she could. The teenager mumbled something about her not having to help, but Rachel had to do something.

Once she'd finished stacking, Rachel tugged

her blouse back to rights and stared at her darling traitorous daughter.

Poppy's eyes were closed. Occasionally, her lips worked the pacifier and she chugged in a snotty breath.

"You don't have to look at me as if I'm dressed in red tights and have been treed by Ferdinand." Ben spoke softly, rubbing Poppy's back. "I'm not your enemy."

"Aren't you?" Rachel murmured. She could use a back rub. Or a foot rub. Or a plain old hug with whispered reassurances that she hadn't put her trust in the wrong man.

Ben studied her expression the way she imagined he studied legal precedent, committing it to memory for later use and analysis. "You look like you could use something to eat and a coffee." He hooked the fingers of his free hand into the shopping cart and tugged it toward the front of the store. "Just don't ask me to change diapers unless you want to give me a crash course. I seem to recall putting Chance's diapers on backward."

Rachel bit back the urge to ask Ben what he'd been searching for at the county recorder's office, tamped down the curiosity about him being fired and followed his conversational lead. "With only two years difference between you, I bet you didn't change your little brothers' diapers often." She followed behind Ben, wrapping her arms around her waist instead of taking control of her cart, her case, her heart.

"Well, I wasn't supposed to," Ben allowed. He wore a dark suit. He looked tall and imposing. Handsome. Worldly. Reliable.

Love tried to blossom in her chest. It tried to squelch the doubts she had about his intentions.

No-no-no-no-no.

Her gaze fell from his shoulders to his groceries. "Why is there nothing in your basket but fruit?"

"Fruit is a healthy snack." Ben glanced back at her cart contents. "Why is there nothing in your cart but baby food?"

"I spend every evening at the Double T, helping run the ranch. Mom makes me dinner." She spotted infant cold medicine and grabbed a small package.

"I'm envious." He turned back toward the checkout stands, now within sight. "Can we take Poppy to the coffee shop?" He let a bit of Western twang color his words. "I'm hankering for one of Edda Mae's pot pies."

Edda Mae owned the Shiny Spur Diner

downtown. As teenagers, they'd spent many afternoons there before going home, doing homework, downing milkshakes and sucking salt off french fries.

Oh, for the days when Rachel didn't have to watch every morsel she put in her mouth.

"I haven't had a pot pie in forever," she lamented, smoothing her stained and wrinkled blouse over her mommy hips.

"How about I buy you a pot pie for old times' sake?" Ben's gaze was warm, encouraging her to trust him.

Rachel the lawyer experienced a twinge of unease, even as Rachel the single mom cheered silently. She cleared her throat. "What are you up to?" Would that he'd tell her.

"I'm up for sustenance." His smile attempted to reassure. "Nothing but the truth, counselor."

How she wanted to believe him.

He continued, "We can go to the diner and you can tell me how you're not going to budge on water rights, while I keep this little one quiet and you get a chance to enjoy a decent meal away from the homestead. It'll give Zoe a little time to settle in on her own and us a little time to talk about…things."

Things.

Feelings, the dreamer in Rachel whispered.

Legal moves, the cynic in Rachel hissed.

Rachel didn't want to hear about either one. "I shouldn't," she hedged, like the little lady she was. "There are a gazillion things to do out at the ranch. Let's stick to the plan of coffee."

"There will be a gazillion things to do tomorrow." Ben's voice dropped. He held her baby more tenderly than Ted ever had. "Let me do this for you, Thompson."

Her heart clenched.

When was the last time she'd had a meal with anyone other than her family? Apart from Ben saying he'd fix the gate, when was the last time anyone offered to do something for her? Rachel couldn't remember.

"Come on. Live a little."

Still, Rachel hesitated.

Ben didn't wait for her answer. He told the clerk at the register to unload Rachel's cart and that he'd pay for everything, the ruined cereal, too.

I'll ask him about the title search at the coffee shop.

And then he'll break my heart.

Rachel straightened her spine. If he did turn

out to be a disappointment, she had no one to blame but herself.

And only herself to pick up the pieces.

CHAPTER SEVENTEEN

"WHAT DID YOU do today?" Ben asked casually. "Were you with Zoe?"

He didn't feel an iota of guilt about kissing Rachel several times over the previous few days, but he wasn't sure she felt the same. She'd been strung out when he'd bumped into her at the grocery store, and she'd looked at him the way she had the first day he'd come back—as if she didn't trust him.

He wanted her to look at him the way she had last night—as if she'd never let him go.

Even as he acknowledged he had deep feelings for Rachel, Ben had no idea what to do about them. His life was in New York. Her life was here.

They sat in a booth in the back of the diner. Ben had requested some privacy, saying the baby might get loud and fussy. The waitress had been more than happy to show them to a table far away from other customers.

The power nap had restored Poppy's good

nature. With Ben's hands supporting her waist, she stood on his thighs. She leaned on the table for additional support, bouncing up and down almost in time to the music playing on the radio in the kitchen. She gummed on cracker bits and barely protested when he swiped at her runny nose with a paper napkin.

"I was," Rachel confirmed briskly. "Zoe's trying to decide what she wants to do about Big E's divorce request."

"Does she have a choice?" At Rachel's scowl, Ben added quickly, "A divorce filed in Nevada is pretty much a done deal. And just to be clear, it was a deal done by my grandfather. I had nothing to do with it." He had to make sure Rachel understood where he was coming from. He was going to tell her everything.

Her scowl became more of a semi-frown. "Big E blindsided her. She loves him." Her gaze dropped from his face to Poppy's and her voice softened. "Whether she has a choice or not, it makes no difference. Big E's treatment of Zoe is sad and demeaning. She didn't deserve to be thrown out like the trash."

Ben refused to enter that discussion.

Poppy banged a spoon on the table.

"Poppy, no." Rachel reached for her daughter. The collar of her black blouse was wrinkled and stained, almost as if little Poppy had clenched the fabric in her fist and then wiped her nose on it.

Ben liked that Rachel didn't appear self-conscious about the state of her work clothes.

"No." Poppy was having none of it. She thrust her nose in the air just as her mama did when she was upset.

Her attitude made Ben smile.

"Please don't let Poppy do that," Rachel chastised, tucking her blond hair behind her ears. "She'll get bad manners."

Rachel's warning made Ben remember his assistant training him in the art of caring for babies.

"Although I appreciate you staying after five," Ben had said to Darcy one night. "I need you to work, not take care of your child." It'd been a heartless thing to say, but Ben had been trained by the firm to sacrifice his heart for the sake of a case.

"She's a baby," Darcy had snapped, handing her over to Ben. "She's just been fed. She'll bounce and kick and blow bubbles. And then before you know it, she'll pass out."

Ben had held Annabelle away from him and stared from her to her mother, thinking about all that needed to be done in the next two hours and all the effort it took to fire and hire a new assistant. "But…"

"Bring her in close to your body." Darcy had blown out a frustrated breath and shown him how to hold her child. "Do a circuit in your office. I hear you complaining about sitting all day long. Go log some steps while I get this work done."

Like Rachel, Darcy was a single mom in her thirties. She was good at her job, able to manage her boss, but more importantly, she'd been a good mom.

Rachel was a good mom, too.

"Give her fifteen minutes or so," Ben said. "She'll be exhausted, and you can eat in peace." And then Ben could broach the topic of water rights and see if he could settle this out of court quickly. And then he'd tell Rachel about the bull-for-land trade. And then he bet that would be the end of Rachel smiling at him with forever in her eyes.

The way Rachel was looking at him now, he'd be lucky if she stayed through the pot pies they'd ordered.

"No," Poppy said louder, waving a hand toward her mother. The little imp clutched the small packet of crackers Ben had opened and swung around to look at him, spilling crumbs over Ben's dark wool slacks. Her thick-soled sneakers ground the bits into his thighs.

"People are looking." Rachel reached across the table for her baby. "Come on, honey."

A quick survey of the sparsely populated café discounted her statement. "People are smiling, Rachel. Except for the people who hate the Blackwells, who are frowning at me."

In actuality, there was only one person frowning at him. Pops Brewster. He'd abandoned his chess game over at the feed store and was nursing a cup of coffee while watching Rachel and Ben. Chances were, the old man's eyesight was so poor that squinting was more likely making him frown more than any disapproval of Poppy's restaurant etiquette.

Poppy fell back against Ben's chest. "Baba." She patted his cheek with her wet crackery fingers. "Ba-ba."

He wanted to hold Poppy close in one arm and Rachel close in the other, the way he'd done in her office after Ted left. He wanted Rachel to give him that dreamy look that said she'd enjoyed his kiss, thank you very much, and wouldn't mind another. He wanted to hear Rachel's burst of laughter and laugh himself when they teased each other. He wanted Rachel and Poppy to fill the silence at the ranch house, out in the pasture and in his apartment in New York.

Ben smiled. He didn't mean to. He wasn't even sure why he couldn't stop his lips from curling upward. It was just... Rachel made him smile more than any woman had in a long time, maybe more than any woman ever had. Including Zoe.

With a sigh, Poppy sank into his lap and reached for the pacifier. It hadn't been fifteen minutes. It might have only been ten.

Ben's smile broadened.

"Stop smiling like that," Rachel ordered quietly. "I'm taking you to court. Don't be nice to me. I'm not going to be nice to you."

"There's no one here to see me smile, Thompson." When had his voice turned that low and soft? "Not Judge Edwards. Not your grandmother. Not Zoe. No one but you." And Pops Brewster, who probably couldn't see this far away. "Your daughter is about to fall asleep on the bench seat over here. I think I've earned the right to smile at you." He wiped cracker crumbs from his cheek.

Rachel swallowed, looking about their table as if she couldn't find the salt and needed it desperately. And then she brought her chin up and her gaze to his. "Why were you fired?"

Ben hadn't thought Rachel could say anything to make his smile fall. He was wrong. It fell so far it felt like it might not return. "It doesn't have anything to do with our dispute." He shifted Poppy until she lay on her side with her back against the bench seat. "And I signed a nondisclosure agreement."

"In theory, you could confide in your lawyer."

"Which you are not." He wished there was a window closer, one he could look out of. He should have chosen a booth by the door; at least then he could have stalled the conversation by saying hello to Sarah Ashley before she went to sit with her grandfather, Pops Brewster.

"In an alternative universe, you and I could have been partners in a law firm," Rachel said with bomb-dropping calm. She stared at him in complete seriousness.

This was interesting. And scary. Ben's heart beat faster. He'd see her bet and raise the stakes. "In an alternative universe, we could have dated in high school." Yeah, he went there. And if that wasn't a sign that his feelings for Rachel were getting in the way of his role as the Blackwell attorney, he didn't know what was.

Without missing a beat, she leaned forward. "Let's say we did. Let's say you and I married, but we stayed here in Falcon Creek. Would you have been happy?"

"No." He'd wanted the status and challenge of practicing in New York.

"So this—" she gestured between them "—whatever this is… It would only work in Falcon Creek."

"Correct." He was answering like a well-trained witness. Short. To the point. Trying to remain calm under duress. Which this was. He loosened his tie.

Rachel continued her cross-examination. "Which makes this a sort of…an alternative universe."

He saw where she was going. "The one where we end up together, practicing law in a creaky shack?"

"Correct." She sat back and raised her eyebrows over a small but triumphant smile.

"Objection." He hated to disillusion her. "Your family, your best friend… They wouldn't let you partner with me, much less marry me." He slipped that last part in, testing the waters.

All of this was a test between them. A mock trial. Like those debate competitions she used to enter where she'd present the best arguments and win. But winning now didn't change anything.

"This is my alternative universe," she countered, without objecting to the M-word. "And in it, there are no obstacles to either pairing." Her gaze might have dropped to his lips, but it returned immediately to his eyes. "You and me. No secrets. No lies. No betrayals."

He knew what she was saying. She wanted to know everything. And when she did, she'd snatch up Poppy and shut him out of her life forever.

So, it made no sense that he'd waste time and risk his heart with a twist on her alternate universe. Ben ran a hand over his hair the way his father used to. "In my alternate universe, we'd have spent time in New York, honing our legal skills."

"Only until my father died and..." She hesitated, twisting around to look toward the kitchen. "Where are those pot pies?"

He was losing her. It was only a matter of time before Rachel bolted. And if she left, he might not ever again work up the courage to tell her the truth.

"Maybe we'd have returned here to *retire* to a slower practice." Ben had no choice but to enter her alternate universe. "To have kids and settle back into our roots." Maybe she'd have kept Ben grounded in New York. "But first, I might have come home from work one night and told you about a case I'd been working on."

Rachel whipped around so fast, her blond hair flew over her shoulder.

"This is all in an alternative universe, of course," Ben said, watching Sarah Ashley hug her grandfather with clear affection.

"Because none of it happened." Rachel was subdued, still. "A discussion about an alternative universe is like a hypothetical."

Ben nodded. "In this alt-universe, you'd know that I worked at a firm specializing in public utilities representation. You'd know that there'd been a gas leak in a suburban neighborhood resulting in losses, both homes and life." His skin felt too tight, as if it was trying to keep his secrets in. But it was too late. They were spilling out. "There were many casualties, including a father of two." He passed his hand over Poppy's blond curls.

"In this…*hypothetical*, I'd know these kinds of cases were common for you."

Ben agreed, although he was unable to look at Rachel and the contempt he expected to see in her eyes. "We have a calculation we perform to determine the settlement with the client's insurance. The income of the deceased times the number of years we estimate he would have worked, with a factor added for raises and cost of living increases. And kids… There's a calculation for that." It sounded so cold. *He* sounded cold.

"Pain and suffering?"

"On a case-by-case basis." Ben stroked Poppy's hair. "You'd know I don't usually meet with those impacted by these accidents. Everything is handled through their lawyer." Everything was designed to be impersonal and avoid involving the courts.

"But this case was different." Rachel reached across the table, her hand palm up. She was offering to comfort him?

Her gaze held no contempt.

Ben took hold of her warm hand. Why wouldn't he? They were playing a game, one where they were married, where touch and comfort were freely given. "Opposing counsel showed up with the widow and her children."

Innocent, big brown eyes that would never know what it was like to see her father's smile, or register the expression on her father's face as pride.

"It sounds like a tactic you'd employ," Rachel said.

"Because it works." Ben's voice was thick with regret. "I couldn't negotiate with babies in the room."

She squeezed his hand. "In that scenario, the suit would move to trial and you'd work your magic."

Ben nodded. "Hypothetically, my client wouldn't take kindly to me pointing out in the pretrial hearing that this was the fifth such accident in three years. Call me a dreamer, but if you supply a flammable product to consumers, you should be maintaining your pipelines and be responsible if you aren't. They have insurance for settlements, but no one should lose a loved one because a certain number of accidents are forecast in some company's ten-year plan." His voice shook. He couldn't help it. "No amount of money will replace your parents." He should know.

"And so you were fired, with charges of misconduct filed." Rachel brought his hand to her lips and kissed it. "You know what I think?"

"No," Ben said in a voice strangled with surprise.

"I think you learned what you needed to

in the big city. I think you should stay in Falcon Creek." Her brown eyes settled something deep inside him. "Grant the Double T the water rights we deserve. Help my family and yours defend our right to use water in ways that will allow the ranches to grow and prosper." She made no mention of the personal side of the fairy tale.

Ben swallowed, staring at their joined hands. "Is this still an alternate universe?"

"Ben." Ben, not Blackwell. She didn't let go of his hand. "Maybe it's time to retire."

To Falcon Creek, she meant. To continue this charade that there was something good and lasting between them. His heart swelled around the thought that he had something to build on here besides the ashes of family loyalty. He had Rachel and Poppy. He had tentative relationships with Jon and Ethan. Zoe would be out of the picture, at least as far as Big E was concerned.

But there was one more secret to tell.

"About the water…"

"Don't tell me you're going to fight me on priority position." Rachel released his hands. "I know you've been researching deeds and titles and probably property lines." Somehow, an edge had slipped into her tone. "What dastardly deed do you have planned, Blackwell?"

Big E had been right. A title search in this remote place could never be secret.

"I have a document signed in 1919," Ben said slowly, reluctant to make things more adversarial between them but having no choice now. "A bull was traded for a small parcel of land."

"You aren't getting an inch of Double T property, Blackwell." She moved to the end of the booth, readying to stand.

"You've got it all wrong." Ben drew a deep breath. "It was a Thompson bull. The Double T's acreage expanded."

Rachel held herself very still, one hand on the straps of her diaper bag and purse. "*We* have more land? *We…*" She grimaced and rubbed one side of her neck. "Tell me it's the land you've been irrigating. The pasture with that bull you're so fond of."

He shook his head. "It's the road. The road to the river."

"The road…" Her slender brows drew together and then blossomed apart. "The aquifer?"

Ben nodded. "But before you get excited, you should know that the trade was never recorded and the Blackwells have been paying taxes on that land for nearly a hundred years."

"I don't care." Rachel leaned forward, not to comfort but in a posture of strength. "The water is mine. Aquifer water can't be regulated by the state."

Poppy stirred, perhaps roused by the anger in her mother's voice.

"Wait." Rachel's eyes narrowed. "If the trade wasn't recorded, how did you find this document? You've spent two days with the county recorder and probably as many at the library." Understanding dawned. Her eyes opened wider. "How long have you known about this?"

"It's not that simple." It was a weak attempt to soften the blow, to keep the alternate universe alive.

Rachel stood. "When? When did you find that document?"

"Big E—"

"Don't you blame this on your grandfather." Rachel's voice was hard, but there were tears in her eyes.

Poppy pushed herself up, blinking sleepily.

"Give me my daughter." Her voice was as hard as the steel girders holding up the Freedom Tower. "Give me my daughter and tell me the truth."

"Big E had it five years ago." There. He'd said it. But he hadn't said enough.

"You mean *you* had it five years ago."

"Yes." His cheek stung as if she'd slapped him, but it wasn't breaking, like his heart.

A tear tracked down her cheek. Her eyes were wide with shock. "I should have known. I should have known you'd cheat."

He gathered Poppy into his arms. "Rachel, I'm sorry."

"Don't." She shook a trembling finger in his face. Her features wavered between a meltdown and fury. "You always apologize and I'm just now realizing why. You feel guilty for everything you've done. And you should. You have no honor. You steal water from hardworking ranchers and you penny-pinch settlements for grieving widows. I hate you. I hate you." Another tear spilled over her cheek. She let it fall and snatched Poppy from him, grabbing the handles of her purse and diaper bag.

Poppy whimpered but was still half-asleep as Rachel ran out of the diner.

Everyone was staring at Ben.

He slid down in the booth until his neck

rested on top of the seat back, and ran both hands over his hair.

She'd confirmed what Ben already knew. He'd crossed a line professionally five years ago and his meager attempt to make things right for a widow and her children a few weeks back wouldn't make up for who he'd become.

A sellout. A liar. A thief.

The waitress slid two steaming chicken pot pies on the table and quietly left him alone.

Ben poked at the pastry with his fork, releasing steam. He wished he could do the same. His emotions felt bottled up inside of him. Telling the truth hadn't solved anything.

Ben took a bite of the pot pie. It didn't taste as good as he remembered.

This must be why Big E never looked back.

CHAPTER EIGHTEEN

"YOU SHOULD DROP me off here." Zoe clung to the truck's windowsill as they passed the turn for the Blackwell Ranch. She'd changed into blue jeans and an off-the-shoulder red blouse. "I can search Big E's office for that paper Ben was talking about."

Ben.

Rachel felt the same gut-wrenching disappointment she had five years ago. Except this time, there was also the heartbreaking feeling of the loss of something that might have been special. Her body ached with it. "As your attorney, I refuse to condone breaking and entering."

"I put my heart into that place." Zoe's blond hair whipped in the wind. "I studied ranches that were doing well in other parts of the country. At first, I wanted to branch out into alligator farming, but Big E wouldn't have it."

Big E might be a sneaky old man, but he

knew what he was doing when it came to ranching in Montana.

"I'm not sure alligators would have liked the climate," Rachel said patiently. Not to mention they might have eaten the other livestock.

"But the guest ranch... That works with or without snow." Zoe stared straight ahead. The tears in her eyes threatened to dislodge her false eyelashes. "I hope the guests are having a good time. I hope... I hope Big E remembers his meds and to stay away from fatty foods. He can be so stubborn."

Rachel chose not to comment. She turned down the Double T's driveway, parked and got out, picking up the baby and her diaper bag. After the most embarrassing time of her life with Ben this afternoon, she'd changed into comfortable old jeans and a plain blue T-shirt. She'd texted her mother and asked her to make macaroni and cheese.

But no amount of cheesy pasta was going to mend her broken heart.

Henry walked between the old homestead and the barn, carrying a shotgun. He nodded Rachel's way and kept walking.

"That's not normal." Rachel transferred Poppy and the diaper bag to Zoe, who held the baby in extended arms as if she had poopy pants, which she did not. "Take her inside. I need to check on Henry." Rachel hurried around the corner of the barn, calling the foreman's name.

He turned at the gate to the road, the same gate where she'd kissed Ben just yesterday, the gun in the crook of his arm.

"What are you doing?" No lie, the sight of the gun made her jittery. It wasn't hunting season.

"Sometimes, you have to put trouble out of business." Henry pointed to the pasture and what looked like the troublemaking heifer.

Rachel laughed once, awkwardly. "You're not going to shoot her."

"I am. I fixed the pickets today." Henry raised the rifle and seemed to be taking aim. Not that he stood steady as a rock. He swayed a bit, as if there was a stiff breeze, which there was not. "That piece of beef is going to cost you. She won't stay up-country with the herd, which means she won't get pregnant. Might just as well eat her, little lady."

"No, Henry." Rachel was close enough now that she could put a hand on his gun barrel and lower it. "That's not how we do things at the Double T. And I'd like you to stop calling me little lady. That's not me anymore." The words were freeing.

"I'm sorry, li… I can't keep up no more." He sniffed and shuffled back a step, an old man coming to grips with the limitations of his age. He gestured toward the heifer. "Not if we keep stock like her. I'm letting your father down."

"Henry." Rachel took the rifle and put the safety back on. "The gate is fixed." Thanks to Ben. "That heifer can't get in. Your pickets will be safe. And my dad would be grateful of the help you give me." Her father would also be proud of how Rachel was transitioning to ranch life. She might not do things the way her father did, or as efficiently, but she was getting them done. And she could only get better every day.

"I spent a lot of time on that fence." The old man wiped at his nose.

"And I appreciate it." Rachel hugged him. "Come on. Let's get you back to your shows." Rachel escorted Henry to the homestead, making a mental note to adjust Henry's workload.

Afterward, Rachel trudged up the steps. Ranching was a full-time job. As was legal work. Since Nelly's judgment, she'd gotten three calls for representation. She felt as if she needed to make a choice. It was just that the ranch couldn't break even without her small legal fees. She refused to decide about the ranch until the court decision on Friday.

"We didn't hold dinner for you," Mom said when Rachel came inside. She was sitting on the couch, a TV tray in front of her. "Because of the movie."

The movie.

The afternoon heat sank beneath Rachel's skin. They must not have canceled the cable service as Rachel had requested.

Nana Nancy had a similar tray in front of her, but she sat in a kitchen chair. "Before you get your panties in a bunch, we're watching television with commercials. It's why we couldn't wait."

Rachel sucked in a breath and realized there was macaroni and cheese on Nana's plate. *Comfort food...*

"*Love, Actually.*" Zoe held Poppy in her lap but near her knees, as if she was afraid to get close to the little thing. "It's one of my favorites."

"Ha!" Mom pointed at Nana with her fork. "Your grandmother is trying to convince Zoe that Jamie and Aurélia are the best storyline, but she doesn't have anything to bribe her with."

"Colin Firth's character learns Portuguese for her." Nana's fork clattered on her plate. "A man doesn't love you unless he gives something up for your heart."

Zoe made a sound like a cat coughing up a hairball, startling Poppy, who reached for Rachel with a tentative wail. Zoe handed her over and swiped Nana's napkin to blow her nose.

Her distress went unnoticed by Rachel's mother. "Your grandmother would choose Colin Firth if he was an animated voice in a cartoon."

"That's because he has talent," Nana said staunchly.

"That's because he's adorable," Zoe said tearfully. "Men who are adorable steal a woman's heart."

That statement got through to Mom. She searched Zoe's face and then Rachel's, before rising and carrying her dinner dishes to the kitchen. "Seems we could all use some chocolate chip cookies."

"Nana, do you remember anything about a land trade with the Blackwells? It might have happened a hundred years or so ago."

"That would have been the time of Seth Thompson, my grandfather. He was rumored to be a drinking man. Fell off his horse bringing back the herd and broke his neck. My mother called him a ne'er-do-well."

"Nothing about a land trade, though?"

"Nope. Now, shush. Here comes Colin." She focused on the television.

Rachel wandered into the kitchen. Poppy bounced on her hip and held out a hand for her grandmother.

Mom turned at the sink to face Rachel and took the baby. "What's wrong? You've got that sad look in your eye, the same one you had that time you lost the debate competition at the university."

"Surely, I had that look some other time," Rachel muttered. A time that wasn't associated with Ben. "If we're going to keep the ranch, I'm going to need you to help."

Her mother bristled. "I do help."

Rachel refused to be baited. "I'll teach you how to do the accounts, so you can see where the money's going and where it's needed."

Her mom's chin shot up. "Are you going to give me an allowance, too?"

Rachel peered in the pot and then stirred the macaroni and cheese. "You decide if you can afford any extras."

Without warning, Mom wrapped Rachel in a one-armed hug, balancing Poppy on her hip.

"I'm so proud of you, honey. I'll make you proud of me."

"We'll both make Dad proud," Rachel said, words roughened with emotion. She slipped free and dished up some cheesy comfort food. "Dad used to talk to Chris Hannigan, didn't he?"

"The state representative?" Almost without looking, Mom held a Cheerio to Poppy, who accepted it greedily. "They'd talk every fall in election years. Chris always wanted a donation. Why do you ask?"

"I think I'm going to need friends in high places."

Mom's face paled. "Is it that bad?"

Rachel nodded. It was that bad.

And it would take a long time to set the ranch and her heart to rights.

"You're a hard man to track down, Ben." Ethan was leaning over Blackie's stall door, staring at him, on Thursday night. "We thought you'd be sitting in the kitchen, using that laptop of yours."

"Since you're the one who called this family meeting—" Jon joined Ethan at the door "—we thought you'd be easier to find."

Ben had taken the tall Thoroughbred out

for a ride and was cleaning Blackie's hooves. He'd tested fate by riding the road to the river one last time and taunting Ferdinand, who ignored him, as if the lawyer on the tall horse was no threat.

Without Rachel, that's how Ben felt. He'd spent the past two days preparing for court, but he had no heart for it.

His brothers stood tall and silent on the other side of the stall door. Their dark hair gleamed in the LED lights Zoe had upgraded to. Everything was clear in the barn. Nothing could hide from the brightness. Not a mouse and not a man's desire to leave.

Nearby, Jon's twin girls were cooing over Butterscotch's foal and begging their dad for a chance to get into the stall to pet her. Butterscotch was content to have the girls give her attention. That horse and Ben's mother had shared the same patient, loving temperament. Never had a horse and rider been so well suited. That personality was why everyone trusted Butterscotch to this day.

Ben had always been more like his grandfather—territorial, standoffish with strangers, ready to stir the pot without knowing exactly what would happen if he did. Few people trusted Ben. Heck, few people *liked* Ben.

And after he argued the family's case tomorrow, that number would dwindle even further.

Jon caved in to his daughters' demands and went to supervise their visit to the foal.

Blackie nudged Ben with his big nose, pushing him out of the stall, more than happy to be rid of him. Or more accurately, impatient to be given some oats. Ben slid the bolt home on the stall door, picked up the nearby bucket and held it high for Blackie to eat his treat.

"You've developed quite an attachment to that horse," Ethan noted, not unkindly. "Not to mention an affinity for my clothes."

Since he'd told Rachel the truth, Ben had raided the stash of clothes Ethan had left in the ranch house more than once. "You'll get your clothes back on Saturday." Ben stroked beneath Blackie's forelock. "As for Blackie... He and I are a lot alike."

Jon backed into the center of the barn where he could keep an eye on his daughters and his brothers. "Meaning you both stand high above everyone else's problems."

"I don't know what you're talking about." Ben hung the empty bucket outside Blackie's stall, avoiding Jon's look. His brother had tossed out a similar observation after dinner on Saturday.

"I'm talking about you buying a plane ticket to go home this weekend." Jon's voice took on that you-better-behave tone that had served him so well as the older brother to four boys. "I'm talking about you leaving when we need you here."

"You won't need me anymore after tomorrow." His gut clenched, not from dread at the upcoming court case, but from dread that tomorrow would be the last time he'd see Rachel.

"Don't think I don't remember what you did when Mom and Dad died." Jon should have been a judge. He never forgot anything and he always—*always*—knew how to hit at a man's vulnerable side. "You took off on your horse with a bedroll. I searched half a day trying to find you."

"I thought you'd been swept away by the river." There was no joke in Ethan's tone. He'd been scared.

When Jon had brought Ben back, Ethan had been waiting at the barn. As soon as Ben got off Rodrigo, Ethan had slugged him in the shoulder and then hugged him the way Ben had wished he could hug their parents.

If he could have hugged them one last time before they died.

"I wanted perspective." Ben had wanted to be alone. To look down on the Blackwell Ranch and see what it would be like without the two people he'd loved most in the world in it. But the bridge had been out, so he'd ended up at the end of the river road, staring at the Rockies until Rachel had joined him.

He'd gotten no perspective. But the foundation of friendship and love with Rachel had been built.

"And after Zoe eloped with Big E," Ethan said, still using that neutral voice, still looking at Ben with understanding in his eyes, "you didn't even spend the night here. It was off again to New York."

The twins giggled softly, the way ranch kids did because they knew not to startle the stock with loud noises. Jon had raised them to belong to the land the way their father had raised the Blackwell brothers.

A shaft of longing pierced Ben's heart. He wanted someone to give Poppy that love of the high plains, that respect and love for animals that made it possible to live up here without time clocks, billable hours or security desks.

"I'm wondering why you came home now," Jon said carefully. "You never answer the phone when we call. You rarely reply via text. And all of a sudden, you call Ethan back? You come out here? You don't help around the ranch, but you take off on that animal as much as you can."

"You're questioning why I came?" Ben made to move past his big brother.

Jon caught Ben's arm. "No. I'm asking you to question yourself. When will you settle down and be happy?"

Never. Happiness without Rachel… Ben lifted his chin. "I am happy."

"You're wearing a polo shirt with blue jeans, Ben." Ethan apparently felt the need to jump back in to the conversation. "You're straddling two worlds."

"And which world would you have me in? *This one?* There's no place for me here."

"There could be," Jon said, which was rich considering he wanted to sell the Blackwell Ranch, too.

"There's no place for me here," Ben repeated, speaking with a finality that should have overridden the sickening churn in his gut. But he was a lawyer and used to forcing his emotions into a small little box that he rarely opened. He slammed the lid now. "And if we're selling, there'll be nothing for me in Falcon Creek. You do want me to sell, don't you?"

His brothers exchanged glances the way Ben and Ethan used to, communicating without speaking. About what, Ben had no idea.

And then Jon nodded and said, "Why did you call us out here?"

"I want you to attend court tomorrow. Nine thirty. I'm going on record with the truth." He swallowed and stared at his toes. The toes that felt comfortable in Ethan's boots. "I just want you to know what I did wasn't your fault. It was mine. And it was wrong for me to wrap up my hurt over Zoe leaving with my guilt over being gullible. This time…when I leave…if you call, I'll pick up the phone."

His brothers closed in for a group hug.

It was good to clear out the dirt and darkness from his past.

He only hoped his words tomorrow cleared the way for the Thompsons and the Blackwells to have a better future.

CHAPTER NINETEEN

"ALL RISE FOR…"

Rachel stood, smoothing her slacks over her thighs and wishing she could smooth out the jangle of nerves inside her.

She'd spent years arguing cases in this building. It was like a second home to her. But today she felt out of sorts. Today, she was taking on the Blackwells and nothing was how it should have been.

Because it wasn't just any Blackwell. It was Ben. And Ben was unpredictable.

He'd put his career on the line to do what was right for strangers in New York last month, and yet he hadn't done right by Rachel five years ago. She'd had three days to prepare for this meeting, but her preparations were nothing like Ben's. She hadn't spent hours researching past water cases. The past… What Ben had done… What Big E had done…

It was time to move forward.

The courtroom was full this morning, not

sparsely populated with a few people wait-ing their turn at justice. People had come to watch a show.

Including Rachel's family and Zoe. They sat behind Rachel. Mom held Poppy and was slipping her Cheerios to keep her quiet. Nana was knitting.

Rachel's neck twinged. She couldn't let her family down.

The opposition had his own group of fans. Ethan and Jon sat behind Ben, and Katie one row behind them.

Ben stood in his charcoal gray suit with his perfectly knotted blue silk tie. He probably had no idea the color of his tie made his blue eyes seem electric.

"I'm disappointed, but not surprised, that you two couldn't come to an agreement be-fore seeing me today." Judge Edwards settled behind her bench. "Failed out-of-court set-tlements are becoming a trait of yours, Miss Thompson."

"We tried, Your Honor." Rachel attempted to make the lie sound sincere. From the start, she hadn't been willing to negotiate anything. And now, it was all or nothing.

Judge Edwards turned her attention to opposing counsel. "Mr. Blackwell, I hear you have something to say about this matter."

"Objection," Rachel nearly shouted.

"Good girl," Nana said.

Judge Edwards raised her brows.

"I…" Rachel slanted Ben a glance that didn't quite reach his face "I'd like to present first in this matter."

"I was told Mr. Blackwell has a statement that could resolve this issue," Judge Edwards said. "Overruled. Proceed, Mr. Blackwell."

Rachel sank into her seat, prepared to leap out of it the moment Ben got even a hair out of line.

"This is better than *Oprah*," Nana said, earning her a hard look from the judge.

"Thank you, Your Honor." Four words, and Ben sounded like he had no doubts as to the outcome of the day's proceedings. "Five years ago, a decision by the county court regarding water rights between the Blackwell Ranch and the Double T was made in favor of the Blackwells, despite the Double T being first in time and first in right for the water. Their ranch was founded at least twenty years prior to the Blackwell property, and it is located farther upriver."

What was Ben up to? Rachel's pulse pounded

in her temples, a drumbeat to keep her on her toes. She was hyperaware of the clacking of Nana's knitting needles, the gentle smack of Poppy's gums on cereal and the nerve-jumping creak of the audience shifting in their chairs.

Ben held up a piece of paper with neatly typed columns. "I'd like to invite the court to review the water projections for Blackwell Ranch." At the judge's nod, Ben approached the bench and handed her the sheet. "This shows that the average water use for the Blackwell Ranch can be met by the underground aquifer. And during peak seasons, the secondary river water rights will supplement their needs."

Judge Edwards raised her white brows. "This doesn't seem to defend your water rights, Mr. Blackwell. Are you going to move that I rule in favor of Ms. Thompson?"

"Much as I respect the skills of the opposing counsel—" the look Ben gave Rachel was sincere "—if the court could grant me some patience, I have several aspects of this case to go through, which I hope will clarify the water rights between these two ranches, once and for all."

Rachel leaned forward in her seat, ready to

catch Ben in a lie the moment he tried to cover up the land trade.

"The court awaits your clarity with bated breath." The judge instructed the clerk to log in his water projections as an exhibit.

"Thank you, Your Honor." Ben held up a yellowed scrap of paper next. "This document indicates the land above the aquifer, the land that supplies the Blackwell Ranch with much of its water, was traded by Mathias Blackwell to Seth Thompson in 1919 for a prize bull. This strip of land is currently a road that lies between the two properties."

The audience shifted in its seats, filling the courtroom with wood-straining creaks.

Ben was telling the truth? Rachel sat back in her chair.

"Is there record of this?" Judge Edwards scribbled something on her notepad.

"No," Ben said. "But I believe it to be real, because there is no second piece of paper canceling the transaction or trading it back. That said, there's a history in this valley of ranchers trading breeding rights back and forth like gift cards at Christmas. And, for what it's worth, Seth Thompson may not have had time to document a trade back. He died a few weeks after he signed this."

Ben's brothers exchanged whispers, but they didn't look surprised or displeased that Ben was setting the record straight.

"Where did you find this document?" The judge gave it to the court clerk, who examined it, logged it in and passed it to Rachel.

"In a family safe rarely opened, Your Honor."

"Again, Mr. Blackwell—" the judge leaned forward on her elbows "—you are doing your cause no favors by bringing this forward."

"I want the truth to be told." His gaze, filled with remorse and determination, caught on Rachel, before returning to the judge. "And if truth be told, the Blackwells and the Thompsons have been exchanging their cattle studs and sharing water for decades, if not generations. Possibly going back as far as 1919."

"I thought he was supposed to be a good lawyer," Nana said.

"Order," Judge Edwards warned with a pound of her gavel. "If the public cannot be quiet, they will be removed."

Rachel turned to her grandmother and held a finger to her lips. The peanut gallery didn't look like they were going to be silent observers. Nana shrugged. Poppy grinned. Zoe was smirking. Katie looked worried, and Ethan and Jon exchanged more whispers.

Ignoring them all, Ben stood in the middle of the courtroom and spoke directly to the judge. "The land involved in this trade is more commonly referred to by both parties as the road to the river."

He stood without defense of his silver briefcase. He stood on the merits of an argument alone. His shoulders were back and his voice rang with confidence.

"The road to the river is currently used almost exclusively by the Blackwell Ranch via a gate. From this Blackwell gate to the river—" he held up his hands to indicate a distance from Point A to Point B "—the road is just dirt. Nothing much grows, because it is well used. Now, from the Blackwell gate to the gate leading to the Double T property—" he shifted his hands to the left "—there are weeds blanketing the road, indicating the property is used infrequently, if at all."

"Objection." Rachel stood. "The Double T does use that road. *I* use that road."

"One person, Your Honor," Ben said without turning.

"Is there an easement in existence?" The judge glanced up to include Rachel in the question. "In either party's possession?"

"No, Your Honor," Rachel and Ben said in unison.

"Overruled, Miss Thompson."

Rachel sat down hard, her knees weak with defeat. She knew where this was going. There were laws about property ownership versus possession by use, and it appeared the Blackwells could establish the Double T didn't use the road over the aquifer.

Ben walked toward the empty jury box, as if it was filled. "Let's assume that the bull-for-land trade in 1919 occurred, despite it not being recorded with the county. In that scenario, the land would belong to the Double T. But tax receipts show that the Blackwells have been paying taxes on that land for decades." Ben turned and captured Rachel's gaze. "A fact that establishes ownership recognized by both parties."

"Which brings us back to the original claim that brought us here today," Judge Edwards snapped. "Get to the point, counselor."

Ben nodded. "I move the Double T be given back their first position river water rights, plus ten percent."

Everything Rachel was asking for.

"And what's to stop the Double T from suing the Blackwells for the land over the aquifer?" The judge had a shrewd look on her face, almost as if she'd known this was where Ben was going all along.

"The Blackwell Ranch will be filing claims regarding the strip of land commonly referred to as the road to the river, Your Honor. We'll be claiming Easement by Implication, Easement by Prescription, Adverse Possession and Quiet Title."

Rachel's head pounded. "Objection," she said, because the situation seemed to call for some reaction. She stood and glared at Ben. Somehow, he'd managed to hijack her case, the same way he'd done in Nelly's divorce proceedings. He'd given her the outcome she wanted, and yet Rachel felt it was an outcome she hadn't deserved.

"What grounds?" The judge stared down at Rachel as if she'd jumped the gun.

Think, Rachel, think.

"The Blackwells asked for an easement three years ago, one that cut across Double T land to a swimming hole higher upriver." In fact, it had been Zoe who'd asked, right after Big E agreed to build the guesthouse.

The judge's eyes narrowed. "And did the Double T agree to the easement?"

"No," Rachel said through stiff lips. Her father had denied it for the very reasons Ben was using to establish Blackwell ownership—use of the property.

"Overruled."

Ben wasn't smiling. He should have been smiling. He'd tap danced circles around Rachel, controlling everything. "There is no formal easement, no contract, no paperwork granting or protesting the Blackwell Ranch's use of the property." But his words came out almost like an apology.

He's always apologizing. Because he cares about the people court cases affect.

Ben was staring at Rachel with equal measures of love and sadness in his eyes.

A cold, numb feeling spread from Rachel's toes to her hands. *Ben cares. He loves. He loves me.*

He loved her enough to give her this case, when he could have found some other argument to keep the Double T in second position. He wasn't cold and calculating. He was careful and kind.

And she was losing him. She was losing him the moment Judge Edwards struck her gavel.

"You know what this means, counselor?" The judge was looking at Rachel with concern. After all, Rachel should be happy. "Miss

Thompson?" she asked when Rachel didn't respond.

She nodded her head miserably. She knew. She'd won. And Ben would be leaving town.

"The court rules in favor of the Double T. The water positions will be reverted, with the Double T in first position plus an additional ten percent." Judge Edwards pounded her gavel.

Rachel jumped.

The audience erupted behind them. Well, mostly Rachel's family hooted and clapped.

Rachel gathered her files and stuffed them into her briefcase, snapping it shut. She told her family and Zoe she'd see them outside. Jon and Ethan filed out with the rest of the spectators. The court staff exited to the back.

Rachel and Ben were the only ones left in the courtroom.

"I hate you," she said, because she did. She hated that he was such a good lawyer, that he handled the courtroom as if he'd been born here and that he'd willingly given her what she wanted in this case, only to refuse her what her heart wanted.

"I'm sorry." Ben stood between their tables, holding the courtroom gate open for her.

"You're not sorry. You won." She pushed

past Ben and hurried down the aisle, wanting to turn and cling to him. "You won because even though I got what I wanted, you looked like you were doing me a favor."

"I was only trying to help."

"I have to learn to do things on my own." She reached the door and rushed into the hallway.

The middle-aged man Ben had pointed out last week stood a few feet away checking his cell phone. His black leather shoes were just as nice as Ben's. He caught Rachel staring and smiled, stepping into her path.

Rachel dropped her gaze and mumbled, "Excuse me," as she maneuvered past him.

"Just a minute, Miss Thompson." The older man touched her arm.

Rachel's gaze flew to his. "How did you know—"

"Jack Daniels." Ben's voice was sharper than the barbed wire he'd used to fix the fence. "I did a search on you after I noticed your interest in our case."

Of course, Ben had researched the man, not that it had done them any good.

"It's *Danby*. Jack *Danby*." The middle-aged man's smile turned brittle as he held a sheaf of papers toward each of them. "I'm here representing the Falcon County Water Company. We're serving the Double T and Blackwell Ranch notice. Based on growth in the county, we're going to be annexing land along Falcon Creek, and we'll be needing some of your river water rights."

A shaft of dread speared through Rachel. Ben was leaving. She'd have to face this case alone.

Ben put his arm in front of Rachel. "Don't accept anything from this hired gun."

"You know how this goes, Blackwell." Jack tsked. "You're being served. Don't make a scene."

Ben scowled and took both sets of papers, Rachel's and his.

"Not so fast." Representative Chris Hannigan stepped into the circle of conversation with a booming voice and a belt buckle that proclaimed him a rodeo champion. He'd been sitting at the back of the courtroom. Rachel was grateful he'd had the time to fulfill her request to attend. He introduced himself to Ben and the water company's lawyer.

"And I'm Lilith Adams, state water board." A middle-aged woman wearing a checked pantsuit elbowed her way into the crowd. She extended her hand to Ben and then Jack. "We were alerted by Miss Thompson about potential practices we don't approve of."

"Such as bullying local businesses out of their rightful water," Chris said.

Ben was scanning the legal claim Jack had handed him. Their families waited farther down the corridor.

"You might want to rethink filing any claims on that water, unless your client wants to come under review." Lilith arched a slender, expertly lined brow.

"I'm making agriculture a priority in this state." Chris puffed out his chest. "Farmers and ranchers need water to create jobs and feed America."

That sounded like a campaign slogan.

Rachel didn't care, as long as the politician was on her side. She plucked the briefs from Ben's hands and thrust them toward Jack. "I'm going to assume your client wants to rethink filing suit against us."

Jack Danby, Esquire, was left standing in the hallway as the Thompsons and the Blackwells exited the courthouse.

"You brought in your state representatives?" Ben grabbed Rachel's arm and led her away. "That was brilliant."

Fair praise from Ben Blackwell. She stopped

on the courthouse steps and stared at him one last time.

"You're going to be all right, Rachel Thompson." He kissed the tip of her nose. "And don't you forget it."

She wouldn't.

Nor would she forget Ben and a love that was strong in an alternate universe.

KATIE WAS ALREADY pulling away when Ben caught up to Ethan and Jon in the parking lot.

"That was quite the show you put on." Ethan looked on Ben with pride, and then he gave him a hearty hug. "I'm glad you're on our side."

"I'm on the side of justice, brother," Ben murmured as he stepped out of his brother's embrace. "Truth and justice." He planned on representing people impacted by public utility accidents.

And then it was Jon's turn to hug him. "That might have been the best step toward peace between the Thompsons and the Blackwells anyone's made in years."

This felt like goodbye. Theirs anyway.

Ben wasn't ready. Not yet. Something was holding him back, as powerful a feeling as the emotions that had sent him running five years ago.

"Big E won't be happy with the case," Ben pointed out. "And less water makes the property less attractive for sale."

"Big E deserves what he gets," Jon said firmly. "Let him retire to Florida with his next wife and his share of the ranch."

"You haven't got enough votes to sell yet." It was Ethan's turn to scowl. "And who knows? I might convince you to keep the ranch."

"In an alternative universe," Ben murmured, thinking about Rachel.

"It could happen," Ethan insisted.

Jon smirked, settling his cowboy hat firmly on his head. "More likely you'll come around to my way of thinking and want to sell. You always were trouble."

Ethan's lips pulled in a mulish line. "Only because Ben put me up to it. He learned how to manipulate the court system by manipulating me."

"Don't blame me for you being gullible." Ben laughed, although the sound lacked humor.

"You're both at fault," Jon said. "I am so glad I had girls."

"Don't kid yourself," Ethan said. "Those girls excel at finding trouble."

The three men laughed, but when the laughter ended, Ben felt awkward again.

"So, this is it?" Jon laid a hand on Ben's shoulder. "You're going back to New York?"

Rachel drove off in her truck without so much as a honk or a wave goodbye.

Ben's chest felt hollow. "There's nothing to keep me here."

"Is that the truth?" Jon asked, backing toward his truck. He waved a hand toward Rachel's tailgate. "Or when you look back on this, will you have regrets?"

"Don't listen to him," Ethan chimed in. "He's concerned that the guest ranch will fail and when we sell, it'll be worth considerably less. He's going to call Tyler, because he works in marketing."

"Ty will never come back," Ben countered. "He blames himself for Mom and Dad's accident."

Rachel's tailgate was fast disappearing, leaving Ben to wonder...

Was Jon right? Would he have regrets?

CHAPTER TWENTY

UP AT DAWN, Ben took Blackie out for one more ride on Saturday morning.

He'd picked up his mother's repaired bridle from Brewster's Friday afternoon and put it on the stallion for their last ride.

They'd warmed up with a trot around the southern pasture, empty of stock. They'd galloped across the newly constructed bridge to the summer pastures, where they'd paused and watched the herd grazing. And finally, almost reluctantly, Ben headed Blackie toward the road to the river for a final goodbye.

Rachel sat on the viewing platform. She stared at the sun-tipped Rockies with her feet dangling over the edge of the platform.

Her big-boned strawberry roan was tied to a fence post. Ferdinand grazed near the trees lining the river, but he wasn't alone. A familiar white-faced heifer grazed a few feet from him.

Ben hopped off Blackie and looped his reins

around a fence post near Rachel's horse. "Isn't that your heifer?"

"I have a theory." Rachel turned to face Ben, her expression unreadable. "I think Marigold fell in love with Ferdinand, and that's why she's not staying up-country."

Ben walked onto the wooden viewing platform. "Why do I feel like this has something to do with an alternate universe?"

She stared up at him, not yet granting him a smile. "It's a little Capulet and Montague."

"Romeo and Juliet." He sat on the edge of the deck and stared down at the shallow water gurgling over smooth river rock. "Ferdinand and Marigold. And you're not upset."

Her fingers twisted in her lap. "Turns out, Double T heifers have been producing fewer calves over the past three years. I need to infuse some new blood and our records show some of our bulls have been crossbred from Blackwell Black Angus stock."

"You know, in some circles, using a bull for stud without permission might be considered stealing." But he hoped the pairing resulted in a large white-faced bull.

"Hey." Her fingers curled so tight, her knuckles popped. "That'd be just like using your neighbor's road more than they do means you can take possession of it, and the water beneath it."

"Touché." He laid a hand over hers, not liking that she was worried.

Rachel stared at their hands for a moment before continuing. "Besides, it's not stealing if a Blackwell sits by and lets nature take its course."

"Successful ranchers make bold moves." Ben grinned. "See? I told you you'd be all right."

"There's something I need to know." She half turned to face him, her golden hair catching the light. "When we were married and living in New York, did we have an apartment overlooking Central Park?"

Ben nodded. "Only the best for you."

"Did we go to museums and the theater?"

"We were charter members." He'd write checks to support the arts upon his return to New York and credit the donations in her name.

"It sounds heavenly." She leaned against his shoulder.

Ben curled his arm around her, bringing her close. Sitting there together, watching the sunrise, it felt natural, as if they'd been married for years.

"Do you know what I think?" Rachel glanced up at him.

"No," Ben said in a voice strangled with longing.

"I think you should give that alternative universe a try." She laid her head back on his shoulder. "I think you should retire to Falcon Creek, find yourself a good woman and have a couple of kids."

"Thompson?" He drew back from her. "What are you saying?"

"I'm thinking ahead, like any good lawyer would." She clung to his hand in a most un-lawyer-like way. "And saying what you won't let yourself say. We were meant to be together in an alternate universe, and in this one. I don't know how it happened or when it happened, but I know that I love you and the thought of you leaving when I can't breaks my heart."

"Thompson—"

"Don't you make light of this. I need you."

"Consider what you're saying...*Rachel*." He smoothed a strand of hair from her face, and held his breath when she ran a hand from his crown to the base of his neck, just like his father used to do. His words came out barely louder than a whisper. "Everything you said about me in the diner the other day is true. You don't need a man like me."

"A man like you." Tears sparkled in her eyes. "A man who helps a woman he doesn't even know get a better monthly divorce settlement? A man who stops a bully from using unresolved custody to get spousal support? A man who fixes gates and fences without being asked? What kind of man does that sound like?" She bumped him with her shoulder, as if they were the best of friends, the closest of lovers. "It sounds like a man who'd make any woman proud to call him husband."

All Ben's arguments bottlenecked in his throat. It had been a long time since anyone had told him they were proud of him. But one argument escaped. "I can never make up for what happened five years ago."

She cradled his face in her hands. "What I'm asking has nothing to do with the past, not with harsh words or bad decisions. It has to do with my heart wanting yours nearby, now and in the future."

He closed his eyes and covered her hands with his. "Looking forward, not back."

"I love you, Ben Blackwell." She pressed a kiss to his lips that was so gentle, it hurt.

"You and I should go down to the courthouse on Monday and get hitched."

"But…" She continued to throw him for a loop. "No pomp and ceremony? No wedding reception? No sparkly white dress?"

"We had that before, both of us. And look how both those marriages turned out."

In his case, it'd been a nonstarter.

"Ben."

The way she said his name, softly, tenderly, full of love and promise and hope. How could he refuse her anything?

"I'll make you a deal," he said with a sigh. "You kiss me right now and I'll marry you on Monday. Kiss me right now, Rachel, and I'll promise to love you forever."

Oh, she kissed him all right. Rachel kissed him as if she might not get another chance, putting her heart and soul into it, telling him with more than words that she loved him as deeply as he loved her.

And then she pulled back. "I just wish…"

"What?" he asked. He'd grant her any wish. He'd take her to New York and show her the sights she yearned to see. He'd take the money from the sale of the Blackwell Ranch and invest it in the Double T.

"Don't think this is stupid, but I have one

teeny, tiny regret." She plucked an imaginary thread from her jeans. "I wish that your name started with a T. The Double T was founded with a husband and a wife, and my sister wants nothing to do with it. But I do, Ben. I want to make the Double T our home. I suppose we could change the brand…"

"Ah." Ben brushed a silky strand of hair behind her ear. "You don't know what my middle name is."

"I don't." She straightened. "What is it?"

"Trustworthy."

Their laughter startled the birds in the nearby trees, made Blackie whicker and Ferdinand snort.

It was a great beginning to the kind of love that was often only found in dreams and alternative universes.

And here. At the road to the river.

EPILOGUE

June 30th, Las Vegas, Nevada

IN THE PAST two weeks, Elias Blackwell had driven through the gates to the Las Vegas retirement community and driven right back out four times. But this time, he didn't turn around without stopping.

It's time. He stopped.

In fact, it was long past time. He'd made such a fool of himself, chasing after women instead of chasing after the unraveling thread of love that had once bound his family together.

He parked in front of a tidy duplex in the section of the retirement community that offered additional medical care and traversed the walk in the early morning heat that was summer in Vegas.

When he'd begun this journey several months ago, he hadn't fully comprehended the emotional toll it would take to bring his boys back to the ranch. There was joy, to be sure, in hearing Ethan and Ben had returned to Falcon Creek, at least temporarily. A measure of peace in finally recognizing that Jon had chosen the right path. But there was hardship and loneliness, too. Another failed marriage. This one he'd chosen to leave after realizing Zoe needed someone younger who'd give her the children she longed for.

And now...

His knuckles hesitated, seemingly floating in the air in front of the door. This might be his hardest task to check off his bucket list yet, because it involved more than one broken heart.

Big E knocked three times. Once, a long time ago, they used to hum the chorus of *Knock Three Times* to each other instead of saying "I love you" out loud.

The door swung open to reveal a vision. The same deep blue eyes. The same long braid of hair. No longer a rich brown, but now a bright white.

"You," Dorothy said. There was more than enough *be gone* in those words to make them sound truly disheartening. She moved to slam the door.

He may have been old, but running a ranch had kept his reflexes sharp. He slapped a hand on the door, looked his first wife in the eye and said, "You may not want to see me, Dorothy, but if you still have Brenda's letters, the boy needs them back."

* * * * *

*Turn the page for a sneak peek at
the next installment of the
Return of the Blackwell Brothers in*
The Rancher's Fake Fiancée
*by Amy Vastine,
when Tyler Blackwell arrives back
in Falcon Creek!*

"For the love of all that's good in the world, would you please call your brothers back?"

Tyler Blackwell glanced up at his obviously infuriated employee. Tucking her wavy blond hair behind her ears, Hadley Sullivan's scowl meant she was serious this time.

Tyler's gaze returned to his computer screen. Regardless of her ire, finishing the presentation for Lodi Organics was a bit higher on the priority list than his bothersome brothers. "Which one?"

Hadley let out an exasperated sigh. "Take your pick. That was Ethan just now, but Ben has bombarded the office with at least a dozen calls this week and Jonathan phoned yesterday while you were at lunch. I know you know this. We put all the messages on your desk."

Tyler had seen the notes and promptly tossed the slips of pink paper in the recycling bin because he was nothing if not ecologically minded.

"From now on, when they call, tell them I can only be reached on my cell."

"The same cell they've called five hundred times already?" Hadley paused even though it was a rhetorical question. "They've caught on to the fact that you'll decline their call, Tyler. They've resorted to harassing the people in this office who actually answer their phones."

Clicking Save on the Lodi Organics file, Tyler ran a hand through his thick hair. He'd successfully made himself too busy to return a hundred phone calls from his overreacting brothers but also too busy for a much-needed haircut.

"I'll talk to Kellen about hiring a real office manager who will help us screen all of our calls."

Hadley wasn't appeased. "Maybe I should talk to Kellen about how your personal issues are beginning to negatively impact the entire company."

Tyler wasn't Hadley's favorite person at 2K Marketing. He wasn't sure why that was. He thought she was competent at her job and often asked her to do things for him because he knew she'd get them done. It seemed strange that she was so bothered by his brothers' constant calls. They weren't really her problem. They were all his.

"They've got to be close to giving up," he said.

"Ethan said it was an emergency."

"That's what they keep telling me." For the last three months. He dropped his chin to his chest. These calls were literally a pain in the neck. He gave it a rub.

First, their grandfather ran away from home. The way Tyler saw it, Big E was a grown man with every right to go where he pleased. That was hardly an emergency.

Jonathan and Ethan came to the rescue and managed to get the guest ranch ready for the summer rush. Obviously, they wouldn't be able to manage it forever. Jonathan had his own ranch to run and Ethan couldn't do it on his own. If that meant they had to get rid of the Blackwell Family Ranch, so be it. Tyler wouldn't shed any tears over the end of it.

"Maybe they haven't been able to get things settled with the water," Hadley offered. She'd been privy to more information than she needed because she didn't have the option of hanging up the phone when they called. "Maybe they need your help with that."

Emergency number two had to do with

water rights and bad deals that Big E was most likely responsible for orchestrating. Tyler had replied via text that he was way too busy at work to talk about something he had no control over. "Ben's the lawyer, not me. From what I heard, they got it settled."

"Knock, knock." Tyler's business partner pushed open the door. Kellen Kettering clearly had more time on his hands and less stress than Tyler did, given his perfectly coiffed hair and easy smile. "Is this a bad time?"

Hadley sighed as if relieved. "You're back."

Kellen gave her a crooked smile and adjusted his black-framed glasses. His salt-and-pepper hair was hidden under his beanie. "My flight got in early. I hear I've been missing all the fun around here."

"If by fun you mean work, you are correct," Tyler said, leaning back in his chair.

Kellen had the title of company president while Tyler was the executive creative director. When they started the business five years ago, the two of them worked on every project together. In the last year or so, their accounts had almost tripled. It could have been more, but it seemed the harder Tyler worked, the more Kellen pushed him to slow down.

"Well, I'll let you two catch up," Hadley

said to Kellen before turning her baby blue gaze on Tyler. "Call your brothers back, Ty. I'm begging."

Kellen picked up the shadowbox of arrowheads Tyler had on display on his bookshelf. Tyler resisted the urge to wrestle them away. They had belonged to his father, one of the few mementos he had from either of his parents.

"I heard you accepted a meeting with Rockwell's Hardware," Kellen said, setting the box down. "I thought we agreed we weren't going to take on any other clients until we cleared a couple projects."

"It's a simple rebrand."

"I'm not sure Eric's ready to take on another rebranding account. He's still trying to get his bearings here."

"I'll do most of the work." If he didn't bother sleeping, he'd get it all done easily. Tyler didn't have any other choice. Eric would most likely never find his bearings.

Kellen sat down across from him. "Tyler, you know I appreciate your drive. It's why I partnered with you. But we can't overextend ourselves. We run the risk of choosing quantity over quality."

Tyler tried to sound reassuring. "I got this. Don't worry."

"You sent me thirty-two emails between the hours of 9:00 p.m. and 6:00 a.m. I hate to say it, but you've got to slow down."

This was how Tyler worked. People appreciated hard work. If he wanted to get noticed in the competitive world of marketing, he had to rise above the rest. "All of this will be worth it. We're going to make the top twenty advertising agencies in Portland list this year."

"Tyler." Kellen rested his elbows on his knees. "Maybe after the Lodi Organics presentation, you should take some time off. Relax. Get away for a couple weeks."

Tyler's brow furrowed. He must not have heard Kellen correctly. "Are you suggesting I take a vacation?"

"I'm not suggesting. More like telling you. You need a break. We all need a break." Kellen sat back and seemed to struggle with the right words. "Let me be straight with you. There's been some grumbling. People are feeling... stressed."

"Like who?" Tyler looked out at the office cubicles. The eight-person staff all scurried around, refusing to make eye contact.

"Like everyone."

They had planned this. They had gone to Kellen behind his back.

Get 4 FREE REWARDS!

We'll send you 2 FREE Books plus 2 FREE Mystery Gifts.

Love Inspired® books feature contemporary inspirational romances with Christian characters facing the challenges of life and love.

FREE Value Over **$20**

Get 4 FREE REWARDS!

We'll send you 2 FREE Books
plus 2 FREE Mystery Gifts.

Love Inspired® Suspense books feature Christian characters facing challenges to their faith... and lives.

FREE
Value Over
$20

YES! Please send me 2 FREE Love Inspired® Suspense novels and my 2 FREE mystery gifts (gifts are worth about $10 retail). After receiving them, if I don't wish to receive any more books, I can return the shipping statement marked "cancel." If I don't cancel, I will receive 4 brand-new novels every month and be billed just $5.24 each for the regular-print edition or $5.74 each for the larger-print edition in the U.S., or $5.74 each for the regular-print edition or $6.24 each for the larger-print edition in Canada. That's a savings of at least 13% off the cover price. It's quite a bargain! Shipping and handling is just 50¢ per book in the U.S. and 75¢ per book in Canada*. I understand that accepting the 2 free books and gifts places me under no obligation to buy anything. I can always return a shipment and cancel at any time. The free books and gifts are mine to keep no matter what I decide.

Choose one: ☐ **Love Inspired® Suspense**
Regular-Print
(153/353 IDN GMY5)

☐ **Love Inspired® Suspense**
Larger-Print
(107/307 IDN GMY5)

Name (please print)

Address   Apt. #

City   State/Province   Zip/Postal Code

Mail to the Reader Service:
IN U.S.A.: P.O. Box 1341, Buffalo, NY 14240-8531
IN CANADA: P.O. Box 603, Fort Erie, Ontario L2A 5X3

Want to try two free books from another series? Call 1-800-873-8635 or visit www.ReaderService.com.

---

*Terms and prices subject to change without notice. Prices do not include applicable taxes. Sales tax applicable in N.Y. Canadian residents will be charged applicable taxes. Offer not valid in Quebec. This offer is limited to one order per household. Books received may not be as shown. Not valid for current subscribers to Love Inspired Suspense books. All orders subject to approval. Credit or debit balances in a customer's account(s) may be offset by any other outstanding balance owed by or to the customer. Please allow 4 to 6 weeks for delivery. Offer available while quantities last.

Your Privacy—The Reader Service is committed to protecting your privacy. Our Privacy Policy is available online at www.ReaderService.com or upon request from the Reader Service. We make a portion of our mailing list available to reputable third parties that offer products we believe may interest you. If you prefer that we not exchange your name with third parties, or if you wish to clarify or modify your communication preferences, please visit us at www.ReaderService.com/consumerchoice or write to us at Reader Service Preference Service, P.O. Box 9062, Buffalo, NY 14240-9062. Include your complete name and address.

LIS18

HOME on the RANCH

Get 4 FREE REWARDS!

We'll send you 2 FREE Books plus 2 FREE Mystery Gifts.

FREE
Value Over
$20

Both the **Romance** and **Suspense** collections feature compelling novels written by many of today's best-selling authors.

YES! Please send me 2 FREE novels from the Essential Romance or Essential Suspense Collection and my 2 FREE gifts (gifts are worth about $10 retail). After receiving them, if I don't wish to receive any more books, I can return the shipping statement marked "cancel." If I don't cancel, I will receive 4 brand-new novels every month and be billed just $6.74 each in the U.S. or $7.24 each in Canada. That's a savings of at least 16% off the cover price. It's quite a bargain! Shipping and handling is just 50¢ per book in the U.S. and 75¢ per book in Canada*. I understand that accepting the 2 free books and gifts places me under no obligation to buy anything. I can always return a shipment and cancel at any time. The free books and gifts are mine to keep no matter what I decide.

Choose one: ☐ **Essential Romance**   ☐ **Essential Suspense**
                   (194/394 MDN GMY7)   (191/391 MDN GMY7)

Name (please print)

Address   Apt. #

City   State/Province   Zip/Postal Code

> **Mail to the Reader Service:**
> **IN U.S.A.:** P.O. Box 1341, Buffalo, NY 14240-8531
> **IN CANADA:** P.O. Box 603, Fort Erie, Ontario L2A 5X3

Want to try two free books from another series? Call 1-800-873-8635 or visit www.ReaderService.com

---

STRS18

Get 4 FREE REWARDS!

We'll send you 2 FREE Books plus 2 FREE Mystery Gifts.

Harlequin® Special Edition books feature heroines finding the balance between their work life and personal life on the way to finding true love.

FREE
Value Over
$20

YES! Please send me 2 FREE Harlequin® Special Edition novels and my 2 FREE gifts (gifts are worth about $10 retail). After receiving them, if I don't wish to receive any more books, I can return the shipping statement marked "cancel." If I don't cancel, I will receive 6 brand-new novels every month and be billed just $4.99 per book in the U.S. or $5.74 per book in Canada. That's a savings of at least 12% off the cover price! It's quite a bargain! Shipping and handling is just 50¢ per book in the U.S. and 75¢ per book in Canada*. I understand that accepting the 2 free books and gifts places me under no obligation to buy anything. I can always return a shipment and cancel at any time. The free books and gifts are mine to keep no matter what I decide.

235/335 HDN GMY2

Name (please print)

Address _____ Apt. #

City _____ State/Province _____ Zip/Postal Code

Mail to the **Reader Service:**
IN U.S.A.: P.O. Box 1341, Buffalo, NY 14240-8531
IN CANADA: P.O. Box 603, Fort Erie, Ontario L2A 5X3

Want to try two free books from another series! Call 1-800-873-8635 or visit www.ReaderService.com.

*Terms and prices subject to change without notice. Prices do not include applicable taxes. Sales tax applicable in N.Y. Canadian residents will be charged applicable taxes. Offer not valid in Quebec. This offer is limited to one order per household. Books received may not be as shown. Not valid for current subscribers to Harlequin® Special Edition books. All orders subject to approval. Credit or debit balances in a customer's account(s) may be offset by any other outstanding balance owed by or to the customer. Please allow 4 to 6 weeks for delivery. Offer available while quantities last.

Your Privacy—The Reader Service is committed to protecting your privacy. Our Privacy Policy is available online at www.ReaderService.com or upon request from the Reader Service. We make a portion of our mailing list available to reputable third parties that offer products we believe may interest you. If you prefer that we not exchange your name with third parties, or if you wish to clarify or modify your communication preferences, please visit us at www.ReaderService.com/consumerschoice or write to us at Reader Service Preference Service, P.O. Box 9062, Buffalo, NY 14240-9062. Include your complete name and address.

HSE18

READERSERVICE.COM

Manage your account online!

- Review your order history
- Manage your payments
- Update your address

We've designed the Reader Service website just for you.

Enjoy all the features!

- Discover new series available to you, and read excerpts from any series.
- Respond to mailings and special monthly offers.
- Browse the Bonus Bucks catalog and online-only exculsives.
- Share your feedback.

Visit us at:

ReaderService.com